THE ISCARIOT AGENDA

Book Three of the Vatican Knights Series

By Rick Jones

Table of Contents

CHAPTER ONE

Twenty-three years ago

Senator Joseph Cartwright, an ambitious man whose weighted arrogance was so often exhibited at the podium on the Senate floor, knew he was about to die at the hands of the very monster he created.

Inside the study of his residence, the senator closed the blinds against the inconstant flares from the evening's lightning storm and moved as quickly as possible to his desk to bundle together some special dossiers.

There were eight in all, the documented pieces of the creature he helped assemble into a single, unstoppable mass that was forever at the beck and call of the man holding the highest political seat in the land.

In haste, the senator bound the manila folders together with rubber bands with his arthritically challenged hands moving with surprising deft while hoping that his death would serve as the beginning of the end of something that had gone terribly wrong.

Closing his eyes and clenching his teeth as he leaned over the files, Senator Cartwright couldn't help the pang of regret that tormented him for believing that he was untouchable, which allowed his conceit to carry him too far by pushing certain dignitaries too hard, too fast, or without giving any measurable thought of the terrifying powers they wielded.

Now with his senatorial tenure about to come to a quick and deadly finish, the man struggled in hindsight and wished he kept himself from challenging those whose scepters of rule were loftier.

Beyond the louvered windows of his estate, a staircase of lightning struck close by. The lights in the study winked, died, the house then succumbing to darkness as deep and vacuous as a celestial hole.

Feeling his heart misfire to an unsteady beat, the senator realized that the Pieces of Eight were coming for him.

At best he had a minute, maybe two.

5

Hunkering next to his desk with the dossiers held within his twisted hands, the senator pressed a shoulder against the desk's side panel and gave a nudge. The panel slid inward, then upward, giving approach to a small compartment the size of a breadbox. It was an area where he had kept the untold secrets of others and often used the information against them as an aid of blackmail to reshape, retool or destroy the political lives of those who affronted his views.

Now he would use it one last time, hoping that someone would discover the dossiers and use them to destroy the Pieces of Eight and the man who drove their reins.

After the files were placed inside, the senator pulled down on the interior panel and secured it, the seams of the wood matching so closely that the divide of the partition was barely perceptible.

Laboring to his feet with pain beginning to cinch across his chest to the point of crushing the breath from his lungs, the senator placed his knuckled hands against the desktop and steadied himself.

Where are you?

Beyond the blinds, another stroke of lightning flared: a quick and dazzling flash of pure, unadulterated light that poured in through the edges of the closed blinds and bled hotly across the area, the quick strokes catching movement across the room.

The senator stood and waited, expecting the punch of a bullet to end his life.

Instead, he received a comparable blow equal to a bullet's impact; it was the voice of a preadolescent child crying out to him. "Grandpapa?"

Oh, no!

In the mix of his fears, he had forgotten about his grandson, the only living tie to his bloodline and the only family left. If the child were discovered by the Pieces of Eight, they would kill him without mercy by the same protocols he created.

The senator got to a bended knee and beckoned his grandson to rush into his outstretched arms. Pulling his grandson close, his gnarled hands caressing the child, the senator kept repeating 'I'm so sorry,' and wept into the wild tangle of the boy's hair.

"Grandpapa, are you afraid of the lightning, too?"

The child sounded so innocent that the impending nature of what was going to happen to them crushed the senator's blighted soul.

"I'm so sorry," the senator whispered as he buried his face against

6

the crown of the boy's head. "I'm . . . so . . . sorry."

At that moment, he noted the shared features of his daughter within the boy as he appraised him, the child possessing the eyes and lips of his mother, beautiful and petulantly full. "You look so much like your mother," he told him. *Oh, how I wish she were here to see how much you've grown.*

Two years ago, his daughter was driving along a causeway when a drunk driver caromed off a barrier and struck her vehicle head-on, killing her the moment her body made its trajectory through the windshield. In the tragic aftermath, the coroner painstakingly pieced her together. But it was not enough for the aesthetic appeal needed for an open coffin viewing.

It was also the first time in the senator's life where he'd been rendered completely powerless to reshape the outcome of an event. Even with all his command, the senator quickly realized that he was limited in capacity with resurrection regrettably not one of his strengths; therefore, this painful lesson drove him back to the status of a mortal with perceived weaknesses.

But as a man of steadfast conviction, he tempered the loss of his daughter by burying his remorse deep and regained momentum, his power going unchecked as his sense of invincibility rose once again to the surface with the senator becoming a political demigod who ruled over others without the impression of impunity or consequence.

Until now.

The old man closed his eyes and rubbed a hand adoringly along his grandson's back.

Then taking on a more sobering appearance, the senator grabbed the child firmly by his triceps to let him know that anything less than undivided attention was unacceptable. "Markie, I need you to listen to me and I need you to listen good and hard. Do you understand me?"

The boy nodded.

"I want you to find a hiding place," he told him. "I want you to hide from the lightning and the thunder. And no matter what, no matter what you see or hear, you are not to come out from your hiding place. Is that clear?"

"Grandpa—"

"Is that clear, Markie?"

"Yes." The boy was frightened, and his chin shook with a gelatinous quiver that prompted the senator to pull him into a hug.

"I love you, Markie. Never forget that. I love you more than life itself." And then he drew back and held his grandson in regarded appraisal for the last time, wondering what kind of man he might have become if granted the time to live.

From the area of the entryway came a sound, the tiny snicker of the bolt being drawn back, and then the subsequent following of the study's doorknob turning slowly in the darkness.

The senator directed the child with a mild goading toward the darkest area of the room. "Quick, Markie. Hide. And don't come out."

As the child ran towards the darkest shadows of the study, the senator labored to his feet with the stiff joints of his knees popping off in protest, and then he waited with a warrior's stoicism as he held his chin brazenly outward in defiance.

The moment the door swung slowly inward on its own accord a silver-mercury flash of lightning exploded throughout the entire estate, divulging an empty doorway before the flashes died off.

The senator swallowed because his throat was as dry as old parchment.

Then, in a warbled tone that sounded unlike the voice of a poised senator, he said, "Show yourselves."

Upon the utterance of his final word a stroke of lightning flashed on cue, igniting the world in a flare that revealed the Pieces of Eight.

Each master soldier stood as still as a Grecian statue before him.

In their unique design, they were eight elite commandos with each one possessing a very particular skill. Collectively, they were a deadly ensemble of skilled assassins better known to the Joint Chiefs of Staff as the Force Elite.

They were spread across the room, one soldier a facsimile of the other with waxy faces and stone-cold deadness in their eyes.

No one moved.

No one spoke.

Their military issue was black adornment with unpolished boots and a black beret bearing the team's insignia of two crossing tantos serving as crossbones beneath a grinning skull wearing the same assigned beret.

My children . . .

Once the lightning died off, the Pieces of Eight became one with the darkness.

"How can you do this to me?" The senator took a step back as an act of self-preservation. "I created you! I created *all* of you!"

Outside, a loud report of thunder sounded off, which soon melted away to an awkward silence that seemed to last countless moments.

And then with the bravado of an all-powerful senator, Cartwright said, "I demand you answer me!"

The louvered blinds did little to block out the light as lightning once again lit up the study with a spectacular burst that was ethereal in its effects. In that brief moment, the senator saw his assassin's face inches from his, then he felt the shallowness of the man's breath graze against his flesh and noted the profound hollowness within his eyes.

He never heard the assassin approach, nor did he hear the others leave the room.

He was alone with his killer.

"Where have the others gone?" he muttered, his head searching his surroundings. Was it possible for the Pieces of Eight to move so quickly, so quietly, and so fluidly without leaving so much as a trace that they had been there at all?

"You know the protocol," the assassin told him. "No one is to be left behind."

"Then they'll be disappointed," he answered, "because there's nobody else here."

"There is the boy." The assassin proffered this so coldly and without feeling or remorse, the senator knew they would complete their mission with unbiased obligation and kill anyone under an executive order, even a child.

"My grandson is not here," he reported too quickly.

Another stroke of lightning, the starburst moment providing a glimpse of the face of the man that held nothing more than indifference. His features were young and seamless, his skintight over angular cheekbones and an even firmer jawline; he was tall, standing six-four with a physique engineered in the weight room with arms, chest, and shoulders defined by long hours in the gym. He was also a prodigy in a line of killers and the most junior of his team.

"Please," the senator whispered. "I created you. I created the entire team. Without me, the Force Elite would be nothing."

In the darkness, the senator could hear the slow draw of a combat knife being pulled from its scabbard.

"You overstepped your boundaries, Senator."

"So now you see it fit to be my assassin?"

"I'm simply following orders from higher command. You know that . . . And you know why."

The senator backpedaled with his hands held up in front of him in supplication. "Please don't hurt my grandson," he pleaded in earnest. "All I ask of you is to let him be."

"If I did that, then I would be remiss in my duties."

"He's a six-year-old boy, dammit!"

"He's also a threat."

The room flared up once again. In the assassin's hand was a KA-BAR knife, a keen edge on one side of the blade, a serrated sharpness on the other.

"I found you—made you what you are today," the senator said. "Will you destroy the one who made you the very heart of the Pieces of Eight and the lead commander of the Force Elite?"

The assassin said nothing. He merely edged closer, the blade poised to strike, to slash, to kill. Then, "As a courtesy to you, Senator, I'll make this a quick kill." With that, he swept the KA-BAR in a horizontal arc and cut the senator's throat, a deep gash that parted like a second horrible grin, the blood a pronounced color of red in the subsequent flashes of lightning as the senator brought a gnarled hand to his neck in eagle-clawed fashion. The other hand swept the darkness for the purchase of the desk's edge, his world spiraling in a maelstrom of pooling shadows with a greater gloom meeting him from the depths.

Just as he found the edge, the senator fell to his knees and drew his bloodied hand across the panel. It was his last act before dying, the mark a final score as a tenured politician.

The moment the senator's life bled out at the feet of his assassin; the killer began his search of the study.

Those dossiers, he knew, had to be here somewhere.

The child had heard the exchange from his seated position within the cabinet space beneath the library bookshelves—had heard his grandfather plead for his life. And then he heard the horrible sound of a man trying to breathe through the wetness of his fount that arced through the ruin of his throat.

Soon thereafter the silence became terrifying to the young child, the idea of not knowing what was going on beyond the cabinet door bringing a need to cry out to his grandfather, despite the old man's warning.

And then the footsteps: soft, light and weightless across the carpeted floor, the footfalls coming closer to the bookshelves, toward the cabinet door.

Grandpapa?

Surrounding doors opened and closed, encouraging the child to bring his knees up into acute angles and flush to his chest. And then he folded his arms across his legs to draw himself into a tighter mass. The act, however, was not just an exercise of self-preservation; it was also a futile measure as the door to the cabinet opened.

The child looked over his kneecaps, his cheeks wet with coursing tears, his tiny chest heaving and pitching with silent sobbing.

The assassin looked at him pensively for a long moment, their eyes meeting.

In the whitewash of lightning that lit the study, the boy saw his grandfather propped idle against the side of the desk with his eyes at half-mast, and the front of his shirt glistening with the redness of candied apple. Following the child's gaze, the assassin noted that the boy's sight was alighting upon the senator. And then he returned his focus to the child.

As the assassin looked in, as the child looked out, lightning strokes engaged in swordplay that seemed to light up the area longer than usual. In the assassin's hand was the knife, which the boy directed his attention on. And then he understood: the knife, the senator's blood-stained shirt, the man wielding the weapon.

And then the boy shook his head violently from side to side in a gesture of 'no-no-no-no-no.'

At that moment, the assassin reached into the recess, placed a soothing hand on top of the child's head, then he brought it down to gently caress the boy's cheek. Without saying a word, the assassin withdrew his hand and softly closed the door, leaving the boy to wonder.

The boy was allowed to live.

Several hours after the storm subsided, with the morning sky the color of slate gray and filled with the promise of more rain, the child emerged from the cubbyhole of the cabinet and crawled his way toward his grandfather, who lay against the blood-streaked desk.

"Grandpapa?"

The child grabbed the old man's arm, felt the stiffness of rigor settling in.

"Oh, Grandpapa." And then he began to weep, feeling entirely alone.

After the child cried himself emotionless, he noted the bloodstain across the desk panel which had become his hiding place so many times he and his grandfather played games of hide-and-seek. It was the panel of secrets.

Moving the panel, he saw tied folders within, eight in all, the secrets of monsters. Pulling them out one by one, he studiously peeled back the pages of the folders and committed the photos and histories of those within to memory.

Even at the age of six, he vowed that he would never forget their faces.

CHAPTER TWO

Present Day, Vatican City

Monsignor Dom Giammacio was the Vatican's counselor for clerics who wallowed in the self-doubt of their waning faith. Most often they went to him to reaffirm their own 'unconscionable' belief that questioning the existence of God was not a fatal sin. And perhaps with some pro-pious readjustment could fall back into His Fatherly graces. In the monsignor's point of view, if they feared Him on some level, even in their queried state of mind, then it could be logically stated that they at least believed Him to some degree. After all, why fear something that did not exist?

But today was marginally different, as was every Monday at this time.

In front of the monsignor sat an obtrusively large man who fiercely raked the cleric with cerulean blue eyes whenever the priest attempted to open a dialogue with him, the man always an unwilling participant in the course of such examinations. But at the direction of the pontiff, the man appealed to the wishes of His Holiness by addressing underlying issues regarding his constantly warring subconscious.

He was large and tall with a wide expanse of shoulder and chest. His massive anatomical design was even more pronounced by the tight fit of the cleric's shirt he wore, the cloth stretched to its limit. And though he wore the Roman Catholic collar as a symbol of his faith, he struggled at the core of his divine devotion.

Unlike others, he was not a priest or a cleric or a man of pious nature, but a Vatican Knight in the service of the pope who was delegated to preserve the interests of the Holy Roman Church. When necessary, he and his elite force of commandos would perform black op missions selected by the pontiff and six of his most trusted and ascribed cardinals known as the Society of Seven. Outside the 'Society,' the monsignor was one of few beyond the circle who knew

13

of their existence and thusly informed to keep matters confidential. Not only were the Vatican Knights to remain a secretive conclave of elite commandos in service to the Church, but they were also to remain so exclusive that they could not even be considered as mythology. Never will the Vatican Knights be made public, since their efforts to achieve the means were sometimes less than charitable. War, after all, possessed a dark side.

Quietly lighting a cigarette, the monsignor let it burn in the ashtray as a lazy ribbon of smoke drifted into the air. After tenting his fingers and easing back into his seat, he turned to Kimball Hayden who sat opposite him. The glower he received from the Vatican Knight was quite communicable: *Let's get this damn thing over with.* The sentiment in the man's expression was quite explicit in that he did not want to be here holding psychological counsel. But neither man had a choice, due to the appeal from the pope.

For a moment they stared at each other waiting for the other to start the session. But over time it had become a battle of wills with the monsignor always giving in. It was a game he never won.

"Let's begin, Mr. Hayden, shall we?"

Kimball sat there appraising the little man with the bad comb-over, which never failed to bring a preamble of a pretentious smirk to Kimball's lips.

"Mr. Hayden—"

"Kimball," he said. "I want you to call me Kimball." He really didn't, but it was a power play on his part to establish authority.

"All right, Kimball. If that's what you want."

He arched an eyebrow. "It's what I want."

The monsignor left his cigarette smoldering in the ashtray as they pinned each other with unwavering stares.

"And how would you like to start with today's session?" the monsignor finally asked.

"As I do at the beginning of every session," he stated. "By saying, I find this to be a huge waste of my time."

"Then why don't you tell that to the pope? Or do you lack the courage?"

Kimball eased back into his chair, impressed that the monsignor had challenged him. For the moment, the Knight conceded. "Please accept my apology, Monsignor. I guess you don't want to be here anymore than I do," he answered.

14

"It's not a matter of what I want," he returned. "It's a matter of you finding what it is you seek, which is the truth of faith versus fate . . . You're no different from anybody else who walks through my door."

Kimball closed his eyes in resignation while his once obstinate will was bleeding away by the inches, which was a promising sign to the monsignor.

So, the cleric led the Knight into a conversation. "Several months ago," he began, "you aided in a mission to save the pope's life, yes?"

Kimball opened his eyes, nodded.

"And in the process of engagement with opposing forces, you had to kill, yes?"

Another nod—a small tilt of his chin in affirmation.

The monsignor leaned closer. "Now, you're conflicted because what you did is inconsistent with Church doctrine regarding the killing of another, yes?"

Kimble hesitated.

"And now you are afraid that what you did for your government so many years ago as an assassin and what you do now for the Church, bears no difference and that the Lord has already condemned you with no chance for salvation, yes?"

A nerve had been struck. Kimball's line of sight made a slow and downward trajectory to the floor.

The monsignor grabbed the burning cigarette and wedged it between his fingers, the smoke rising in tight, corkscrewing trails. "I know you seek salvation for past actions," he told him. "And I know the redemption you seek seems impossible to obtain with your current actions contradictory to what the Church calls for, which is to be the salvation for others when, for this to happen, you sometimes have to kill so that others may live. Therefore, in your mind's eye, if you go on killing, then how is it possible for you to gain deliverance and passage into Heaven? Are these not the questions?"

The monsignor hit another mark in Hayden's view.

"Are these not the questions?" he repeated.

Kimball nodded.

"Then why do you do it?"

Kimball sat in reflection as his eyes took on a detached gaze and stared at an imaginary point beyond the cleric, his mind focusing on a mental illustration of something past. "I'm sure what I'm about to say you probably already know since I'm sure you read my file. But I'm going to tell you anyway." There was a brief hesitation, his focus turning back to the reality of the moment with cerulean blue eyes so clear it enabled the monsignor to see secrets in their depths. What he saw was the constant warring between solemn regret and subdued rage, one emotion trying to best the other.

"Several years ago," Kimball said with sorrowful inflection, "while on a covert mission for the United States government, I was dispatched to Iraq to eradicate a top official within the Iraqi government . . ."

The monsignor didn't press him. He simply waited for Kimball to choose his moment.

And for that moment Kimball seemed to have difficulty trying to articulate his thoughts to words, but ultimately continued, his eyes moving toward the ceiling as if his memories were somehow scribed there in the text, a written aid to refer upon. "While in Iraq I came upon two young boys herding goats," he said. "And they saw me . . . So, I took the only available action to keep them from compromising my position."

"So, you killed them." This was not a question, but a confirmation of what the monsignor already knew.

"That night after I buried them, I looked into the sky and saw so many stars—something I never did before—and wondered if there was anything beyond this place." He then raised his hands to indicate his surroundings. "And then I looked for the face of God, looking for any sign or suggestions that He truly existed. The only thing I saw was the stardust glitter of designs and constellations. And then it occurred to me that I had become what the government made me out to be— something without conscience, remorse, and without feeling. It was a label I was proud of until that very moment."

"Perhaps the face of God came in the essence of enabling you to confront the truth about yourself by discovering your conscience. After all, the true design of God is not how we see Him, but how we imagine Him to be," said the monsignor. "For it is said that God has many faces, but only one voice. In you, Kimball, your epiphany was God's embracement of you, don't you see? You did not see Him, but your soul heard Him."

Kimball didn't answer.

"Sometimes, Kimball, epiphanies come in the strangest ways. The killing of the children was the enlightenment to your true nature."

"Then tell me this," said Kimball. "How can God condone the

16

killing of children?"

The monsignor stared back for a moment before answering. "Do you feel repentant for that action?"

"Of course."

"Then that's your answer. God forgives those who are truly repentant for their sins. And because of your true repentance, He embraced you on that night."

Kimball gnawed on his lower lip. It was amazing how such a heinous act could be so easily explained away and justified. It was no different than the mindset of suicide bombers.

"Kimball?"

Hayden met the monsignor's gaze.

"Do you feel that saving the pope on your last mission was in the interest of the Catholic nation?"

"I do."

"Do you feel that Pope Pius is a good man?"

Kimball didn't know where the monsignor was going. "Yes, of course."

"And those who took him, do you consider them to be good men?"

"Not in my opinion."

The monsignor nodded. "So, you took action against *these* men" — The monsignor lifted his hands with a cigarette still burning between the fingers of one hand, and with his middle and forefingers of both hands flexed the digits in a gesture of italics when emphasizing the word 'these'— "to save the life of the pontiff who has nothing but peace as his primary goal, yes?"

Kimball sighed. "Are you coming to a point?"

"My point, Kimball, is a simple one. Before the incident in Iraq with the two shepherd boys, you killed men because it was obligatory and because you *wanted* to. Am I right so far, at least from what I know of your past as a government assassin?"

Kimball hesitated, then, "So far."

"But in killing those men to save the pope's life, was it because you *wanted* to? Or was it because you *had* to?"

Kimball considered this for a moment as the monsignor homed in with careful study, his spectacled eyes reminiscent like the lenses of a microscope, his demeanor that of scientific appraisal.

While working as a black-op assassin for a group attached to the CIA, Kimball killed out of commitment. In the sense of Vatican convention, however, he killed if a peaceful solution was not soluble and self-defense his only option.

"And there's the difference," the monsignor intuited. "You *used* to kill because you were amenable to the opportunity. But the moment you became an emissary of the Church as a Vatican Knight and staying true to your epiphany and remaining repentant for past sins, you now take life not because you want to . . . but because you *have* to. Saving the life of the pope can only be viewed as a necessity borne from goodness, despite the harsh methods taken to achieve the means. Even God sees the right of good men to champion the cause as a savior for those who cannot defend themselves against uncontested evil."

For a brief moment, Kimball's emotions vacillated from gratefulness to subdued anger. Gratefulness because the monsignor justified Kimball's actions as a necessity of the Church if the actions were conducted in a principled manner. And subdued anger because terrorists conduct their deadly missions under the same so-called principled banner of their God, easily justifying their heinous crimes the same way the monsignor was easily explaining away Kimball's killings as justifiable. It was all in the matter of viewpoint and perspective of what one faction's principle should be. But Kimball saw no difference since one thing was certain in war: both sides always believed to be correct, even though their principles were miles apart. How easy it was to explain things away and justify them at the same time, he thought.

"I don't think salvation lies at my end," he proposed.

The monsignor fell back into his seat and stamped the cigarette out in the ashtray, his gaze remaining studious as he again tented his hands in steeple fashion. "Salvation lies at everyone's end," he told him. "And the mystery of what lies beyond will be answered upon the moment of death for everyone. But you have to have faith, Kimball. You need to start believing in the good in yourself, rather than dwell on a past laden with the sinful wage of pride. Now I believe you when you say you're truly repentant for past sins, but yet you can't seem to forgive yourself in your own eyes when you have already been forgiven in the eyes of God."

"That, Monsignor, is because I don't believe that anyone can justify terrible acts with simple faith in what we believe God thinks is right. I believe it goes much deeper than that."

"And that, Kimball, is why you need to see beyond the box and realize that you need to step further away from the darkness you lived in for so long, and step closer to the Light. You may be a high-ranking member in the eyes of Vatican principals, but you are also a man who is very detached from God."

"That's because I have seen too much of the real world, Monsignor. And I participated in many things I'm not proud of, things that will make me a castaway on Judgment Day."

"Perhaps, Kimball, you need to put aside your doubts and open up to Him."

"You try to make it sound so easy, Monsignor. But it's not."

"At least give it a try," he said. "Go back to your chamber and open up to Him. Pray to God and ask Him to hear you out."

Kimball shook his head in a nonplussed manner. "Can I ask you something?"

"Yes, of course."

"Have you ever killed a man?"

The monsignor's eyes widened into a brief flare, the question catching him off guard. "Lord no, of course not."

Kimball leaned forward. "When you do, then you can tell me the secret of keeping the memories of those you killed buried so deep they'll never show up in the middle of the night as horrific images while you're sleeping, and then drive a scream from your throat."

The monsignor's shoulders dropped. "Kimball, I can't perform magic. And I'm not going to make that you see a new direction within a few sessions. That's understandable. But you have to help yourself as well. Although repentance is the first step, you need to open yourself up to Him and embrace Him." He undid the steeple of his fingers and reached for a cigarette. "All I ask is that you open yourself up and pray with true conviction. That's all I'm asking . . . Just for now. Let's start with that."

Kimball sat idle, unwilling to state whether or not he intended to try. He truly didn't know at this point.

"A week from today," said the monsignor. "Same time as usual. And please don't be late like you were this afternoon."

Kimball stood, his towering frame looking down upon the monsignor's bad comb-over until the monsignor got to his feet and offered his hand, which Kimball took in a crushing grip.

"Good luck, Kimball. If you take time to forget the past rather than reliving it, you may find the Light."

"I'll take prayer into consideration," he finally said.

"Good. And can I ask you one more thing?"

"Sure."

"Can you stop shaking my hand? You're hurting it."

Kimball released the cleric's hand and left the office, leaving behind a lobby filled with clerics waiting to see the monsignor.

CHAPTER THREE

Kimball's chamber was located next to the Tower of San Giovanni at the west end of Vatican City, approximately 200 meters west of St. Peter's Basilica. The room itself was small, the ceiling high, with the walls made of slump stone the color of desert sand. It was so spartan that the room bore little else except for a cross that hung above a small window that overlooked the magnificent Lourdes Gardens. Against the far wall lay a single-sized bed with a nightstand, light, and shelves lined with military texts and journals. Closer to the door was a kneeling rail and votive rack for prayer, the candles had gone unlit, and the kneeling rail unused. Although exclusive of luxury comforts, it was still home to the Master of the Vatican Knights.

Closing the door behind him, Kimball crossed the floor with myriad thoughts swimming in his head after meeting with the monsignor, and sat on the edge of the bed, the frame bowing slightly beneath his weight. For the first time, he had taken the session to heart, the monsignor's insight bearing the frank truthfulness that the Light was not going to come to him, but he must make a viable effort to go to the Light.

Closing his eyes and raising his chin, the muscles of his jaw working, Kimball decided: He would pray. He rose from the bed and went to the kneeling pad before the votive rack and got on his knees. After striking a match, he lit two votive candles in homage to the two Vatican Knights who lost their lives during an earlier mission. He lit the candles for Hosea and Malachi, lost friends and comrades.

Closing his eyes and clasping his hands in an attitude of prayer, he tried to recite the 'Lord's Prayer,' only to forget the words after the preamble of the first six words of the prayer were spoken. So, he tried his hand with the 'Hail Mary.' But after forgetting the words beyond the first sentence he subsequently gave up, considering himself to be the worst Catholic in the world since he couldn't recall a simple prayer.

21

And then he opened his eyes and noted the serene curl of black smoke rising from the candles' wicks. Their motion was gentle and fluid, like the composites that once made up his friends—yet the flames could be caustic when need be. And then he wondered if the former Knights made it to the ethereal Light, then questioned if there was a Light at all. What Kimball needed to believe in was to see something far more wonderful beyond the pain and madness of killing, something well beyond the darkness in which he had spent his entire life.

What he wanted was peace.

Closing his eyes, he once again prayed. Not in idle words that were written on the pages of text to be recited without feeling or emotion, but words from his heart and soul. He spoke in whispers and hushed tones, wondering if He was listening, and asked for forgiveness for the lives he had stolen without remorse.

However, in the aftermath of prayer came the passage of silence.

No feathers floated down from the ceiling, thunder did not sound off in the clear blue sky, nor did he receive any sign that God was even listening. Believing his fate had been determined, he surrendered his attempt of good faith by blowing out the candles.

"Well, so much for praying, Monsignor. At least I tried."

Getting to his feet, Kimball crossed the short space to his bed and fell onto the mattress, the bed whining in protest beneath his weight.

With strong light coming in through the window, he lay on the bed with his hands behind his head and stared at the pieces of leaded glass that formed the colorful figure of the Virgin Mother, who reached out to him with outstretched arms that glowed in the mid-day light.

With silence filling the room, Kimball Hayden turned away from the image and fell into a much-needed sleep.

CHAPTER FOUR

Manila, Philippines

Twelve years ago, his legs had been taken above the knees.

Twelve years later, Marshall Theodore Walker, who was once an assassin with the Pieces of Eight, went commercial after the Force Elite disbanded.

In a small apartment five stories above the busy and chaotic streets overlooking Manila, Walker awoke in a wild tangle of sheets that had gone unwashed for several weeks. Through the windows, he could hear the busy Filipino marketplace below, as vendors sold butchered strips of meat, gutted fish, and fruit.

Sitting up in bed with his hair naturally unkempt and his eyes at half-mast, Walker stared at the stumps of his legs and recalled the exact moment of their loss.

As a consultant with a private military company in Iraq during the onset of the war, he was riding point during a recon mission in the Al Anbar Province, when the vehicle he was in tripped an IED. In a fiery flash, the floor of the Humvee buckled upward into the cab as shrapnel as keen as surgical steel sliced through everything, including the bones of his legs in such neat precision that there were no ragged tears, mutilated muscle or jagged bones—simply perfect saw-blade cuts.

When he came to, he found his team dead, sliced and burned, the vehicle twisted around him like a protective capsule. Where they had died, Walker had lived. And often he found himself wishing he had followed his comrades to Glory.

Closing his eyes, he sighed in the way of regret, the memories as vivid as the day the IED took his legs. The pain, the phantom itches, none of it fading or going away, the scars—real and imagined—a constant reminder of that life-altering moment in the Province.

Living mainly off a small government allowance, he pissed away most of it on cheap booze, low rent, and Filipina whores, all the sum of his life. And now he awoke with a headache, an empty bottle of some indigent liquor he couldn't even pronounce on the nightstand beside him.

Scooting down along the bed, Walker maneuvered himself into position, propped himself into his wheelchair, and made his way across a room that was a fetid wasteland of dirty clothes and empty bottles.

When he got to the kitchen, he felt something that had been lost to him that day in Al Anbar—that impression of an animal sensing great danger.

In the center of the kitchen, he paused, waited, and listened.

Nothing but the Manila crowds in the streets below plying their wares.

And yet: *I know you're here.*

With his head on a swivel, his eyes aware, Walker reached for a Glock taped beneath the kitchen table.

But the holster was empty.

Clever creature, aren't you?

In a movement that was so swift and from shadows so dense, something moved across the room with such speed and poetic grace that the action was gloriously beautiful.

It was also the last thing Walker considered before being rendered unconscious with a blow to the head.

When Walker came to he found himself face down on the kitchen table with his arms draped over the sides and his wrists bound to the table's legs with duct tape. He was bound so tightly that he was rendered immobile and, having partial legs, had no leverage to move.

He rolled his head to one side, kept it there, his eyes trying to tune in, to focus, his world now coming to a crisp clarity, the things around him beginning to take on definition and form.

A man he did not recognize sat next to the table, watching. His eyes were so dark they seemed without pupils, yet they were studious and patient and somehow terrifyingly omniscient. His face was highly rawboned with a lantern jaw and powerful chin.

The man, seeing Walker's eyes coming up to meet his, held up an 8x10 photo. "Do you know what this is?"

Walker passed a dry tongue over parched lips. "Who are you?"

24

"Do you know what this is?" the man repeated.

Walker studied the photo and recognized it as a photo of his old unit, the Pieces of Eight. In it he was much younger and whole, everyone hamming it up for the camera except for Kimball Hayden, the man presumably without a conscience or a sense of remorse.

"What do you want?"

The man held the photo close. "Take another look."

Walker noted that he and two others were circled with a red marker. "Yeah . . . So?"

"The other two, I know they're working for a private military outfit as consultants here in the Philippines. I need to know where they are. And you're going to tell me."

"You think so, huh? Well, you can just kiss my fat ass. How 'bout that?"

"Where are they, Mr. Walker?"

"You know something, you little punk? You're a real tough guy taking on a cripple, you know that? If you took me on when I was in the condition that I was in in that photo, you'd be a dead man."

"I'm well aware of the Pieces of Eight and I hardly doubt, Mr. Walker, even during your prime, that you'd be able to match my skills as an assassin."

"Tough talk coming from a man who's whole. How about you undo the tape so we can see how well you fare against a cripple not tied down? Or are you too much of a pussy to find out?"

"Mr. Walker . . . where are they?"

"And why should I tell you?"

The man remained tolerant, and then in monotone, "Look at me, Mr. Walker." From the cargo pocket of his BDU uniform, he pulled out a silver cylinder and depressed a button. A pick shot out like the blade of a stiletto. Its tip keenly pointed and honed to a razor's sharpness.

"Is that supposed to scare me?"

"No, Mr. Walker, it's a tool, really—a writing pen, as you will."

"What?"

The man held the blade over Walker's naked backside.

"What are you doing?"

"Please, Mr. Walker, remain still." The man set the pick's tip against Walker's shoulder blade, the embedded point drawing a bead of crimson. "This will only take a moment." And then he drew the pick across his back, a neat slice running from shoulder blade to shoulder blade.

Walker arched his back against the pain, his teeth clenching in protest until the muscles in his jaw worked furiously.

But he refused to cry out.

"Very good, Mr. Walker, a true warrior never shouts out in pain, does he?"

"Oh, you son-of-a-bitch! Untie me and take me on like a man!"

The assassin held the photo towards Walker. "Mr. Grenier and Mr. Arruti—tell me where they are."

"What do you want with them?"

"Isn't it apparent, Mr. Walker? I want to kill them."

Walker laughed condescendingly. "Are you out of your mind?"

The man carefully placed the point of the pick against the center point of the horizontal slash, and drew the sharpened point downward along the spinal column to the small of his back, the drawing cuts forming a perfect T.

Walker arched again, his face as red as the blood that coursed from his wounds and onto the table, the veins of his neck sticking out in cords. "YOU . . . BASTARD!"

"That was close to crying out, Mr. Walker. Not the true sign of a warrior, is it?"

"Piss off!"

"Arruti and Grenier, where are they?"

Walker laughed.

"Mr. Walker?"

His laughter escalated.

"Very well, then." The man placed the tip of the pick against the small of Walker's back and drew a horizontal line, the three slices now forming the letter I.

Walker's body tensed against the pain. And then through the set of his clenched teeth, he said, "You want to know where they are?"

The man waited patiently with the point of the pick stained with red.

"I'll tell you. I'll be glad to tell you . . . And do you want to know why I'll be glad to tell you?"

The man held the pick high, the steel cylinder throwing off a mirror polish.

"Because they're going to rip you to pieces," he told him. "It doesn't matter if they know you're coming or not. They'll smell you. They'll sense you. They'll feel you . . . And then they'll kill you."

"Where are they?"

Walker was fading, his voice weakening. "You'll find them in Maguindanao consulting against the terrorist factions there."

"Thank you, Mr. Walker."

"I'll see you in Hell."

"That's unlikely." The man placed the point of the pick at the base of Walker's skull and forced the point upward through the opening of the brain stem and into the brain, killing him.

As Walker's body deflated, the man expelling a final breath that cleared his lungs, he soon fell into the gentle repose of death.

The man, after watching Walker transition from life to death, pressed the button on the cylinder. The pick quickly retreated into the tube faster than the eye could see.

Placing the weapon into a cargo pocket of his pants, the man removed a red marker, wrote the letter 'I' in the circled picture of Walker, and left the photo behind.

The assassin would be in Maguindanao Province within hours.

CHAPTER FIVE

Cotabato City, Philippines

Cotabato City in Mindanao is a municipality of roughly a quarter-million people with a high Muslim population. It is also a city of growing insurgency where al-Qaeda and the Taliban were taking root—the area becoming the 'New Afghanistan' of the Pacific Rim.

Five years ago, when The Blackmill Corporation became employed by the Philippine government as a freelance consulting firm from the United States, the government was hiring high-tech mercenaries to help counteract the spread of revolutionary idealism that was becoming a blight to the small island nation. And Cotabato City, which bordered the guerilla strongholds thirty kilometers to the south, served as the company's command post.

In a small, smoke-filled bar that smelled of sweat and cheap cigarettes that did little to mask that stench, War Consultants David Arruti and Sim Grenier sat at a table in the back of the establishment knocking back a few shots of whisky.

Although in their forties they remained in good shape, keeping their bodies regimentally fit. Of the two Arruti looked more like the aggressor with a handlebar mustache, shaved head, and powerhouse arms that were exposed from a sleeveless shirt. Sim Grenier, however, looked like the corporate thinker—a man of good dress, even though a huge Rorschach moth of perspiration spread out to meet the overflow from his armpits of a neatly pressed shirt—who always kept his hair nicely coiffed in such high humidity.

Whenever they banded together, they spoke little of the past when they were a part of the Pieces of Eight. Instead, they spoke of the future and about guerilla insurgencies in Mindanao. They often spoke of strategies and counter-offensives, as well as the beneficial possibilities their success may bring to the people of the Philippines.

But little did they speak of the past.

On the opposite side of the room, a male wearing a camouflaged boonie cap sat alone at a table with a glass of water. He appeared to be focused on a Blackberry-type device, punching buttons with a stylus, his surroundings oblivious to him.

However, he did not go without notice.

Grenier kept a watchful eye on the man who appeared without concern.

"Yeah, I saw him too," said Arruti. "He's been here for about an hour, and he hasn't taken a sip of his water."

"He's not a part of our units?"

"No."

"Tell me, what is a Caucasian male doing this close to the Mindanao territory knowing full well he could become a target for kidnappers?"

"Maybe he doesn't know."

"There're government warnings posted everywhere, especially for travelers."

Arruti kicked back a shot of whisky. "Not my problem if people want to be stupid."

At a nearby table, two Filipinos began to argue in earnest about the outcome of a card game and the pot, about thirty cigarettes. As the yelling subsided, Arruti and Grenier turned and immediately took note that the man was gone. The glass of water was still there, untouched. Beneath the glass was a photo, an 8x10 glossy.

They scanned the entire bar, necks craning, turning. The man was gone like a wraith, becoming a part of the cigarette smoke that was everywhere, thick and cloying.

"Curious," Arruti murmured.

When the barmaid went to clean the table, she picked up the photo, scrutinized it, looked at the two consultants, and then headed for their table.

With a beautiful smile, perfectly lined teeth, and cocoa-tanned skin, she approached them holding the face of the photo in their direction. Even from a distance of ten feet, they could see it was a picture of their old unit, the Pieces of Eight.

The Filipina, who was adorably cute and doubled as a bargirl who enticed the Blackmill employees for American dollars to screw on a stained mattress in the upstairs loft, handed the photo to Grenier. "Mr. Sim, on the back it says to give to you."

Grenier took it, and then passed it off to Arruti who examined it long and hard. He and Grenier were circled in red marker. Walker had been X'ed out.

The barmaid began to rotate her hips in sexual innuendo, and then she began to run a tongue over her luscious lips. "Maybe when I'm done, you can take me upstairs?"

Grenier feigned a smile. "Not tonight, my love. Maybe some other time."

The barmaid offered a petulant pout and then smiled. "OK, Mr. Sim. Some other time, then." With an enticing swagger to her gait, she returned to the table and began to clean it with a filthy rag.

Grenier watched her movements from the waist down as Arruti continued to examine the photo.

And then from Arruti, in a voice sounding so definite and so evenly calm that there was no doubt of the certainly in his statement, said, "We're being targeted."

Grenier sighed. "We need to check on Walker."

He flipped the photo to the tabletop. "He's already dead."

"We don't know that."

"Maybe you don't, but I do." Arruti got to his feet, all six-foot-four of him, and reached for a Glock that was situated in the back of his beltline and racked it. "He's calling us out, Sim."

Grenier stood and checked his weapon, a Smith and Wesson .40, then felt for the sheath of the KA-BAR knife straddled to his right thigh. "Then let's not disappoint him."

The streets of Cotabato City were well lit beneath the multiple coils of neon lighting. Yet there were recesses deeply shadowed, alleyways opening into complete and utter darkness.

It was also a place of opposites: light and dark, good and evil, life and death, all within a span of a few blocks.

Standing beneath a circular pool of light, Grenier and Arruti openly screwed suppressors onto their weapons.

"You take the left side and I'll take the right," said Arruti. "And don't kill him. I want to question this guy."

Without adding a word Grenier took the left side of the avenue, his weapon held firmly against his thigh.

Arruti did the same on the right side, his weapon ready for the quick draw.

As they moved slowly through the dense Filipino crowd, Arruti came upon the mouth of the alleyway.

Approximately twenty feet in, where the light of visibility ends and a wall of darkness began, someone stood at the fringe of illumination, watching.

"Simon Grenier." It was the Caucasian's voice. "Or would you prefer that I call you Sim?"

Grenier took a step forward, the Shape a step back, deeper into darkness.

"What are you afraid of, mate?"

"Hardly a fair fight when you're carrying a firearm."

"You mean the same kind of fairness you showed Walker?"

"Walker's fate was written the moment the IED took his legs."

"That's your justification for taking out an invalid?"

Grenier took another step forward, his hand working to better his grip on the Smith and Wesson. The Shape retreated another step.

"Tell me something," said Grenier. "Who are you?"

The Caucasian remained silent, and then he gracefully fell back into the shadows until he was eclipsed by them.

Grenier felt uneasy knowing he was completely exposed, the Smith and Wesson having little value when his target went unseen—a target Arruti wanted alive. In feline motion he went for the nearest point of salvation, a recess steeped in gloom, and hunkered down. He was now in his element, he thought—that of Stygian darkness. And because of this, he felt the advantage now belonged to him.

He waited and listened.

And then he began to level his weapon, the point coming up slowly.

And then something ripped through the darkness.

A three-bladed star slice through the air, point over point, like a wheel rolling, with the edges so sharp they could be heard cutting a swath through the air as it made its way towards the target point. With marked precision the star hit the barrel of Grenier's weapon and knocked it from his hand, the weapon skating off into the shadows.

Grenier looked at his open hand in astonishment, fingers flexing, undamaged. And then he turned toward the darkness, the absolute darkness, his one-time friend now holding something far more dangerous.

From its depth, something came forward, a figure that was blacker than black.

"Not so tough without your gun, are you?" The Caucasian's voice was mild.

"I'm tough enough," he answered. Then he withdrew a long-bladed knife from his sheath and fell back to the mouth of the alleyway, and toward the light.

The Caucasian moved closer with his features marginally visible in the feeble lighting.

Grenier held the knife tight. "Who are you?"

"Does it matter?"

"You think you can take me?"

"What I'm going to take, Mr. Grenier, is your life." The Caucasian removed the silver cylinder from his pocket, held it up, and then he depressed the button, causing the pick to shoot outward.

"You're kidding, right? You plan to take me out with an ice pick?"

"What I plan to do, Mr. Grenier, is to kill you with this. And then I'm going to use it to leave a message for the remaining members of the Pieces of Eight."

Grenier nodded as the sudden enlightenment of the assassin's presence became all too clear. "So that's what this is all about, the Pieces of Eight. You're here as the mop-up man for the government to cover up past political transgressions, is that it? After all this time?"

The Caucasian began to spin the cylinder skilfully between his fingers as easily as a majorette spins a baton, the motion truly aesthetic in its performance. "Mr. Grenier, this will be a quick kill. I promise."

The corners of Grenier's lips curled slightly into the beginnings of malicious amusement. "You're cocky, kid. I'll give you that much. Maybe even a little overconfident thinking you can take me down." The former assassin began to move his blade in circular motions. "You have no clue as to what I can do to you with this KA-BAR, do you?"

"Your skills, Mr. Grenier, don't even begin to parallel mine."

"You *are* cocky. But I like that in a soldier, even if you are a green-ear compared to me."

"Please, Mr. Grenier, I will make this quick and painless."

"Yeah, well, unlike you, kid, I'm going to make this *quite* painful for you . . . But not before you tell me what I want to know."

Both men began to circle one other, both grossly intent as they drew a bead on the other while waiting for the opportune moment to make the kill strike.

"Tell me, whose little boy are you?"

The Caucasian did not answer.

Talk was over.

And the time to kill was now.

In a move so deft, so swift, and so clean, the Shape advanced on Grenier with the speed of a wraith, and with the point of the pick zeroing in.

And as promised, the former assassin's death was quick and painless as the pick found its mark with a single piercing.

At the mouth of the alleyway, a crowd gathered.

Filipinos spoke in agitated tones, pointing, Arruti cutting his way through the crowd while stuffing his firearm in his waistband, then pulling out the tail of his shirt to conceal the weapon.

When he forced his way to the front of the crowd his stomach clenched into a slick fist, a feeling he had not felt since he was a newbie drawing blood from the throats of his enemies while conducting his first mission.

Laying face down on the pavement was Grenier in a prone position. The blood from a hidden wound spread outward around his head in a perfect halo, slowly, the fluid as black as tar and as thick as molasses in the quasi-shadows. His shirt was torn and parted. And carved into the flesh of his back was a poorly scribed S, something that looked like the insignia lightning bolt drawn from Himmler's SS, the *Schutzstaffel*. The single engraved bolt was cut into the skin from the scapula to the small of his back. But this mark was not engraved by a Neo-Nazi.

This was just a crudely drawn S created in haste.

Pulling back into the crowd with his head on a swivel, Arruti waded through the masses and raced back to the comfort of his safe house.

At least there he would have the advantage over the assassin, should the assassin decide to follow.

CHAPTER SIX

Arruti was feeling every bit of his forty-five years of age, the run back to the safe house a harsh one given the humidity of the Philippines. Even though he was still in excellent shape, he knew he could not fight the clock forever.

With his soaked shirt clinging to his skin, Arruti leaned against the wall of his one-bedroom apartment and waited for calm. As his chest heaved and pitched in controlled breathing to slow the pace of his rapid heartbeat, he also bore the heavy burden of the loss of a close friend.

After pulling his gun from his waistband and placing it on the counter, he then went to the window and slightly parted the drapes.

Nothing below, nothing above—the streets were often empty in this part of Cotabato.

After letting the curtains fall back into place, he went to the icebox and pulled out a soda, yanking the tab clean. However, when he closed the door, he saw the photos attached to the door. The initial shock caused him to drop the can, the soda spilling everywhere on the yellowed and cracked tile.

The added photos were centered among three of his personalized photos. One of him and Grenier smiling as they held their weapons high in a display of macho attitude, and two with him and Grenier standing alongside a smiling and legless Walker, who sat in his wheelchair. It was a small collage of a Band of Brothers.

The three additional photos were somewhat vulgar in their display. One was of Walker lying tethered to the table with his life having bled out, and the letter 'I' had been carved into his back. The other was of Grenier, a stilled photo capturing the bolt of the 'S' that was sliced into his flesh. The last photo was an old black-and-white glossy of his old unit, the Pieces of Eight. Walker and Grenier had been circled in red marker, the letter 'I' within Walker's circle, the letter 'S' in Grenier's. His face was also circled, but no letter filled its emptiness.

Yet.

Arruti quickly pivoted on the balls of his feet and reached for his weapon on the counter. But the weapon had been broken down. The magazine had been ejected from the weapon and lay on the countertop; the ammo lined up in a perfect roll. The barrel's slide had been separated from its grip and lay on the counter as well, side by side, the weapon now independent pieces rendered inoperable. Oddly enough, the disassembly work was accomplished within a few feet away from him in absolute silence, and all within moments.

How is that even possible?

Behind the counter stood the assassin, watching, his face betraying zero emotion, the face of a killer.

"How did you get in here?"

"Does it matter, Mr. Arruti?"

"No, I guess not."

In a sudden burst of speed that caught the assassin off guard, Arruti circled the counter and extended his leg in a kick that caught the assassin's chest, sending the man in flight until he came crashing down onto a coffee table, smashing it, papers and magazines flying everywhere as the assassin rolled onto his hands and knees, then got to his feet.

"You think you can just walk into my home and take me out?"

When Arruti charged the assassin was ready.

This time, when Arruti threw a sidekick to catch the killer in the temple, the assassin trapped his leg, held it, then threw a quick knuckle jab to Arruti's groin, sending Arruti to a bended knee.

The assassin then took to the air in a gymnast's somersault with his body spinning in a clockwise motion with his leg cutting downward like an ax-blade and catching Arruti on the shoulder. The impact snapped the collar bone and rendered the man's arm useless. In a follow-up motion, the assassin came up and over with his opposite leg and connected with the other shoulder, the bone snapping with an audible crack.

As white-hot pain coursed through Arruti, he clenched his teeth and fell to both knees, his shoulders hanging in awkward angles, both arms useless. "You son of a bitch!"

The assassin calmly took to the couch, rubbing his chest. "There comes a time, Mr. Arruti, when a man's life must come to an end. I will give you a moment to reflect upon yours before it's taken away."

"Who are you?"

"Who I am is of no importance."

Arruti appeared spent. "Then tell me why."

"All I'll say, Mr. Arruti, is that you have exactly one minute to make peace with your god for all the transgressions you committed in your life."

"What are you talking about?"

The assassin leaned forward. "I'm talking about your roll in the Pieces of Eight."

"Ah, an assassin coming to kill an assassin. Seems a little hypocritical with what you're about to do, don't you think?"

The assassin reached into the cargo pocket of his pants and pulled out a silver cylinder. Depressing the button, a pick shot outward and upward. "You have forty-five seconds, Mr. Arruti. If you believe in God, then you may want to start asking Him for forgiveness."

"What I want to ask is this: On whose behalf are you doing this for? A senator? A past president, maybe?"

"Thirty seconds, Mr. Arruti."

"You're good. I'll give you that."

"You're wasting time."

"It's my time to waste."

"Twenty seconds."

Arruti swallowed, his eyes beginning to dart from side to side searching for an avenue of escape as self-preservation began to kick in.

"Pray, Mr. Arruti, it'll give you comfort in your final moments. You now have fifteen seconds."

"Look. I have money. I'll just go away. Whoever you work for will never have to know, right?"

"Wrong. Ten seconds."

Arruti sighed in resignation. "No god will forgive me for the things I've done."

"Maybe you should have thought of that twenty-three years ago."

At the last second of the countdown, the pick found its mark, killing Arruti instantly.

The assassin was true to his word.

Raising the tail of the dead man's shirt and exposing the back, the assassin then sliced a crude C into the man's flesh.

His work in the Philippines was complete.

CHAPTER SEVEN

One Week Later

Kimball Hayden sat in Monsignor Giammacio's office, another tedious session, sitting quietly as the Monsignor sat across from him with a cigarette in his hand.

"And we were making such promising strides on your last visit."

"Look, Padre, I'm not much of a talker. I never was. Things like this make me feel awkward."

"Kimball, we have twenty minutes left. I suggest we make the most of it. Would you like me to lead, then?"

He shrugged. "Whatever."

The Monsignor tapped the ash from his cigarette into an ashtray. "In your last session, it was clear that you seek salvation for past actions. Yet you seem to believe that no matter what you do, you do in vain. No matter how hard you seek the Light, the Light will not be there for you on the Day of Judgment. Is this correct?"

"Look, Padre—"

"Am I right, Kimball?"

Kimball sat erect, unknowingly taking on a defensive position. "Um, well, yeah, I guess."

"No matter what it is you do in the eyes of God to redeem yourself?"

Kimball leaned forward; his voice laced with frustration. "Look, I kill people. It's what I do. It's what I'm good at."

"But we've discussed this matter already, haven't we? The way you killed to save the life of the pope and the lives of the bishops within the Holy See. Did we not cover this in detail?"

"Padre, I killed two children."

"And in seeking redemption for this action, have you not since saved the lives of other children?"

Kimball fell back into his chair and reflected.

Vatican Knights were chosen young when they're waifs and orphans with little promise of direction but possess the tools to excel in character and physical dexterity. To possess the tools of a warrior, then one has to have the hunger to be learned and engage fully in academics and self-examination. To see oneself is to see Loyalty above all else except Honor.

At the Hilbert Institute, an academy for wayward boys too old for adoption, Cardinal Bonasero Vessucci stood beside Kimball and was dressed down from wearing cardinal attire by wearing a simple cleric's shirt and Roman Catholic collar. Kimball remained true to the Knights' attire—wearing a cleric's shirt, collar, black fatigues, and boots.

Standing on an upper-tier walkway overlooking a basketball court, resting their elbows along the top of a railing, both held little interest in the ongoing game. What they locked onto was the player sitting on the bench, a third-stringer, and a child whose sneakers never touched the court.

"Picking a Knight, Kimball, takes an objective eye no matter how much you empathize with the child. This boy has no ambition, no skills, and according to the administrators, he's so withdrawn from society and has no friends. And that is by his choosing." He turns to Kimball. "He does not have the tools to take on the responsibilities of a Vatican Knight, come fifteen years from now."

Kimball stood back to evaluate the child from a distance. The boy was gangly and pale and far more interested in drawing imaginary circles on the floor with the toe-end of his foot than watching the game.

"What he needs is a mentor," he finally said.

"What he needs is a miracle worker. There are far more children out there who hold the standards to become a Vatican Knight."

Kimball leaned forward on the railing. "You know who this kid reminds me of?"

The cardinal smiled. "I suppose you're going to say that he reminds you of yourself?"

"That's exactly what I was going to say. And do you know the person who lent me a hand when I needed it the most?"

The cardinal nodded. "It was me."

"In Venice. You knew all about me, all the horrible things I did. But

you opened up anyway and let me in . . . That was the day I opened myself up for the first time to anyone."

"But you possessed a very particular set of skills that was over and above everyone else."

"Skills I had to learn. You have to remember, we all took awkward steps from the cradle when learning to walk, sometimes falling, then getting back up and doing it all over again until it became an involuntary act."

"I don't know, Kimball. I just don't feel good about this one. And I've been choosing Knights for a long time."

"If I'm to ever choose my team and future teams, then you have to trust me. Otherwise, why am I here?"

"To learn and see in those who have what it takes to serve best on the pontiff's behalf."

Kimball sighed. "I can reach him."

The cardinal turned back to the bench, to the child, who continued to draw imaginary circles with his foot. "Some people cannot be reached, Kimball, no matter how hard you try. And I'm saying this child is too far gone."

"And I'm saying he's not."

There was a silent moment between them.

"Despite what I think," said Vessucci, "you're not going to budge, are you?"

Kimball nodded. "Not on this little guy. No. All I ask is that you allow me to be this mentor, his guide, and I guarantee you he will become one of the best Vatican Knights the pope could ever hope for."

"That's a lofty goal, Kimball, considering what you have to work with. It takes more than you realize to reach a child on an emotional and psychological level if they're too far gone."

"If nothing else, then we at least gave a child-in-need an opportunity for something better than what he has right now—and that isn't much."

It was something the cardinal couldn't refute or deny. "Touché. But all I ask is this: Are you sure it has to be this one when there are so many more with the same need for salvation?"

Kimball nodded and pointed at the child. "It has to be him."

The cardinal saw the conviction in Kimball, the obsessive need for Kimball to commit to the boy, and then faced the child who sat alone. "Then we will call him . . . Ezekiel."

39

"Kimball?" The Monsignor dashed his third cigarette out in the ashtray. "You're saying that you tried to save this boy as—shall we say—redemption for taking the lives of those boys in Iraq?"

"I didn't say that."

"But your actions are."

"If that's the way you want to see it, then go for it."

"Then tell me. Why this particular child when Cardinal Vessucci was so adamant against it?"

"I have my reasons."

"Would you like to expound?"

"Expound?"

The Monsignor gestured with his hands. "To develop or explain more in detail."

"Then why didn't you just say that?"

"Would you like to expound?"

"No."

"Then tell me about Ezekiel, now that he's a man."

Kimball hesitated while the Monsignor reached for another smoke, and then. "I reached him as I knew I would, and he became solid."

"Solid?"

Kimball moved his hands in mock gesture imitating the Monsignor. "To develop a person until he is pure, unadulterated, genuine."

The Monsignor smiled. "Then why didn't you just say that?"

Kimball returned the smile.

"Time's up, I'm afraid," said the Monsignor. "Next week we'll take up where we left off, with Ezekiel."

"There's not much to say about him other than he turned out to be one of the best in the league of the Vatican Knights."

"Not about him as a person, but what his redemption means on a psychological level."

Kimball stood and offered his hand, but the Monsignor refused it, smiling congenially. "You almost crushed my hand the last time. I don't have to be slapped twice to learn my lesson."

As Kimball lowered his hand a feeble knock sounded off the thick wooden door that was pieced together with black iron bands and rivets, an ersatz design of medieval times.

When the Monsignor opened the door, a bishop stood at the threshold with his hands hidden beneath the sleeves.

"I'm sorry to disturb you, Monsignor, but the pontiff has requested the presence of Mr. Hayden. He said it was quite urgent and that he was to be summoned to the pontiff's chamber."

"That's quite all right," he returned. "We just finished our session."

The Monsignor held the door wide and gestured his hand in a way of showing Kimball the way out. "Next week, Kimball, and I know I say this all the time, but you continue to do this anyway, but please don't be late."

"I'll be here at the top of the hour, Doc."

The Monsignor sighed. "I'll believe it when I see it."

CHAPTER EIGHT

The pope's chamber was laden with veined-marble flooring that shined like the surface of ice, and scarlet drapes with scalloped edges and gold fringe covered the floor-to-ceiling windows. Polished brass sconces surrounded six-foot portraits of past popes, the gallery lining the walls in the chronological order they served the Church. The chamber held the sizeable dimensions of a ballroom that served as the nerve center of papal activity.

After Kimball entered the room, the enormous wooden doors closed behind him with mechanical slowness. His footfalls echoed throughout with the poor acoustics as he neared the pontiff's desk, which bore the ornate carvings of angels and cherubs on the mahogany panels.

Sitting in a button-studded chair made of Corinthian leather sat Pope Pius. Beside him stood Cardinal Vessucci, wearing the normal vestments of the simar with scarlet trim and a scarlet biretta. The cardinal appeared to be holding photos, obviously engaging the pope of the matter in hand before Kimball entered the chamber.

Pope Pius fell back in his chair and gestured for Kimball to take one of the two chairs before his desk. "I'm glad you could make it, Kimball. My deepest apology for interrupting your session with the monsignor, but the situation requires your immediate presence."

Kimball sat down. "We were done anyway. How can I be of service, Your Holiness?"

Pius turned to the cardinal, a cue to Vessucci to take over. The cardinal then handed three 8x10 glossies to Kimball. "We just received these from Vatican Intelligence," he told him.

Having diplomatic relationships with more than ninety percent of the world's countries, the Vatican's Intelligence Service, the *Servizio Informazione del Vaticano*, better known as the SIV, was created to counter early 19th century efforts to subvert the power of the Vatican. So, the Church saw the need in creating an "unofficial" security agency to solve problems by conceiving a system of confidential communication and information gathering. But with the growing threat of extremist groups, the SIV had grown to a major organization since the attempted assassination of Pope John Paul II.

As Kimball examined the photos his shoulders began to soften and slump. "I know these people," he said. "They were a part of my old unit, the Pieces of Eight."

He inspected the glossies further, noting the dead faces, the whites of their eyes holding at half-mast.

"The photos you're holding were taken in makeshift morgues in the Philippines. These, however," he handed Kimball three additional photos, "were taken at the scene where the bodies were found."

The bodies were facedown, unrecognizable, with their shirts ripped and parted, and a letter carved into each man's back. He also noted that Walker was tied to the legs of a table, though his legs were missing.

"Somebody cut off Walker's legs?"

"No. Mr. Walker was apparently—for lack of a better term—a mercenary who lost them in an IED attack in Iraq. Misters Grenier and Arruti, however, were operating a military agency in the southern Philippines while looking after Walker, who remained in Manila."

"A band of brothers," he whispered. And then he took notice of the carvings. "Symbols?"

"Letters," Vessucci immediately stated.

"Are you sure? One looks like a lightning bolt and the other looks like a sideways V, like Greek runes or something."

"At first glance—yes, but the SIV has concluded that they're nothing more than crude carvings. It's been determined that the bolt is an S, and the sideways V—as you put it— the letter C." He handed Kimball another photo, this one of his old units posing for the camera's lens. Kimball was kneeling in the bottom roll, the last one on the right, his face maintaining the appearance of cold fortitude in a time that seemed so long ago. In the top roll the faces of the Pieces of Eight—Walker, Grenier, and Arruti, who stood side-by-side from left to right—were circled in red marker, the letter 'I' in Walker's circle, the letter 'S' in Grenier's, the letter 'C' in Arruti's.

"I-S-C. Whoever's doing this is spelling out a message, that's clear."

"But what? And even more disturbing, why?" asked the pope.

Kimball traced the photo with a glancing trail of his finger over the fourth member, Ian McMullen, an Irishman who lived up to his stereotyped billing by loving his alcohol as much as he loved his AR-15. An empty circle was drawn around his face. "This guy isn't very subtle, is he?"

"Kimball, these photos were sent to the SIV by whoever is doing this to these men. And he's working toward the final member in the photo . . . And that's you. Whoever sent it knows you're here."

"That's impossible," he said heatedly. "Everybody attached to that unit, including the United States government, believes I'm dead."

"Apparently not," said Pius. "Otherwise, there would be no reason for this murderer to be sending these photos here."

Kimball considered this. Reasonably speaking, the pontiff was correct. "You're right, but what concerns me is that Grenier and Arruti were sharp commandos. It's hard to believe that one guy could take them on and beat them both."

"Whether it is one or many, this has to be dealt with before he, or they, decides to bring their war to the Vatican."

Cardinal Vessucci rounded the desk and sat on its edge, facing Kimball. "The problem, Kimball, is that Leviticus and his team are in Brazil, and Isaiah is in Colombia with his. Ezekiel, Job, and Joshua are on their annual sabbaticals and won't be back for another two weeks."

"You're telling me I'm on my own?"

"We'll do whatever it takes to find Ezekiel, Job, and Joshua. The SIV will find them."

"That could take days." He turned to the photo; saw the circled face of McMullen. "I already have a team," he added.

The pope leaned forward. "You're not talking about your old unit, are you?"

"Why not? There're five left. That's more than enough to accomplish the means."

"Kimball, these men," the cardinal pointed to the photos of the murdered men, "were mercenaries killing for the highest bidder. Are you sure you want to reconnect with the ways of old?"

"Let's put it this way: Let's see how far I've really come with a little temptation in my life. Let's see if I miss what I was . . . Or if I'm pleased with what I have become."

"Kimball—"

The Knight immediately raised a halting hand. "Bonasero, please, this man" –He pointed to McMullen's image— "saved my life on two occasions. Obviously, he's next on the list, which means I have to get to him before they do. My time is limited."

Pope Pius sighed. "I'm not comfortable with this, Kimball," he said. "But I cannot allow someone's life to hang in the balance under any circumstance. Nevertheless, I will have the SIV look into the whereabouts of the Knights on sabbatical and, once found, have them reconnoiter with your position as soon as possible."

"Understood. But I'll need to leave right away and re-team with my old unit. I just need the current dossiers of the remaining members. And I'll need to know where they are."

"The SIV will have the information available by the time you're ready to leave," said Vessucci.

Kimball stood. "I appreciate it."

"And Kimball." The pope rose, donning his full vestments. "This temptation you speak of about turning back to the ways of old once you return to those who chose to remain in darkness, I have all the faith that you will stay true."

"Yeah, well, somebody has to, I guess."

"Kimball," the cardinal placed a gentle hand on Kimball's shoulder. "Be careful, please. It's hard to fight something unknown, unseen, and uses the shadows as camouflage."

"If it exists, then it can be found. They found me, didn't they?"

"Be careful, Kimball," said Pope Pius. "And may God be with you."

Kimball nodded. *I'm certainly going to need Him for this one,* he considered. Not due to the danger to his welfare, but because of the dangers of falling back to the ways of old. Would he like the taste of taking a man's life simply because he could, the same way an alcoholic needs a single taste to fall off the wagon? Or would he be able to remain guided, taking life only because he had to with killing as a final option?

After giving the cardinal a good-bye pat on the shoulder and kissing the Fisherman's Ring on Pope Pius's hand, Kimball made his way toward the massive chamber doors with his footfalls echoing throughout the room in haunting cadence.

CHAPTER NINE

The Vatican secured an immediate flight on Alitalia Airlines from Rome to Las Vegas, Nevada, with a stop in Boston for refueling. On his journey, Kimball carried clothing and, in a secured panel of his luggage, dual KA-BAR commando knives. On his person, he carried a false passport, which was provided to him by Vatican officials to protect his identity in the States since he was an absconder presumed dead by the United States government. If it should be discovered that he was still alive and holding secrets regarding the reprehensible dealings of past presidential administrations—the murders, the in-house assassinations, the monolithic political cover-ups—Kimball would most likely end up at the wrong end of a Company man's Glock and disappear forever.

Sitting alone in one of the two seats in the first-class row, Kimball sat in the aisle seat. An open manila envelope lay beside him in the other. In his hands were the dossiers of the surviving members of his old team. And Kimball had to wonder how detailed information was gathered so quickly by the SIV.

And then he looked up, his eyes starting with enlightenment: *They have a file on me*, he realized. *All this information was already in my file.*

Giving a sidelong glance for a cursory view outside the window, Kimball saw the choppy waves of the Atlantic below, the frothing mounds churning up specks of white against a plain of ocean blue, as the jumbo jet made its westbound trajectory to the United States at a clip of five hundred sixty miles per hour.

He checked his watch: another four hours to go before landing in Boston, then another six to Las Vegas; more than enough time to glean information from the book-thick dossiers.

Turning back to the folder in hand, he took note of the before-and-after photos of the next target and then closed his eyes, biting softly on his lower lip.

What Ian McMullen had become from what he was could not be considered anything less than a fall from grace. In a photo taken within the last two years, according to its timestamp, the former commando appeared to be thirty pounds less with an aged and crestfallen face that looked thirty years older than what he was. Obviously, he had given himself totally to drink and had become a man who no longer possessed a soul, ambition, or hope.

For years he'd been living from shelter to shelter in the hot, sweltering Las Vegas streets. The climate sapping his body dry the same way his past had sucked his will to press on.

Kimball opened his eyes and saw the earlier photo of a man with a strong jawline, thick neck, and the red handlebar mustache bracketing Irish lips. What he saw was a man whose face had slimmed to hatchet thinness, now dirty and soiled, with unkempt hair mostly matted, and eyes that had gone from the color of bottle green to drab olive.

What Kimball was looking at was the photo of a vagrant who had no hope of returning to his former self as a top-of-the-line soldier, no matter how hard he fought. The man was too far gone in a battle he could not fight or win. And just like that, Kimball's team had dwindled from four to three.

Placing the photo aside, Kimball picked up the presumed target after McMullen, a man by the name of Victor Hawk, a Native American Indian of the Mescalero Apache Nation in New Mexico. Apparently, he returned to his people after he served the American government, collecting a retired federal stipend, and using his time to raise horses on a ranch just outside the reservation.

As a soldier the man was brutal, specializing in stealth kills by combining the immaculate expertise of his people and training of a soldier, then plying them as part of his skill set as an unseen assassin. With his unit branding him 'The Ghost,' it was said that Hawk's target would see nothing but jungle, then a flicker, and then the target would be dead as the Apache drove a knife across his throat or a garrote around his neck.

Now having aged with his face growing heavier and jowls beginning to form, with raven hair beginning to show streaks of silver and a belly beginning to show a paunch, Kimball could only wonder if anybody in his team remained in fighting condition.

Placing the photos aside he picked up the dossiers of the last two members with a little more hope and optimism. Jeff and Stanley

Hardwick, both crazy in a reckless sort of way because of their never wavering lust for danger and their constant need for an adrenaline rush, looked well-muscled and cut today, as they did years ago.

Known as the Brothers Grimm, one being a world-class sniper and the other a demolitions expert, they both exceeded in other areas of expertise including martial arts and double-edged weapons play. But they also had a proclivity for being insubordinate, the brothers often teaming up against other members due to their My-Way-Or-The-Highway mentality.

Currently, the brothers ran an Army and Navy surplus store in Baltimore and possessed a lengthy record of misdemeanor convictions for Drunk and Disorderly, Disorderly Conduct, and the Obstruction of a Public Officer.

Kimball nodded. *Some things never change.*

Placing the materials aside, and then rubbing the fatigue from his eyes with his thumb and forefinger, Kimball attempted to formulate a plan. But how do you do that with a vagrant, an aging Indian, and two out-of-control maniacs who never really grew up?

More so, how do find someone who doesn't have a face or name?

That's easy: You let them find you.

After taking in a deep breath and then letting it out with an equally long sigh, Kimball picked up the photo of McMullen and considered this: *When this assassin comes looking for you, I'll be there.*

The plane continued on its westward flight.

CHAPTER TEN

Las Vegas, Nevada

The Entertainment Capital of the World always lived up to its billing. Lights and glitter, hotels built as facsimiles to Paris, Monte Carlo, Hollywood, and Egypt, others to Mandalay, New York City, and The Greatest Show on Earth, the carnival setting of Circus Circus.

However, where there is light there is darkness. Just beyond the downtown section of The Experience on Freemont, and less than a mile away, were homeless shelters and soup kitchens.

Sidewalks were cluttered with makeshift shelters, the homeless, and individuals in need of psychotropic medications. Gutters were filled with trash and refuse, the surrounding buildings old and empty, like the people who surrounded them. In the background, the skyline of downtown Las Vegas can be seen, such as the towers of Lady Luck, the Golden Nugget, and Union Plaza.

On Owens Street, a man exits from a soup kitchen whose walls are covered with gangland graffiti and heads east towards the Boulevard. He is wearing a moth-eaten overcoat, and though it's unbearably hot, he wears it because it's his prized possession. He wears fingerless gloves and grease-stained pants. His hair is long, matted, and in a wild tangle. And his face hangs with the looseness of a rubber mask that has yellowed with the sickness of a dying liver. To look at him no one would have guessed that he was once one of the deadliest warriors to have walked the planet.

Instead, Ian McMullen was now a vagrant in the twilight of his life.

After reaching the Boulevard, he turned toward the downtown area to secure a spot to panhandle enough change to buy a bottle of cheap wine.

After passing the streets of Washington and Bonanza with downtown in his sight, McMullen could feel something that had long been latent, that feeling an animal gets when sensing great danger.

Stopping, and then turning, his body having arched to the shape of a question mark over time, McMullen took in the non-descript faces of tourists and locals, probing micro-expressions that may give them away as somebody on a potential hunt.

Scanning and appraising for that give-away tic, he cited nothing but people laughing and smiling, people lumped together in this city where sin reigns and morality nothing more than an afterthought.

McMullen chortled in self-chastisement. Not only was he aging exponentially, but he was becoming paranoid.

Standing in the crossway where Freemont and the Boulevard after the sun had settled and the Vegas lights dazzled as did Paris did along the Seine at night, McMullen began his ritual by holding out his hand to receive coins. "Please, can anyone spare change for a veteran . . . Change for a vet . . . Any amount will help." And then he would recite this all over again, word per word, with the same pitch and tempo.

But for the most part, Ian McMullen was hardly noticed.

"Please, can anyone spare change for a veteran . . . Change for a vet . . . Any amount will help."

While halfway through his chant a man slapped a bill into McMullen's gloved hand. "For a few moments of your time," he told him. And then the man curled McMullen's fingers over the money, hiding the amount of its denomination. "All I ask—if you'll grant me the privilege—is a few moments of your time."

McMullen withdrew his hand and opened his fingers. Inside was a crumpled fifty-dollar bill.

McMullen quickly evaluated the man who was rugged in appearance with strong features that were rawboned and angular. Around the neckline of the man's shirt was the pristine white collar worn by the clergy.

"And what can I do you?" He placed the fifty into the side pocket of his overcoat.

"Please," said the clergy, "I have a parish on Fourth Street. Can we talk there?"

"I'm no trick, man."

The cleric smiled. "It's not like that."

"It better not be."

The cleric gestured his hand in the direction for McMullen to take. "Please."

Both men began to walk.

"So, what is this about since it's worth fifty dollars of your hard-earned money, Father?"

"Insight," he said.

"Insight? That's it?"

"That's it."

"Well, Father, you're in luck. Today I have a special. Fifty dollars for all the insight you want."

The cleric smiled. "Then let's begin with why you have chosen to live as you do."

The Irishman hesitated as if searching for the proper words. Then, "It's not as much of a choice as it is fate," he finally said.

"So, you're a fatalist?"

"I believe a man creates his fate by the actions of his past. And sometimes a man has entrenched himself so deeply that no matter what, he can never dig himself out."

"I see. So, what you're saying is that you're so deeply entrenched that hope and salvation are well beyond your reach."

"That's exactly what I'm saying."

They walked slowly towards Fourth Street, a quiet moment passing between them.

"May I then ask why you gave up the right to seek redemption—to better yourself?"

McMullen shrugged. "I'm not a good person."

The cleric stopped. "Why do you say that?"

The one-time assassin stared him directly in the eyes. "If somebody says that they wished they could turn the clock back and do it all over again, then they haven't lived life the right way. A day doesn't go by without me wishing I could do it all over again."

"But isn't life full of struggles?"

"True. But my life, Father, jumped the shark years ago."

"Jumped the shark?"

"It's a term that means that something has lost its way and no matter how hard you try, there's no real way back."

"So, you're lost?"

"For some time now—yes."

"You do know that confession is good for the soul, don't you? It opens the doorway to redemption."

"Yeah, well, even God turns away those who don't care or give a damn." He faced the clergyman. "I've done horrible things, Father. So

51

horrible that God Himself would send me to Hell on a first-class ticket without so much as to look at me."

"Nobody is that far gone."

"Really." The vagrant stepped closer to the priest, the stench of his body rising off him like a battery of heat lifting off the pavement on a hot summer day. "I killed people, Father. I killed innocent people because they were in the way. And I did so without impunity. And you want to know something else?"

The clergyman stood idle.

"I liked it," he said. "I liked it a lot."

The priest raised his hand slowly, gesturing to McMullen to continue the walk.

"What? No comment."

The priest sighed. "Even people who kill do not choose to live like this."

"I told you, it's not so much of a choice as it is fate."

"So, you have no remorse? None at all?"

McMullen faltered with a hitch in his step. "I did in time," he finally said. "And I found my salvation in a bottle. I still do."

"Alcohol is no substitute for God."

"It is for me." He stopped once again, looking at the priest. "It got to the point when I saw the faces of those I killed, the terror in their eyes, the sobs of their pleading; it ate away at me like cancer. Mind you now that I always liked my booze, but it came to a point when becoming addled with alcohol washed away the images, made it OK for me to get buy." He began walking. "And that's why nobody wants to give a lush like me a job or an opportunity. Nobody wants to hire somebody who can't make it through the day without imbibing. I'm simply trading the demon of alcohol for the demon of my conscience."

The parish sat on the corner of Bridger and Fourth. Yards away an alley separated the church from a defunct wedding chapel.

"The alleyway will take us to the back door," said the priest.

"How much insight do you want?"

The clergyman remained silent as they made their way to the rear of the parish, which was gated.

"I'm afraid I don't have a key," said the priest.

"Then I guess we're done."

"Actually, we're not," he said. From his back pocket, the clergyman pulled out a silver cylinder and held it up to display. "A man who truly feels repentance for the things he's done gives him the right for redemption."

The pick shot upward and outward.

"What are you doing?"

The priest moved closer. "I'm going to allow you the opportunity to meet God and to ask Him for salvation."

"Are you nuts? You're a priest!"

"Actually, I'm not."

And as promised, he allowed McMullen to ask God for the chance to enter His Kingdom of Light and Loving Spirits.

CHAPTER ELEVEN

Vatican City

Pope Pius stood before the mirror in the bathroom. His face was pale and pasty like the soft, white underbelly of a fish. The lines along his forehead, the countless intertwining creases along his face appeared longer, darker, deeper, a scrimshaw account of the burdens he carried over the past several years. In the whites of his eyes laces of red stitching interlaced throughout, giving them that thick, rheumy look of fatigue.

After a cursory examination of his depleting reflection, the pontiff turned the handle of the faucet and watched water pour from the mouth of a polished-brass spigot in the shape of a large-scaled fish, and into the basin. After spooning cool water onto his face with cupped hands, and then patting himself dry with a towel, Pope Pius made his way back to his chamber in a gait that was disturbingly labored, his steps short, shuffling, the movement of a geisha girl.

Sitting before the papal desk with a manila envelope in his hand sat Cardinal Bonasero Vessucci, who waited patiently.

The pope entered wearing his everyday dress which included the full-buttoned cassock of the floor-length *sottana*; a sash; the hooded cape of his *mozzetta*; red slippers, the *pantofole*; and the skullcap of his *zucchetto*. However, the garments seemed to weigh the man down, the fabric hanging loosely as if the material was too large for his frame.

"Please, forgive me, Bonasero. The amount of work I've been putting in is beginning to wear on me." He positioned himself over the seat and let his legs buckle, the pontiff falling into the cushion of soft Corinthian leather. He pointed to the envelope in the cardinal's hands. "Is that from the SIV?"

Vessucci nodded and opened the envelope. Inside were 8x10 photos of a crime scene in Las Vegas. He placed the photos in front of the pontiff.

What the pope was seeing was a spread-out gallery of Ian McMullen in the pose of death. There were several photos taken from different angles of the man lying prone on the pavement with his arms aside—but not quite in mock crucifixion—with the material of his overcoat ripped from the tail to the collar and parted, revealing the man's naked back. The letter 'A' was carved into his flesh.

"Ian McMullen," said the cardinal. "He's the last man in Kimball's unit positioned in the top row of the photo. He is the letter 'A.'"

The pope sighed, examining the photo in earnest. From left to right the red circles surrounding the faces of Kimball's old unit were filled in with the letters I-S-C and now the letter A, leading to the reasonable hypothesis that the assassin would now begin the final leg of his journey by killing those on the bottom row, beginning with a Native American and ending up with Kimball.

"That's four down," the cardinal said dourly, "with four to go."

The pope tented his fingers and bounced them nervously against his chin. "I'm worried about Kimball," he said. "Has the SIV found any of the knights on holy sabbatical?"

"Not yet, Your Holiness. But they're using every possible means to find them."

"I would feel much more comfortable, Bonasero, knowing that he had the support of the Vatican Knights, rather than the backing of his old unit."

"We could always call in Leviticus or Isaiah."

The pope nodded. "They're committed to the salvation of innocent people elsewhere. To call them back when the citizenry of the Church needs us most would be a grievous sin not only on my part but also on the part of the Church. No, Bonasero. As much as I would like to, I can't take them away from their rightful duty as Vatican Knights . . . I'm afraid Kimball's on his for now."

The pope grabbed the photos and spread them out on the desktop before him: Walker, I; Grenier, S; Arruti, C: McMullen, A.

"I know what he's spelling," said the cardinal.

The pope nodded. "So do I." He traced his finger over the photos. "I-S-C-A," he said, and then fell back into his seat. "He writes of the one who betrayed Jesus for thirty pieces of silver."

"Judas Iscariot."

"Judas Iscariot," he confirmed.

55

"But why?"

Pius shrugged. "Does a madman ever need a reason?"

"Or perhaps madmen. We have no idea how many are involved in this. All we know is that whoever did this is probably in Las Vegas. He, or they, may even be waiting on Kimball."

"When does he land?"

"Within the hour," he answered. "I've got somebody waiting for him the moment he arrives to apprise him of the situation."

"Let's just pray that Kimball doesn't walk into anything he's not prepared for."

"Kimball's elite. It's in his blood to be attentive."

"He's also alone." The moment the pope gained his feet he wobbled in his stance and fell forward, his world a dizzying spiral as he used the desk as a crutch to hold him upright.

Cardinal Vessucci reacted quickly, aiding the pontiff back into his seat, the pontiff's eyes seemingly detached, distant, and lost. "Your Holiness."

The pontiff reached out with a hand that appeared as feeble as a bird and laid it upon the cardinal's forearm. His breath was labored as though he had committed himself to a long sprint. "I'm fine, Bonasero. Really. I just got up too quickly, that's all."

And then Pius went into a chain of coughing as his lungs sounded wet with a phlegm-like rattle, his face then going crimson, and then his eyes bulged and became teary as he coughed into the sleeve of his white *sottana*. When his coughing subsided, he could only stare at the sleeve blankly. It was marked with splashes of blood.

Cardinal Vessucci took a disjointed step forward. "My dear Jesus," he said. "That's not good."

The pope faced him. "Get me to Gemelli."

CHAPTER TWELVE

McCarran Airport. Las Vegas, Nevada.

To the child, the man was like a mist that broke apart then coalesced, always in three places at once, the shadows his camouflage.

"Again!" The voice was harsh and authoritative, that of a mentor who expected nothing less than perfection.

From the shadows to the boy's right, the blade of a wooden katana shot forth and struck the boy across the shoulders, then disappeared back into the darkness as quickly as it appeared. The strike in itself was hardly perceptible against the child's skin, but the noise of the wooden blade striking his flesh sounded off like slapstick.

"Again!"

The boy turned toward the point of attack holding his wooden katana, frightened, the shadows pooling around him.

This time, from his left, came a similar strike, extremely fast, the wooden blade striking the small of the child's back.

The boy pivoted on his feet, listening. Straight ahead he heard something move—the mere shuffling of a foot being drawn across the floor, something close, the figure using the darkness as camouflage. Then in a quick reaction, the child struck out with his blade, after he centered on the location of his attacker based on the spot of the sound.

From the wall of darkness, the blade of the wooden katana shot forward and deflected the child's blow, blades colliding with a clack that echoed throughout the darkened chamber beneath the Vatican. And then his mentor's blade disappeared beyond the fringe of light that was granted by the flames of distant torches.

"Very good, Ezekiel," came the mentor's voice, that of pride. "Always rely upon other senses where others fail you. What you can't see, then you must listen. What you can't hear, then you must smell. What you can't understand, then you must reason."

The boy held the katana straight before him in a firm grip, waiting and listening.

His mentor once more moved through the shadows, gearing himself to strike.

And the child listened, shuffling upon his feet but maintaining his balance, his blade ready to defend.

"Good, Ezekiel, you're showing excellent poise. However, I'm behind you."

The mentor's blade struck once again from the wall of darkness, this time a glancing shot across the boy's back in a slashing motion, a kill strike.

Disgruntled, the child tossed the wooden katana to the ground and fell petulantly down onto his backside, sobbing in defeat.

Kimball watched the child from the shadows for a long moment before treading carefully to Ezekiel and taking to a bended knee beside him. With a sweeping motion of his arm, he pulled the boy close to him. "It's all right, Ezekiel. You're doing fine."

"I suck!"

Kimball couldn't help the smile. "No, you don't." And then he took a seat on the concrete next to him. "I've been in this arena training kids a lot older than you. And do you want to know what?"

Ezekiel looked up at Kimball, the lines on his face dancing eerily with the movement of the torches' flames.

"Believe it or not," said Kimball, "you're showing me incredible skills of self-defense far above those who are much older than you."

A slight grin surfaced upon Ezekiel's tear-streaked face. "Really?"

Kimball nodded. "Absolutely. In a few more years you'll be an expert. I guarantee it."

The boy's shoulders slumped in defeat.

"What?" asked Kimball.

Ezekiel sighed. "By then I'll be twelve or thirteen. I'll be old."

Kimball laughed. "What you'll be, Ezekiel, is a fine young man who will be at the top of his game. Just be patient and never give up, OK? Remember what we talked about earlier about quitters and losers."

The boy nodded. "Quitters never win, and winners never quit."

"That's right. And you're a winner, right?"

"I guess."

Kimball mimicked him sportingly. "I guess." And then he grabbed the wooden katana and handed it back to the child. "Quitters never win, and winners never quit."

The boy looked briefly at the sword, sighed, and then gained his feet holding the katana before him in a firm grip. "Quitters never win, and winners never quit."

Kimball got to his feet and receded into the shadows. Once he was eclipsed by darkness, he shouted one word. "Again!"

And the child attacked.

The moment the plane touched down at McCarran Airport in Las Vegas, the images of him mentoring Ezekiel in the early stages of the boy's life had vanished. And perhaps the monsignor was right after all by assessing the fact that Kimball was trying to absolve himself of his sins by usurping the life of this child and nurturing him in compensation for the lives of the children he had taken as an act to gain redemption. Take a life, raise a life.

After disembarking, Kimball grabbed his luggage and made his way to the taxi queue. Standing outside, with the heat hitting him like an oven blast, even at night, was a diminutive man with a conservative haircut, black-framed glasses, and the cleric's outfit with the white band of a Roman Catholic collar around his neck, hardly a warrior.

The man approached Kimball who stood out like a beacon with his cleric shirt, Roman collar and, military-style pants and boots, an odd combination. "Mr. Hayden? Kimball Hayden?"

Kimball faced the priest. "Yes."

The man pulled out his wallet and flipped the cover, showing his ID as a member of the *Servizio Informazione del Vaticano*, the Vatican Intelligence, or the SIV. "I'm Father Michael Sebastian. I have a car waiting."

The men made their way to the moving walkway that led to the short-term parking area of the garage. Just as they secured their seatbelts and got the vehicle in motion, Father Sebastian handed Kimball a manila envelope. "I'm sorry to say that you will not like what you'll find there in those photos." And then, "I'm sorry about your friend."

Kimball withdrew photos of a crime scene—that of a man lying face down on the pavement with an 'A' carved into his back.

"Your friend, Ian McMullen, was found dead not too long ago. I was able to intercept those photos a few hours ago from the County Coroner's Office."

The cleric drove out of the garage and onto Swenson, making his way toward Tropicana.

Kimball, with photos in hand, showed little emotion. "Same MO for death?" he finally asked.

"It appears to be. It's some kind of pick-like device, like an awl or something. But we're not quite sure as to what the mechanism is. But the strike is a single blow to the head area—a kill shot that's instantaneous."

Kimball examined the picture and wondered if the photo was that of McMullen. The man lying prone seemed wasted with the outline of his ribs pressing against the skin of his backside. The knolls of his spine appeared too prominent and the man too skinny. Even thinner than the man he examined in the photos of the dossier.

"Are you sure this is McMullen?" he asked.

"It's him all right. The alcohol ate him down to nothing."

Kimball sighed and looked out the window as they went west on Tropicana. The Pieces of Eight were dwindling at a rapid pace. Only half the team remained.

Then from Father Sebastian, "We believe the assassin is still in the area since McMullen has been determined to be dead not more than four hours."

"A man can be anywhere in four hours."

And this was true, which is why Father Sebastian remained quiet.

"By the way, where are you taking me?"

"To a parish on the west side of town," he answered. "You'll be safe there."

"Actually, I'll need to get to New Mexico as soon as possible. Can you arrange that?"

"I can. But you need rest."

"What I need is to get to New Mexico to reach The Ghost before the assassin does. If he maintains one step ahead of me at all times, then there will be no one left."

"It's late. Ticketing kiosks and flights won't reopen for another few hours. The red-eye flights are already gone."

"Then rent me a car."

"With all due respect, you'd have to drive through Arizona and half the way through New Mexico. It would take you longer to drive to your destination than to wait for ticketing to reopen and fly."

Kimball drew a mental image in his mind of the map of the US. Sebastian was right. New Mexico, especially Albuquerque, was far from Las Vegas. By flight it was nothing. The moment the plane leveled off, then it would be time to descend. Kimball just couldn't stand the lapse between now and then.

"Perhaps you should rest."

It was a good notion, but Kimball was too hyped up.

He looked out the window and at the lights that made up the Las Vegas Strip. His eyes took on a hypnotic gaze. Out there, he considered, was the man who killed his friends. Out there, in the blaze of neon glory, was the man who was targeting him with the presumption to take him out.

The lights were incredible.

"Perhaps you should rest," Father Sebastian repeated.

But how could he? Wondering if the killer was within the city limits of Las Vegas, or if he already had a leg up and was on his way to kill The Ghost.

"Just get me a flight as soon as possible. And have a car waiting for me when I get there. I'll need it to get to the reservation."

Father Sebastian nodded. "I understand."

CHAPTER THIRTEEN

Rome

Pope Pius rested comfortably at Gemelli Polyclinic; his bed raised so he could better view the television. Beside him sitting in a chair was Cardinal Vessucci.

"Bonasero." The pope reached out to him with a bony and frail hand, and Vessucci grabbed it with ease. "You're a good friend and favored by the College to succeed me—"

"Let's not talk about this, Your Holiness."

"Bonasero, death is only a new beginning. It's a way of life."

"Of course. it is. But yours is far from over."

Pius smiled, becoming passive. And then: "I've lived a good life, my friend. But we both know that I'm in the twilight of my existence. I don't need a doctor to tell me that. I know just as you do." The pontiff sighed and laid his head against the pillow, their hands still clutching. "It's time to see my Heavenly Father," he added.

"Amerigo—" The cardinal cut himself off.

"Bonasero, you're my good friend and the College favors you to succeed me. You have the tools to win the masses, and the gift to give hope when hope is needed the most. Use them wisely."

The cardinal relented. "If I should succeed you if the College of the Cardinals deems me fit to sit upon the papal throne, then I will not disappoint."

The pope smiled. "I know that." And then the pontiff fell into a severe coughing fit, more blood, his face growing crimson. Red flecks ended up on the back of Pius's liver-spotted hand, which the cardinal wiped clean with a tissue.

Within moments the pontiff eased back into a calm repose with a hand to his chest as his breathing fell into a more rhythmic, a more normal pattern.

"On my passing," he told the cardinal, catching his breath, "you'll need to fill the vacant seat within the Society of Seven. There are those who are too conservative to see the need for the Vatican Knights. But there are some who recognize the Church's right to protect its sovereignty, its interests, and the welfare of its citizenry. Choose wisely, Bonasero, to avoid an insurrection by conservative factions within the Vatican, those who are most politically minded."

The cardinal nodded in agreement. "The secrets of the Knights will be well kept and held to the Society of Seven. There are many within who recognize the right of the Church to protect itself. So don't worry, Amerigo. I'll find someone to fill the void without a setback."

"What about the status of the Vatican Knights?"

"Isaiah and Leviticus are meeting with marginal resistance and no collateral damage, but far from being relieved of duty to aid Kimball. We still haven't found those on sabbatical."

Pius sighed. "And have you heard from Kimball?"

"No. But he did land safely in Las Vegas where he was met by SIV who informed him of Mr. McMullen's fate. From what I understand he's now on his way to the next perceived target."

A man of Lincolnesque statute, tall and lanky with wispy limbs beneath his medical coat, entered the room wearing a feigned, if not uneasy, smile. As he stood at the foot of the pontiff's bed the man wrung his hands nervously.

With an encompassing smile magical enough to soothe the man, the pope put the doctor at ease. "And how are you today, Doctor Simonelli? Blessed, I hope?"

"Your Eminence—" The man took a step closer, the pretend smile gone. "Your Eminence, I'm afraid I have some rather disturbing news regarding your condition." The physician hesitated for a brief moment, the lapse of time, however, seemingly long and surreal. "I'm afraid you have cancer."

"Advanced?"

"Yes, Your Holiness, I'm afraid so. Your cancer has metastasized to tissues to both lungs and neighboring organs. You're at stage four."

"Stage four?"

"I'm afraid it's terminal."

There was another pregnant pause, the moment awkward.

And then: "How long?"

"I'd say anywhere from three to six months. It all depends upon how your body responds to chemo and radiation."

"There'll be neither," he said. "I'll simply let nature take its course."

"But, Your Holiness—"

Pius raised a halting hand. "No, Bonasero, God is calling me home. There is no need to prolong the inevitable."

"Are you in any pain?" asked the doctor.

"No, only tired. I thought I was just overworking myself."

"If you want, Pontiff, I can prescribe morphine."

"There's no need, Doctor." He turned to the cardinal. "I'll need around-the-clock care until I can perform no longer. You're the secretary of state, so I'll need to groom you to cover my duties until my passing. From then the Cardinal Camerlengo will take over the duties upon the moment I die and continue those duties until a successor is chosen."

The cardinal nodded sadly. "Of course, Your Holiness."

The pope laid his head against the pillow and stared at the ceiling. "I'm going home."

CHAPTER FOURTEEN

The assassin had no idea that Kimball Hayden had just driven within fifty feet of his location as he holed himself up inside a cheap franchise motel along Tropicana. Behind the drawn drapes the assassin sat on the edge of the bed going over aged dossiers of the Pieces of Eight. The dossiers of Walker, Arruti, and Grenier were closed out, the files bound by an elastic band and sitting on the nightstand between twin beds. The five remaining dossiers sat on his lap. The profile of McMullen was open, the aged photos yellowing at the edges, the detailed information regarding the one-time government assassin spelled out in seventeen pages.

Taking the photo of the Pieces of Eight, the assassin traced a finger over the face of McMullen where the letter 'A' was scribed within his circled head.

I-S-C-A, the top row was now complete.

And there was no doubt that those on the bottom row would soon coalesce into a fighting force and strike up a plan for self-preservation, with Kimball as their lead.

But they would be fighting blindly, he considered, the core members not knowing who they were up against—how many or how little—with every sound or moving shadow a possible threat.

The assassin then closed the folder and slipped it beneath the band with the other closed files, then placed the active files on the bed beside him.

The first to fall would be the Indian from New Mexico, he mulled, the one they called The Ghost. And then the brothers who were by nature passionately reckless, with Kimball to be the last to feel the bite of his pick.

The man got to his feet, went to the window, and parted the drapes. The lights of the Las Vegas Strip were truly magnificent; the city the bedrock of dreams of becoming wealthy beyond imagination usually going unfulfilled. It was a place created on romantic illusions of penthouse living, caviar snacks, and champagne brunches, only for the city to spit you out in the end once it bled you dry.

It was a cruel place that took McMullen by the inches. He just finalized the inevitable.

Returning to the bed, the assassin picked up the final folder and peeled back the cover. Inside was an old photo of Kimball Hayden who was young and stoic looking, the man appearing without conscience or feeling. It was the photo of a killer.

The assassin traced a finger over the picture. "After I take those around you and there is no one left, I will take your life before your soul has a chance to find the salvation it so badly seeks . . . I will send you to Hell where you belong."

Closing his eyes, his breathing finding the even rhythm of meditation, the assassin shut the file and found himself at peace.

Kimball Hayden had flown into Albuquerque and rented a car. His eyes were weighted, his entire body fatigued with more than thirty hours of going without sleep. But he pressed on towards the Mescalero Apache Nation.

Around him, the land was made up of multiple color blends in shades of reds and pinks and mauve. The buttes, the rocky rises, all lined with the strata lines formed millennia ago, lent somewhat of a primal, prehistoric look to the terrain. Sage and desert flora dotted the landscape. And the sand was the color of Mississippi mud, red with alluvia lines formed by the push of hot winds rather than the force of running water.

The flight to New Mexico was minimal in time expense. The drive, however, was time-consuming.

By mid-afternoon, he had found the cut-off that led to the reservation. But according to the dossier, Victor Hawk's ranch was on the border between his people and the people he lived with, the White man.

Taking the dirt road, his vehicle kicking up rooster-tail plumes of red earth in its wake, Kimball could see a ranch-style house in the distance and a barn that was surrounded by posts that corralled horses.

Leaning against the corral posting stood a large man. But Kimball was too far to see if it was Hawk.

What he could tell, however, was that the large man was looking right at him.

The Native American leaned his elbow against the corral posting and stood there in leisure, eyeing the vehicle that was making its way down the dirt road to his ranch. Next to him was a German shepherd. A growl rumbled in the back of its throat.

"Dog," said the Indian, "hush." But the shepherd continued his growling.

As the car neared the Indian stepped away from the posts and closer to the road's end. He was tall and broad with the beginnings of a paunch. And beneath the ten-gallon hat, he wore his raven hair was fashioned into a thick braid that went down to the small of his back. His eyes were dark, the edges surrounding them were deeply lined with crow's feet from spending too much time beneath a sun that had ripened his skin to the color of tanned leather.

The shepherd matched him step by step, its growl hardly abating.

"Dog, I said hush."

When the car drove up it was coated with dust. The windshield, however, was marginally clear after a mopping of the wipers. When the driver exited the vehicle, he stood before Hawk with a briefcase in his hand. The first thing the Indian set his eyes on was the Roman Catholic collar, then the cleric's shirt, and then at the military-style pants and boot wear.

"Something I can help you with?"

The driver took a step closer. "It's been a while, Hawk. You still go by Ghost?"

The Indian cocked his head, his mind working with recall. And then his jaw dropped as his eyes flared with incredulous disbelief. "Kimball?"

He smiled sheepishly. "How's it going, big man?"

"You're supposed to be dead. Died before the first war with Iraq."

"Apparently, I didn't"

The dog began to growl.

"Is the dog friendly?"

"When he's not hungry."

The Indian walked closer, appraising Kimball, his eyes staring in wonder.

And then: "What happened?"

"Truthfully, Hawk, I just walked."

The Indian tilted his head. "You absconded?"

Kimball nodded. "I just couldn't do it anymore. I couldn't continue to do all the horrible things we did. Not anymore."

Hawk stood within a foot of Kimball. And after what seemed to be an awkward moment embraced him. "It's good to see you again, my friend. On the word of your passing, I prayed to the spirits for many nights on your behalf. And here you are many years later." He pushed away and pointed to Kimball's white collar. "And what is this? Are you a priest of your people now?"

"Hardly."

"Then, why the collar?"

"It's a long story, Hawk."

"All I have is time. All I do is stand here all day and watch my Appaloosas roam the land."

"They are beautiful," he commented.

In the pen behind Hawk were six horses, all mottled with different patterns in different shades and sizes.

"But enough about my horses," he said. "Why are you here?"

CHAPTER FIFTEEN

As night fell the sky was filled with a multitude of pinprick lights, the constellations alive with the movement of starlit glitter. In the distance coyotes bayed at a moon in its gibbous phase, the canine language causing Dog to raise his head in the direction of the howl, but nothing more.

In the meantime, as a slight breeze blew in from the west, Kimball confided in Hawk the reason why he absconded before the first invasion of Iraq—about the two boys he killed to keep them from compromising his position. He told him about his epiphany and the opportunity of redemption given to him by the Church to seek the 'Light' of his inner self. But he omitted the part about the Vatican Knights since they were a clandestine group, telling Hawk in mention that he served as a low-ranking emissary within the Church's hierarchy.

While they sat on a wraparound porch in wicker chairs Hawk listened, once in a while giving a perceptible nod of understanding as his eyes focused on a landscape that was the color of whey under the watchful face of a semi-full moon.

As Kimball spoke, he did so in a manner and tone that beseeched forgiveness from the Native American for absconding from his duties as a warrior. As a soldier of the Pieces of Eight and an elite commando of the Force Elite, absconding from the unit was considered to be the most magnificent act of cowardice in the eyes of one's brethren.

When he finished, he sat back and remained quiet while waiting on a response from the Indian that never came.

And then: "It's quite peaceful here, Hawk. The way the stars shimmer, the quiet of the surroundings."

"It's the land of my ancestors," he finally said. "It's my home."

Kimball sighed. "You're disappointed?"

"You were an Elite," he answered. "But if your inner spirit cannot commune with the spirits that show you a path you truly do not wish to

69

take, then there is disharmony. Your inner spirit must find its place by following a journey that leads to inner peace. Without that, a man is never whole." The Indian turned to Kimball. "I can tell you that you are still on your journey."

"I am."

"With age comes maturity and wisdom. And I am not without the mindset that we did horrible things, Kimball, things that should never have happened now that I have been wizened by the spirits of my ancestors." The large Indian hesitated, staring out at the scenery. "On most nights, the spirits show me the errors of what I was," he said, "of the things I've done. And every night I see the faces of those I killed, the faces of those who are now the spirits who haunt me." He turned back to Kimball to punch his point home. "But I never ran."

Kimball nodded. "I didn't come here to seek forgiveness, although it would be greatly appreciated. What we did, we did a long time ago. We need to move on."

Hawk turned back to view the landscape with his chin raised; something about him stoic in the way he sat. "Then I will ask you once again: Why are you here?"

Kimball reached for the files sitting on the table between them and grabbed the top folder. "I'm here," he said, "because we're being hunted."

"Hunted?"

Kimball opened the folder and grabbed the top photo. It was of the Pieces of Eight. The faces of those on the top row were circled with letters etched over the faces, I-S-C-A. Hawk was the first one kneeling on the left side of the bottom row, a machete in one hand and an assault weapon in the other.

Kimball handed Hawk the photo and grabbed the next photo in the folder. "A few days ago," he began, "Walker was hit in the Philippines." He handed the Indian the second photo, that of Walker lying on the table, an 'I' cut into his back.

"He has no legs," the Indian said simply.

"He lost them in an attack while serving as a mercenary. In fact, he worked for a militant group that was seated on top by Arruti and Grenier."

Hawk accepted the third and fourth photos, that of Arruti and Grenier lying face down with the letters 'S' and a 'C' notched into their backs.

70

"Both dead obviously?"

"Within a day of Walker's murder."

"They were in the Philippines. It can be a dangerous place."

"You know as well as I do that Arruti and Grenier were at the top of their game. Yet someone had the military sophistication to take them out." He pointed to the first photo in Hawk's hand—that of the Pieces of Eight lined up and posing. "Whoever is doing this is choosing their targets sequentially from left to right, top row first, and presumably the bottom row next. And you, Hawk, are next in line."

"But why now?"

"I'm not sure. But it's somebody who has the connections to send forward an elite military unit as a disposal team. Politicians, a government insurgency group, anyone who believes that we can be a detriment because of the things we know."

"Then my guess would be the powers that be who applied our skills to better promote their rankings. But that was so long ago. So, why now?"

Kimball shrugged before falling back into his seat.

The Indian examined the photos for a long moment before setting them aside. And then he looked over the landscape with a keen eye and nodded once in a while as though he was communing with his inner self. "He's here," he finally said.

Kimball looked out at the desert, seeing nothing but the shadows of distant mountains and the darkened shapes of cacti and saguaros. In the far distance to the west, thunderheads were gathering, and the sky grumbled. "How do you know?"

"I know with this," he said, pointing to his nose. "And also, with this." He then patted his chest over his heart with the flat of his palm. "I was 'The Ghost' because I know the skills of a hunter. I know stealth. And I know every hunter watches his prey before he strikes. Even prey is wary of what he cannot see."

Kimball chalked it up to Apache instinct, the man simply spouting off since it was impossible to tell if anyone was out there or not. But Kimball also knew that Hawk was amazing with his skills of intuiting what others could not.

"He'll watch, and then he'll strike when it's opportune."

"Are you prepared for a defense?"

The Indian looked at him quizzically. "Are you kidding? What I miss, Dog will pick up. And if he—or they—should break the first line of defense, then I'll be there waiting for them. I may be old, Kimball, but I haven't lost my skills."

"I have no weapons."

"I've plenty. Wait here a sec."

The Indian got to his feet and went into the house, the hinges of the screen door whining in his wake as Kimball was left to view the desert wondering if he was caught in the crosshairs of an NV scope.

When Hawk returned, he did so with a minor arsenal. Strapped to his leg was his Bowie, a knife he cherished due to its size, always saying that a sizeable blade provided a psychological edge; bigger was always bad, he would say. Seated on his head was a pair of night-vision goggles with a monocular lens. And in one hand he carried an assault weapon with an attached suppressor that was as long as the weapon's barrel, an MP-5, and in the other hand was a top-of-the-line rifle used by snipers, the CheyTac M200, which was effective for up to 2000 meters.

"This only scratches the surface," he said. "In the back is a hidden room holding all the toys I covet."

He handed Kimball the CheyTac, which had heft to it but was extremely manageable.

"And with these," Hawk lowered the monocular lens over his eyes and switched the unit on, the goggles powering up as the batteries whirled the apparatus to life, "I'll be able to see him coming no matter what point he wishes to attack from. The CheyTac will then take him down the moment he steps out into the moonlight."

"I know I've lost credibility in your eyes, Hawk, but I need to fight by your side on this one."

The Indian smiled. "Like old times?"

"Like old times."

Hawk nodded in approval. "But right now, you need rest. How long has it been since you slept?"

"Over thirty hours," he said.

"You're no good to me unless you're sharp. Get some sleep. Dog and I will watch the compound."

"But if you're right about him—"

"I'll be fine, Kimball. I'm 'The Ghost,' remember? I know what to look for in a predator since I am one myself. If he comes, I'll know it. And once I know he is here, then I'll make sure that you're fighting by my side."

"We'll need him alive, Hawk. Or them. I'm not sure how many there are since I find it hard to believe that one man is capable of taking out Arruti and Grenier."

"We'll soon find out, won't we?"

"I just need a couple of hours, maybe three."

Hawk smiled a wide grin with the wage of pride. "I'm 'The Ghost,'" he said. "At first, you would see nothing but jungle, then the flicker of a shape, and then you were dead by my hand. That's me, 'The Ghost.'"

"Yeah, I remember."

"Then don't worry and get some sleep. I'll need you at the top of your game."

Kimball lay the folders down and got to his feet. His face was beginning to hang with fatigue and his eyes were growing glassy and red.

"Take my bed," said Hawk. "It's comfortable."

"Thanks, man. And, Hawk?"

"Yeah."

"It's good to see you again."

Hawk turned toward the landscape while resting the CheyTac across his lap. "Yeah. You too, brother."

CHAPTER SIXTEEN

The assassin wore a Ghillie Desert suit. At nighttime, the color didn't matter much since the darkness was his camouflage, and the suit looking as much as the surrounding desert sage. From a hilltop overlooking Hawk's ranch, the assassin spied down on them through a night vision monocular.

Sitting on the porch were two men, with the Native American keeping a vigil eye over the landscape with night vision goggles and a rifle across his lap, a CheyTac M200.

So, you were expecting me.

The large man sitting beside him he couldn't quite make out, so he dialed the lens and zoomed in, first catching the pristine white collar and then the man's face.

The assassin's breath hitched. *Well, if it isn't the priest who is not a priest.*

The level of the assassin's jeopardy had just risen tenfold.

Moving slowly across the terrain on his belly, the fabric of his Ghillie suit swaying like grass in a soft breeze, the assassin moved to gain a different vantage point. When he reached a row of thick sage, the assassin had a solid blind that granted him a complete frontal view of the entire ranch. The question was, how was he to encroach with Kimball and Hawk working in tandem? He was sure that he could take down one, but not both. Not when they were members of the Pieces of Eight no matter how far removed, they were from active duty. Kimball Hayden was a testament to that.

But killing Hayden now was not in the assassin's scheme of things, as he wanted Hayden to die in the sequential manner of the way the warriors were posing in the photo: First Hawk, then the brothers, and then Kimball.

But if it was one thing the assassin learned in life was that plans rarely came together due to the unpredictability of the human element. And Kimball Hayden had become that element.

In the west where thunderheads gathered, celestial rumbles sounded off like aged cannons of the Colonial period—something distant with the deep rumble that shook the earth miles away.

Patiently, the assassin waited for the opportune moment, always believing that there was a solution to everything. And twenty minutes later a solution presented itself.

Kimball rose from the chair, spoke to Hawk, then disappeared into the house.

Divide the team, and then conquer. Always level the playing field before engagement.

The moment Kimball left, the assassin moved away from the blind careful not the catch the eye of Hawk through the NVG he was wearing, fully aware that he was time-restricted and needed to act quickly now that the team was separated.

So, inch-by-inch and foot-by-foot, the assassin made his way toward Hawk in a hastened belly crawl with murder as his sole intent.

Hawk sat on the porch with all the ease and content of a retired layman with the CheyTac M200 resting across his lap and rocked leisurely on the curved skids of his chair while looking through his NVG.

The landscape before him was lit up in luminescent green. Everything that was once steeped in shadow was now defined; the saguaros, the brush, the sage—even the outlines of the sandstone escarpments were obvious to where he could see every curvature or indentation of any particular rock or boulder.

Night had become day.

Slowly, moving back and forth on the skids of his rocker with his eyes forward and focused, nothing moved other than the occasional sway of sage branches that moved with the course of a soft breeze.

But because something could not be seen did not mean that it did not exist. Predators often waited for hours for the opportune moment to strike, the reward always the relish of the kill. And no one knew this better than 'The Ghost,' who once waited as long as seven hours to run the blade of his knife across an unsuspecting throat.

A cool breeze came in from the west, along with the soft soughing of the desert wind that sounded like a drawn and distant sigh, almost pleasurable in its tone. In the sky, lightning flashed. Most likely the coming of a storm, he considered, the slight wind an obvious precursor.

On most nights he would delight in such cool weather, but not tonight. Not when strobes of lightning would render the optics of his NVG inoperable.

Not with the assassin a click or two away from his ranch.

Are you out there? he thought.

At the trailing edge of Hawk's thought, Dog responded symbiotically to his master by craning his head off the floor and staring off into the darkness, centering on something only he could see. A deep growl rumbled in the back of his throat, the red flag that Hawk had become accustomed to when they were not alone.

Reaching over, Hawk scratched the dog behind the ears. "He's out there, boy, isn't he?"

The dog remained as still as a Grecian statue, focusing, sensing, the growl abating little.

Hawk then placed both hands on the rifle, then carefully popped off the caps covering the front and rear lenses of the weapon's hi-tech scope.

All he needed was one shot.

In the not-too-distant skyline, lightning flashes were becoming more pronounced, the wind rising to more than just the soft soughing.

Damn!

The brush began to sway and roll with the direction of the growing breeze, the landscape coming alive from all directions.

Hawk stopped rocking.

But Dog continued his growl at a leveled measure as he slowly got to his feet. The hackles on the back of his neck rose the same time the folds of his muzzle lifted to show off canines that were polished and keen.

"Oh, yeah," whispered Hawk. "You're out there all right."

Hawk then spoke in a manner Dog had heard many times before, giving that one order geared to attack an opponent with the intent to kill.

"Get him."

And Dog bounded off into the darkness with his jaws snapping.

The assassin lay quietly in wait. Behind him, coming from the west, a wind began to surge. The brush swayed all around him, the earth coming alive with movement that gave him aid, his Ghillie suit just another part of the living landscape.

Through his NV scope, he could see the Indian sitting serenely on the porch with his dog next to him, the Native American seemingly at ease but was suspicious that he was not alone. Odd, though, that he would sit openly like that knowing he could be in the crosshairs.

And then the dog lifted its head, staring, the creature looking uncannily his way and drawing a bead.

The Indian stopped rocking.

And the dog got to its feet.

What an amazing sense of instinct and intuition, he thought.

Reaching beneath the folds of the Ghillie suit, the assassin worked his way to the hilt of a KA-BAR knife and slowly retracted it from its sheath, turning the weapon over in his hand to get a better feel, and then a better grip.

If the assassin understood one thing, he knew that dogs were full of fight and possessed a courage that was as stout as their loyalty. And that self-preservation was secondary to the welfare of their masters.

He gripped the knife tighter.

And then the dog launched itself in his direction, a straight line— the shortest distance between two points. But most noticeably to the assassin, its jaws were snapping in a manner to rent and tear.

But all he could do was to lay in wait as the beast drew near.

Hawk loved the animal more than he loved most people, its loyalty immeasurable and its companionship always an unwavering joy. From the moment Dog took off from the stoop, Hawk recalled the entire moments of the dog's life from a puppy with a penchant to play to the moment it ran off into the darkness. It was a quick collage of wonderful snippets filled with good remembrances.

A horrible sadness crept over him, but Hawk remained stoic, his face betraying little as his emotions warred for the release of pent-up sorrows in the form of tears.

While Dog served as a distraction, Hawk bolted from the porch and ran into the darkness to set himself up with a vantage point. The strategy was for Dog to locate the assassin so that he could find them through the scope, home in, draw a bead with the CheyTac, and pull the trigger.

Pressing himself against a sandstone block wall, Hawk quickly established himself by mounting the rifle on the ledge, removed his NVG, and placed an eye over the eyepiece of the weapon's scope, searching.

Through the lens, the world became a planet of lime green light as he tried to center his sight on Dog and his target.

And then he saw him, a man in a Ghillie suit waiting as Dog approached him.

Hawk began to draw a bead. "I got you," he whispered and put his finger on the trigger.

The assassin could feel his temples throbbing as adrenaline coursed through every minute fiber of his body and being. His position had been compromised—his mission, his life, everything he worked for now in jeopardy as the dog raced toward him with the intent to do nothing less than to rip his throat free and clear from his body.

The problem was that he needed to focus on the animal knowing that the Indian was maneuvering into position to make the kill. It was a simple choreographic device to provide oneself enough time for a tactical advantage.

And it was working. The assassin knew he could not keep an eye on the beast and an eye on Hawk at the same time. And no doubt the Indian was already on the move as Dog closed the distance between them with its teeth gnashing, and with eyes that gleamed like silver dollars in the faint moonlight.

With his mind and heart racing with the speed of a passing cheetah, the assassin realized that the Indian now had the advantage.

One of the oldest moves ever created, he thought. And it was still effective.

With the knife held firmly within his grasp, Dog approached him with incredible velocity, and then propelled himself toward the assassin by leaping through the air like a projectile.

Hawk watched Dog run straight toward the man wearing the Ghillie suit, the assassin standing to meet his attacker, a knife in his hand.

Beautiful!

Hawk wrapped the crook of his finger across the CheyTac's trigger, the assassin's head dead center of the crosshairs.

And he began to squeeze, slowly, his breath coming in shallow pulls.

Behind the assassin, on the sandy rise where the western sky served as the backdrop, a staircase of lightning crossed the night sky turning darkness into day for the briefest moment, the burst of white-hot light rendering the CheyTac's NV scope inoperable, as the illumination turned the landscape from a marshy green glow to snow-blind white. Everything in Hawk's vision was immediately washed away, the sudden flash sending intense pain to his optic nerves as he errantly pulled the trigger, the bullet going wide.

Dropping the barrel of the CheyTac toward the ground, Hawk quickly began to rub the sting from his eye with his forefinger.

In the distance, he could hear Dog engaged in battle, the animal growling, barking, his jaws snapping.

A shot at this point would be difficult, thought Hawk, with Dog and the assassin fighting each other on the mound in a drunken tango, the masses becoming one.

In the distance, coming closer, thunder rumbled.

Hawk took a quick look through the scope, searching for Dog and zooming in, the land once again a marshy and luminescent green where everything was once again pronounced, the sage, the brush, the saguaros.

But he could not find Dog or the assassin through the lens.

Worse, everything went quiet.

He panned the scope to the left, to the right: Nothing.

The mound where they engaged in battle was now empty.

Hawk quickly turned toward the porch. By the rocker was the assault weapon he left behind in his rush to grab the advantage on the hillside, the MP-5.

Damn!

The CheyTac M200 was excellent as a sniper rifle. And in battle, the assault weapon was the key to survival. And with the MP-5 on the porch, he might as well have been miles away. There was no doubt that he had missed his mark; therefore, *he* was now in the crosshairs.

He then lowered his NV monocular and searched the landscape.

There was nothing but the soft swaying of sage and brush, as the wind continued to march in from the west.

Where are you?

The sound of the wind soughing through the land began to pick up, the song a continuing sigh of gentle whispers.

"You are 'The Ghost,'" he told himself. *You can do this.*

Hawk tossed the CheyTac aside and methodically removed the Bowie, the long blade sliding neatly from its sheath. Hunkering down, Hawk, 'The Ghost,' closed his eyes and called upon the spirits. Although it had been a while, he was confident that the skill of his people was something inborn. Taking down 'The Ghost' was like trying to catch a wispy comma of smoke within the clench of a hand, which is impossible. And Hawk believed himself to be that smoke. He would use stealth as his tool, locate the assassin, and drive the blade across his throat.

After all, he was an elitist on his land and knew every nuance about it, which gave him the advantage.

Low to the surface of the sand, using the NVG as an aid and with the Bowie in his hand casting glints of light whenever the mirror polish of the blade reflected the cold moonlight from the east, Hawk went to find his quarry.

The last thing the assassin saw before the impact was the canine's long teeth. As the dog was taking flight the assassin's world seemed to move with the slowness of a bad dream. He noted its teeth, long and dangerously keen, and the fury within its eyes.

Just before the moment of collision, the assassin heard what he thought was the waspy hum of a bullet missing wide, and then the impact that struck him like a hammer and sending him to his backside, the knife in his hand taking flight.

The assassin held the dog at bay, at least for the moment, watching the silvery threads of drool cascading down from its jaws, snapping— could smell its fetid breath as the gnashing teeth drew closer to the assassin's throat.

The knife!

Where . . . is . . . the . . . knife?

With one hand on the dog, the assassin reached blindly to his right, his hand scrabbling through the sand like an arachnid searching for the blade, the hilt, a stone.

There. In the sand. Was that a glint of steel?

The assassin reached out, stretched his arm, his fingers flexing for the purchase of the handle.

Dog's teeth were closing in on the throat—inches away now, closer, the grazing of teeth against flesh.

The hand found something solid, the end of the knife's hilt, his fingers grazing the tip, but just out of grasp.

The German Shepherd's teeth touched the assassin's throat, the skin parting, but barely, the blood now beading, then flowing.

Dog was now going wild with blood lust.

The tip of the handle—the hilt—was now within his grasp.

The dog, in frenzy, reared his head back for the final blow.

But the assassin brought the blade out and up.

Hawk quickly learned that no man could fight age. Nor was the trait of skillful hunting something merely inbred, but something that must be maintained with constant practice. Since the man had aged without the benefit of rehearsal that would have kept his skills honed, the Native American could feel his confidence wane as quickly as his endurance.

Sweat trickled down the Indian's brow, down his cheeks, the wind doing little to cool his flesh as his heart palpitated in his chest, the rhythm threatening to misfire. And Hawk chastised himself for letting himself go.

Lightning was beginning to flash in strobe fashion, with the subsequent roll of thunder shaking the granules beneath his feet. The storm was upon him, a strong wind brewing.

As the sky flared with incredible brightness, the Indian was again blinded. In frustration he removed the NVG and tossed them, relying now on the skill of Apache stealth.

Hunkering low, the wind buffeting him so that his braided ponytail flagged behind him like the whipping mane of a horse, Hawk approached the position where Dog and the assassin converged.

But there was nothing but the footprints of a skirmish, which were quickly disappearing as the wind began to erase away all telltale signs by rolling sand and dust over the tracks.

The Indian then scanned the area with his head on a swivel.

There was nothing but the wind that was beginning to sough like a nocturnal howl, the wail of a banshee.

Above him, the moon was being eclipsed by scudding clouds, the thunderheads from the west now beginning to stake their claim.

And then another brilliant flash, another staircase of lightning as the world lit up long enough for Hawk to recognize a shape about fifty meters to the south—that of a man?

The Indian got low and drew a bead. When a subsequent bolt crossed the sky, it provided him with enough of a lighted glimpse to see it was a man in a Ghillie suit.

The Apache toyed with the knife by tossing it from hand to hand, feeling its weight, its heft, its power.

Slowly, he approached the assassin from behind, careful not to attract attention.

Thirty meters away.

His temples throbbed with blood lust while his heart hammered deep inside his chest with the beat of a drum roll.

Twenty meters away.

Hawk turned the knife over in his hand, rolling it until he got a white-knuckled grip on the leather-laced handle.

Ten meters away.

Another stroke of lightning, a dazzling display of inconstant lighting as the Indian closed in, hunkering, the point of the Bowie ready to rent flesh.

In front of him was a man wearing a Ghillie suit and someone who was oblivious to Hawk's approach.

I am one with the Earth. I am 'The Ghost.' At first, you see nothing but jungle . . .

He raised the knife in a fashion to stab and drive the blade through.

Five meters away.

. . . then the flicker of a shape . . .

The fabric of the Ghillie suit wavered likes blades of grass in a soft breeze. The assassin had his back to him.

And then the Indian struck, the blade biting deep through flesh, the sound reminiscent of driving a knife through a melon.

. . . And then you were dead.

The assassin watched from behind the sandstone rise as the Indian approached from the north. He was turning a knife over in his hand, the steel glinting against the rays of a disappearing moon.

Then in a deft move, the Indian drove the blade through his intended target.

The assassin did not betray a single emotion as the Bowie found its mark.

Hawk could feel the resistance of the blade driving through flesh again and again and again, the man in the Ghillie suit maintaining his feet.

Impossible!

More stabs, then hacking, the Bowie used like a Roman gladius—the blade slicing, cutting, and slashing.

Hawk stood back, observing, his chest heaving and pitching from lack of exercise, his power diminished.

The Ghillie suit fell away, revealing a small saguaro about six feet high, the trunk badly chopped.

Hawk looked at the knife, saw the juice of the cacti on its blade, then turned back to the saguaro, his face registering an uncertainty.

And then he felt an awful stab in the back of his neck—white-hot pain—as the point of a throwing star found its mark, crippling him, the large man falling to the sand as a boneless heap. At first, his entire body became a tabernacle of pain, of jabs and darting pins and needles, which was subsequently followed by a wave of fire that swept throughout his entirety.

The Indian gritted his teeth but refused to cry out. In his blurred vision, he could see the assassin work against the wind toward him.

The Indian could only move his eyes, but not enough to catch a glimpse of the assassin's face.

"Did you really think you still had an edge after all these years?" asked the assassin. His voice was smooth and hypnotically melodic. "Is that why you did it alone? To prove to yourself that you could still be 'The Ghost' after all these years?"

Hawk grunted, caught himself, and let the pain ride without uttering another groan.

"You're paralyzed," the assassin said. His voice was steady and even, a voice without care. "The blade damaged the column bad enough to destroy the nerves. However . . ." The assassin let his words trail as he produced a silver cylinder. With a quick depression of the button, a pick shot forward. "I can mercifully end the pain and send you off to the land of your ancestors. Or," the assassin leaned closer, "you can spend the rest of your life as a quadriplegic for the next twenty years until your body atrophies to a pathetic skeleton."

Hawk clenched his jaw in response, the disdain apparent.

"Your call, Mr. Hawk. Or, if you like, I will decide for you."

The Indian looked skyward, the repose of his face becoming stoic and unmoving.

"I see," said the assassin, who then grabbed the Bowie from the sand. "I'll need this," he added. And then he placed his hands beneath the large Native American and flipped him onto his stomach. Sweeping the braided ponytail aside, the assassin removed the star and laid the point of the pick against the base of the man's skull, the tip indenting the flesh. "May the spirits have mercy on your soul," he said.

And then he punched the weapon home.

Standing in the doorway of Kimball's room, the assassin held something in his hands. Slowly, as Kimball slept with his chest rising and falling in even rhythm, the man crept silently into the room.

Through the NV monocular he appropriated from Hawk everything appeared green and definable.

Kimball was laying on his side with his knees drawn up and his arms in a manner of self embrace.

The assassin moved closer, his footfalls so silent no one would have known the man was there, even if awake.

Kimball shifted, moving a leg.

And the assassin stilled.

A moment later, when Kimball found his comfort point, the killer moved forward careful not to awaken the sleeping giant, then placed the item that was in his hands on the night table beside the bed.

Through the NV monocular the assassin watched Kimball, his head tilting from left to right as if studying a living cryptogram.

And then he began to retreat, the assassin backpedaling slowly, softly, always maintaining a keen eye on Kimball as he slept.

And then like a wisp of smoke caught within the current of a breeze, he was gone.

CHAPTER SEVENTEEN

Vatican City

Pope Pius lay in bed propped up by a myriad of pillows examining documents through glasses that hung precariously on the tip of his nose. Papers lay scattered across his comforter. And the glow of the mid-afternoon sun rained in through the panes of the floor-to-ceiling windows.

There was a slight knocking on the door. "Come in."

Bonasero Vessucci entered the pope's chamber, softly closed the door behind him, and stood next to his friend's bed. "Are you comfortable, Amerigo?"

The pope removed the glasses and held the stem between his thumb and forefinger. "As good as expected," he answered. "No matter how much I sleep, I'm always tired." He quickly noted the concern on the cardinal's face. "What is it, Bonasero?"

The cardinal sighed. "It appears someone at Gemelli leaked the fact to *Il Messagero* that you have cancer." *Il Messagero* was the leading newspaper in Rome. "The conservatives in the College of the Cardinals are already gathering."

"It's nothing personal, my dear friend, you know that. It's politics."

"Right now, Giuseppe Angullo is politicking his way to be the next server of the pulpit."

Pius waved a hand dismissively. "He won't have the votes from the consensus party no matter how hard he tries to promote his platform. He is too much of a conservative not only to the constituency of the Church but also to the citizenry of its followers. A good man he is, but if he refuses to bend, even if bending is a necessity with a changing world, then he chances the risk of losing the faith of a constituency. Even the Curia will recognize that."

"True. But he has many supporters and is an ally to Cardinal Marcello, who also has a strong camp of followers. Together,

85

Amerigo, they may conform into a single, large camp that would endorse Marcello to take over the post as the next pontiff. *Il Messagero* is reporting this to the people in the columns of the front page."

Pius chewed on his lower lip, realizing where Vessucci was going. Marcello was a powerful cardinal with conservative constituents inside the Church that would never allow the right for the Vatican Knights to exist, deeming them too militant a faction even though there was a need for them. The Society of Seven would disband.

"If his following becomes too strong," said the cardinal, "then the Knights will not have a following. I will not keep them active behind Marcello's back, should he be elected."

"And you shouldn't," he returned. "But you have a strong backing. But more importantly, you have *my* support. I will counter Marcello's followers by calling them to counsel in solitary, if necessary, and garner their favor on your behalf. I will have them commit, as a favor to me."

"It seems so political."

"It's been the way of the Church since its conception," he said. "It's what has kept Catholicism afloat for all these centuries. And right now, it needs strong leadership. And I believe, Bonasero, with all my heart that you can take the Church on the right path in a world growing morally corrupt every day in a time when it needs us most. The Vatican Knights must be a staple to this Church until all men can lay down their swords and live in peace. But until that time, we need people like Kimball and Leviticus to man the front lines when peace is no longer forethought in the minds of men."

The cardinal leaned over and patted a pillow, an attempt to fluff it.

"We knew this day was coming," the pope stated, smiling lightly. "Nobody lives forever, Bonasero, we know that the mantle will be passed to you. All I ask is that you hold it high and make God proud with the way you serve Him."

Bonasero Vessucci nodded and smiled back, but the smile was weak and feigned.

"Now, about the Knights," said the pontiff.

Vessucci nodded. "Leviticus and Isaiah are still tied up with their missions. So far, there are no casualties or collateral damage. They've also managed to pull innocents out of harm's way and are taking them to debarkation points where allied support will take them to safe zones."

"That's good," said the pontiff. "Very good. And what about Kimball? Have we heard from him yet?"

"No. Not since the SIV aided him to get to his New Mexico contact."

"Victor Hawk?"

"Yes. But Kimball hasn't contacted us yet."

"You look concerned."

The cardinal nodded. "Kimball was supposed to contact me over an hour ago . . . But he hasn't."

The pope sighed, and then looked out the window—a beautiful day, sunny, birds taking flight against a perfect canvas of a blue sky. The man had every right to be concerned, he thought, since it wasn't like Kimball not to keep his contact times; unless, of course, he was unable to.

The pontiff closed his eyes. "Dear Lord," he said.

It was all he could whisper.

"Again!"

The wavering light of the torches cast awkward shadows against the surrounding stone walls of the chamber that held no windows. The room was circular with a domed ceiling and a wraparound second tier that overlooked the area. In the center of the room, Kimball was mentoring three of the youngest knights: Ezekiel, Job, and Joshua, with Ezekiel being the eldest at thirteen, and Job and Joshua both twelve.

Kimball was pacing back and forth like a caged animal, his hands behind the small of his back as he watched the boys with careful examination, looking for minute imperfections in style as they went through the motions and techniques of aikido, a Japanese art form of self-defense.

While Joshua and Job employed locks and holds against each other by utilizing the principle of nonresistance to cause an opponent's momentum to work against them, aikido also emphasized the importance of achieving complete mental calm and control of one's own body to master an opponent's attack. There are no offensive moves. Yet while they seemed to be grasping the techniques with fluidity, Ezekiel floundered, the moves and locks mere puzzles to him as he looked awkward in his performances.

When Job attacked Joshua, Joshua grabbed Job by the hand, bent his wrist away from his body, and sent Job into a perfect somersault with the twelve-year-old landing hard on his side on the mat.

"Very good, Joshua. And you too, Job. Both of you did a nice job. Now hit the showers. The two of you are done for the day."

Joshua and Job pumped their fists high into the air and headed off down the stone-walled corridor.

Ezekiel watched them go with hangdog eyes.

And Kimball took a knee beside him so that they were of equal height. "You want to be the best, don't you?"

The boy remained silent. He had been training for years, but seen others progress faster—those who were younger and greener; those with the affinity to do what came to them naturally, whereas he struggled mightily.

And then: "I'll never be as good as them," he finally said. "I can barely tie my shoes."

Kimball smiled. "You'll do fine, Ezekiel. I have faith in you. Sometimes you have to work harder than others to achieve greatness."

"I don't want to work harder. I just want to be good."

"Look, Ezekiel, I will work with you until you get it right. And before too long you will be better than Job and Joshua combined."

"I doubt that. They're really good."

"You doubt it? Well, let me tell you something. Remember a few years back you could barely hold a sword?"

He nodded.

"Well, you said the same thing back then. But look at you now. You're the best I have in Chinese Kenpo in your age group."

Ezekiel sighed.

Kimball brushed a hand across the boy's head, messing his hair. "I'll tell you what," he said. "Tomorrow I'll show you my secrets, how's that? I'll show you things that even Job and Joshua have never seen before."

The boy beamed. "Really?"

"If you promise to show me more heart." Kimball stood and patted Ezekiel on the crown of his head. "Off you go," he said, giving him a little push toward the hallway. "You're going to have a long day tomorrow, so get a good night's sleep."

Ezekiel responded by racing down the stone-arched corridor.

"Tomorrow!" he shouted.

Kimball watched the boy disappear beyond the light of the torches.

"He's quite a project, isn't he?" Cardinal Vessucci came forth from the shadows opposite the hallway.

"How long have you been watching?"

"For a while," said the cleric. And then: *"The boy's struggling, Kimball."*

"He's struggled with everything he's done," he returned. *"But that's okay since success does not come without struggle."*

"Kimball, the boy does not have the natural tools to be a Knight. What you do you do for yourself—not for the boy."

"I'm trying to do the right thing."

"You're trying to right this boy by hoping it will right you. To save him is honorable, yes. But save him some other way. Do not make him a Vatican Knight when he does not have the tools to become one."

"I believe in him."

"Kimball, it's noble to believe in someone who is down, but it's even nobler to let someone go if you know in your heart the truth. If he goes into battle as a warrior for the Church and is weak at his trade, then he will surely be killed. Can you live with that knowing all along that he never really belonged?"

Kimball was heated. *"You took me in believing I could find salvation within myself, yet I still haven't found it. Not yet. So, maybe I don't belong."*

"I see. You demand of the boy what you don't demand from yourself." The cardinal turned and walked to a stairway leading to the second tier that led to an outside balcony. As he climbed the stairs lifting the hem of the robe as he ascended, he continued to speak. *"I believe in you, Kimball, as does the pope and everyone within the Society of Seven. You have given us no reason otherwise."* When the cardinal reached the doorway leading to the outside loggia, he turned and faced Kimball. *"But don't expect from the boy what you don't expect from yourself."*

And then he opened the door, the chamber illuminating with a bright and dazzling . . .

. . . Light.

Beautiful, glorious morning light.

When Kimball's brain registered the light beyond the folds of his lids, he immediately reacted purely on instinct by bolting from the mattress with his hand reaching for the KA-BAR strapped to his thigh. In a skillful move, the blade was in his hand in a firm grasp, his legs parted, knees bent, the man ready to rock and roll.

He knew he had overslept, the fatigue carrying him deeper than he wanted to, the hours slipping by.

"Hawk!"

He checked his watch. He should have been up hours ago when it was still dark.

"Hawk!"

No response—just an uneasy silence.

And then he saw it—on the nightstand. Dog's head sat sentinel with his ribbon of tongue hanging out, his eyes already taking on the milky sheen of death.

He could have killed me, Kimball thought. *He was here, in this room*. Dog's head was a testament to that, a perverse message.

Hawk?

Kimball hunkered low with the blade in hand and his head on a swivel, as he moved slowly from the room and into the hallway.

The front door was open and gave view to a landscape that had been cleansed by rain, fresh and pure and unadulterated.

He moved down the hallway, his senses kicking in, the feeling of not being alone paramount.

And then: *Why didn't he kill me? He was right beside me—had every opportunity. Why didn't he do it?*

The surface of the porch was beaded with drops of rain and the air smelled like ozone, usually the promise of more rain to come, even though the sky was clear.

Kimball carefully scanned the terrain, close and afar, sighting nothing.

Next to the chair was the MP-5 Hawk left from the night before. Kimball picked it up and snuck back into the house for cover, checking the chamber and noting that the weapon was ready for fire action.

He then brought the weapon up until the scope met his eye. With his head on a swivel and his body low to the ground, he exited the house and onto the porch.

With head shifts to the left and right, Kimball pointed the weapon in the direction to the east, and then the west in grid fashion, always moving in case he was caught in the crosshairs, a hard target to hit.

Twenty minutes later he found Hawk lying face down in red clay that used to be sand until it rained. His shirt was torn and parted, revealing the Indian's backside.

Carved into the flesh was the letter 'R.'

Kimball then turned the man over, the wet clay making a perfect imprint of Hawk's face and body. Little clumps of clay stuck to the man's face and Kimball brushed it off. And then he looked out over the desert terrain knowing that the assassin was gone.

He was keeping with the sequential order of the photo, the brothers being next, Kimball last.

If he wanted Kimball dead, then he could have done it when the opportunity availed itself as he lay in bed, an easy kill. It was apparent he wanted him alive to the very end and was probably off to engage the twin brothers to complete the kills sequentially.

Kimball lowered the point of the weapon and stood to his full height.

He was, after all, alone here.

Looking down at Hawk, he recalled that his skin once held the deep, rich tone of tanned leather, but was now the color of ash.

Kimball took in a long deep breath, and then let it out with an equally long sigh. Closing his eyes, he whispered, "Iscariot."

CHAPTER EIGHTEEN

"We were worried about you," said Bonasero Vessucci. "You missed your contact mark."

Kimball hesitated on the other end. And then solemnly, "He could have killed me, Bon. He had the opportunity."

"But he didn't."

"That's not the point," he returned curtly. "I'm slipping. I was too fatigued to hang in there when I had to. I'm not a kid anymore. It's getting harder to fight time."

"Kimball, all that matters is that you're alive—"

"You're missing the point," he said. "He killed Hawk and he could easily have killed me. I don't think I can keep up with this guy, whoever he is."

"Are you sure it's just one?"

"I think so. The rain from last night washed away most of the prints. But I found a pair beneath a precipice approximately four hundred yards east of the ranch where the rain couldn't get at, and again in the barn. The same set of prints from the same pair of boots—G.I. issue."

"Government issue?"

"You got it." Kimball walked by the corral, the appaloosas paying him no attention. "Look, Bon, you got to find me a team and quick. I need them. My old team is dropping around me."

"The SIV is still searching. We're trying to get a fix on them through GPS signals from their cell phones."

"Any luck?"

"We may have found Job in Switzerland, close to Lake Lucerne. Joshua and Ezekiel are nowhere to be found."

"What about Isaiah and Leviticus?"

"They're still tied up with missions."

Kimball sighed. "Bon, whoever this guy is—he's a real pro. I'm starting to feel naked and lonely if you catch my drift."

"Trust me, Kimball. We're not sitting idle on our end. We'll assemble a team as soon as we can put one together. If we find Job before we find the others, then we'll send him ASAP."

"Job's a good man. I'd feel better with him attached to my hip than those crazy brothers I have to track down."

"They're in Maryland, yes?"

"They are."

"Then if we find Job, we'll send him directly to the Sacred Hearts Church one mile east of the Washington Archdiocese."

"I know where it's at."

"Then find the brothers and hold up. Having them is better than being alone."

"I agree. And, Bon, do whatever you can to find my team. I'm running out of time and friends."

Although Kimball could not see him, Bonasero nodded agreement on his end. "I will."

"Thanks."

"And Kimball?"

Yeah."

Another pause, then, "I'm sure you've heard the news by now."

"What news?"

"About Amerigo."

"No. I've been too busy trying to stay alive. Is he all right?"

"It's not good news," he said. "The pontiff's ill—very, very ill."

Kimball could tell by the hefty weight of the cardinal's voice that the situation was dire. "What's the matter?"

"He has cancer," he stated. "Stage four . . . And it's terminal."

Kimball stopped in his tracks, his mouth slowly dropping, and let his hand holding the phone fall to his side. He could hear the cardinal talking, the voice coming through the receiver that sounded tinny and distant from half a world away. Slowly he brought the phone up. "I'm coming home," he finally said.

"No! The pontiff has time. You need to find this assassin, Kimball. If you come home, then the assassin will surely follow you and bring the fight here. We cannot allow that under any circumstances."

Kimball clenched his jaw, the muscles in the back working furiously. "Then assemble my team, Bon. Get them to the Sacred Hearts. In the meantime, I'll take care of Hawk and be on my way to find the Brothers Grimm."

"Who?"

"Just something we used to call them," he said, and then ended the call by closing the lid of the phone.

Kimball was suddenly without sensation, his world suddenly disjointed like the random scatterings of a Pollock design, the kaleidoscopic pieces creating a surreal existence where life appeared to be spinning out of control: There was the assassin. The murders.

The game of sequential killings, the killer taking away everyone he knew.

And now the final curtain call of Pope Pius.

Kimball sat on a corral railing, the log bowing beneath his weight, and brought his hands up to cup his face. He had been bred to deal with combat and confrontations. And seeing friends die around him was a part of battle and war, something to be expected. What he was not prepared for was the hurtful emotion that swept through him regarding a man whom he had come to love—a man who saw in him the Light he did not see within himself.

So, Kimball did something he hadn't done since he was a child.

He wept for Pope Pius.

Kimball Hayden spent the better part of the morning digging two graves—one for Dog, one for Hawk—next to a towering cottonwood tree situated along the bank of a small reservoir less than a hundred yards away from the stables. The view was breathtaking. The saw-tooth mountain range to the west was a deep purple in the late afternoon shadows, the sky as blue as Jamaican waters, and the one cottonwood in the entire valley stood as a behemoth with a widespread canopy, provided a comforting shade over the graves.

Kimball leaned against the handle of the shovel looking over the two dirt mounds—one small, the other large—as a cool wind blew in from the northwest.

The leaves of the cottonwood began to sway in concert, first in one direction and then in the other. Everything seemed to be in peace where there was so much madness—a nice reprieve, even if it was just for a moment.

Kimball examined the landscape, knowing this is how Hawk would have wanted it—to be buried on the land of his people with his canine companion alongside him.

He made no crosses. He said no words.

The man who was 'The Ghost' was now with the spirits of his ancestors.

After returning the shovel to the barn, Kimball released the appaloosas, the horses taking flight as their hooves kicked up dust trails as they vanished somewhere close to the horizon.

The scene was beautifully majestic.

After gathering his items, Kimball left the ranch to begin the final leg of his journey.

He would find the brothers, engage the assassin, and hopefully come out the victor.

But if he failed in his endeavors, then he hoped to be buried somewhere as undisturbed as Hawk's grave, a place that would provide him with the peace and serenity that had eluded him throughout his entire life.

CHAPTER NINETEEN

There was something about the passenger of the four-seated Cessna the pilot did not like. Whenever he asked a question, the man usually spoke in monosyllable answers of 'yes' and 'no.' And when negotiating a set price from Albuquerque to Maryland, the man spoke in a clipped manner with his answers always brief and to the point. Evidently, he had no interest in small or gregarious talk beyond the settled cost.

The man always held his head low, the brim of his boonie cap covering most of his face except for his jawline. Beneath his clothes, the pilot could see that the man kept himself in shape by regimental exercise. On the ground next to him was a drab, olive-green duffel bag, the type used by the military.

Without a doubt the man was evasive. And with the economy the way it was, the pilot was not about to let a willing customer go So, they settled upon a $1,200/hour flight time with a guaranteed minimum of $6,000.

When agreed upon the man paid willingly, in cash, the $6,000 paid upfront.

Once the Cessna was loaded with the man taking the rear seat behind the pilot, the pilot called the tower for departure rights and taxied the plane onto the runway. During this time, the customer remained silent and always kept his head low, the brim of his hat concealing a major portion of his face, as he periodically gave sidelong glances out the window.

The pilot, in his forties, and with grizzled features of gray-brown hair and premature wrinkles, cocked his head and spoke. "It's going to be a long flight—say, six hours. Mind if I smoke?"

"Yes." Again—a monosyllable answer.

The pilot snapped on a few switches on his console. "Whatever."

Within moments they were flying at an altitude of 20,000 feet.

The assassin knew he was being evasive. He also knew that such actions prompted suspicion from most people. But he also sensed desperation in this man who would sell his principles if the price was right.

The price was fixed at $6,000 in cash; all upfront and paid immediately with no further questions and with the clear understanding that the pilot was to fly him to Maryland.

After loading the duffel bag into one of the rear seats, he took the seat behind the pilot, the act in itself telling the pilot that he wasn't interested in camaraderie, talk, or any type of amity.

With his head hung low he often took sidelong glances out the window, the landscape in the distance a primitive horizon of mesas and peaks in blends of reds and oranges, the strata lines running across them marking the ages.

From the front, the pilot spoke. "It's going to be a long flight—say, six hours. Mind if I smoke?"

"Yes."

The pilot then hit the switches on the console in what the assassin took to be an action of someone in a huff.

Then: "Whatever."

Once the Cessna leveled off at 20,000 feet, the assassin ran the palm of his hand against the duffel bag next to him. And by feel, he found what he was looking for. Beneath the fabric, he located the outline of the CheyTac M200's stock, the weapon broke down and neatly packed.

It was something he could not get aboard a commercial flight; therefore, the private route.

After he had taken the life of the Native American, he saw the CheyTac as an asset and took it not as a trophy, but as a necessity since he was about to go up against the Hardwick brothers.

So, keeping his head held low, the assassin remained silent throughout the flight as he kept his palm against the bag as a constant reminder that the weapon would always be within reach.

Kimball Hayden was on a flight path of his under the false credentials afforded him by the Vatican's SIV Unit. He sat in the economy class, the breadth of his shoulders an inconvenience to the two women sitting on each side of him, their space minimized by his size. But neither said a word once they spotted his collar. They only nodded and feigned smiles, a show of politeness to the priest who was not a priest.

After he spoke with Cardinal Vessucci from Hawk's ranch, the SIV immediately set up the next available flight to Annapolis in Maryland. Once there he would head west toward Baltimore, home of the Hardwick brothers, two of the most hedonistic people who were insubordinate, stubborn, and roguish beyond principle, but excellent soldiers, nonetheless.

On the foldout table before him, he had the photos sitting in a neat pile. In his hand was the glossy of his old unit. Everyone who had been terminated had the spelled marking of the letter in the name of 'Iscariot' beside their name except for Victor Hawk. Using a marker, Kimball simply wrote the letter 'R' over Hawk's image, then sighed.

For a long moment, he stared at the images, then he remembered the camaraderie they shared as an elite force, such as their shared arrogance that they were too good to take down because they were unstoppable.

Now, the arrogance had come back to bite them.

There *was* somebody out there that was better, stronger, faster, and far more deadly. And he was taking his team down with seemingly little effort.

For a lengthy moment, Kimball stared at the photo, the team who posed in front of a camera so many years ago. A photo that now had three surviving members. With his marker, he circled the face of the soldier next to Hawk, the person next in line and most likely within the assassin's sights. Jeff Hardwick.

After laying the glossy down, Kimball glanced at his watch. It would be another two hours before he would touchdown in Annapolis. And perhaps another thirty minutes to Baltimore once he rented a vehicle.

And then he wondered one thing: *Was the assassin one step behind or one step ahead?*

Either way, he was about to find out.

CHAPTER TWENTY

Baltimore, Maryland

Jeff Hardwick always killed with impunity because he could. Having been a member of the Pieces of Eight—a black-op unit from the Force Elite—a one-time government wetwork team, he and his brother had found life difficult. At first, when he was given his release for younger, more athletic super soldiers when age became a factor, he was sent off with a pension, an atta-boy pat on the back, and the following parting words: *Oh, and by the way, if you disclose any information regarding the Pieces of Eight or the Force Elite, expect to be buried inside a pauper's grave moments after the divulging words leave your lips.*

Nice! Especially from a government, you served well and without question.

Nevertheless, with his little government stipend, which was pooled with his brother's, they amassed enough to purchase an army/navy store in downtown Baltimore. At first, they struggled by taking over a business that was floundering, trying to rebuild it from the ground up with potential connections in the military field, such as mercenaries in need of special hardware.

The first year was a struggle, most deals falling through until they were contacted by old teammates—Walker, Grenier, and Arruti—who established their militant organization for hire in third-world nations by governments with first-world money.

They had become their sole arms' connection, profiting beyond imagination by supplying items such as claymores, sentry turrets, or RPG's—basically illegal wares of all types.

So, within a year, the store had become nothing less than a front for selling illegal arms.

And the Hardwick brothers flourished.

Now with padded bank accounts in the Caymans, and with vast

sums across countries such as Belize, Brazil, and Costa Rica, Jeff and Stanley Hardwick relished in the fact that there was a profitable market for just about everything.

And *their* market was destruction.

Walking beneath an overcast sky that was uniformly gray, and with his collar hiked up against a mild wind coming from the east, Jeff Hardwick walked as though he owned the streets, the city, the world. With his lofty chin held high he moved with the authority of a man who believed that rules weren't made for him, and everyone else should step aside as he passed them by. It was also this mindset of self-anointing shared by his brother, Stanley, who was eleven months older.

With a conservative haircut and regimental gym-build, the man looked years younger. He was lean with broad shoulders, thick thighs, and massive biceps, and was much like his brother who was his physical facsimile. Neither brother was to be messed with in a one-on-one situation. To mess with one Hardwick brother was to mess with both. And it was this reputation throughout the streets of Baltimore that allowed them to bend the rules without impunity and rule by fear.

If organized crime had a title or name associated with it, it was 'Hardwick.'

Walking east for a stretch before turning south, Jeff moved into an area hardly considered a decent neighborhood. There were aged storefronts with barred windows and cracked glass that was pieced together with strips of duct tape. Fruit vendors kept their produce beneath canopies that were torn at the edges and wagged with the course of a slight breeze. And drug-addled punks often hung out in the mouths of alleyways and street corners, sometimes congregating at the base of stone stairwells that led into apartments infested with vermin, rats, and roaches. But whenever a Hardwick walked by chatter always ceased, as if in homage, until the man walked by.

Grabbing a key ring from his pocket, Jeff inserted a key into the lock and twisted, the bolt drawing back, and then he opened the door, entering.

The foyer immediately lit up from a lamp with a motion sensor, which revealed a second door that appeared firmer, that of cast iron. On the wall was a keypad. He quickly typed in a code—eight characters—and disabled the alarm. Once done he typed in the second set of codes, this time twelve characters, and the keypad mechanically pushed outward from the wall and tilted downward to reveal an optical scan. Placing his eyes against the lenses, the computer read the orb sequence calibrated to read the uniqueness of the Hardwick brothers roadmap of eyes and confirmed his identity. No one else held the right to enter, especially when there was well over a million dollars of illegal arms stashed away in the lower vault.

After scanning his eyes, a massive bolt from the door automatically pulled back and the door swung open with mechanical slowness.

The store was dark with no windows, old uniforms, and military helmets lined shelves that were heavy and laden with dust. Shadows remained unmoving with some shadows darker than others. And when he turned on the lights everything seemed bleak and gray and still, a coating of dust usurping everything.

After all, everything on this level was a prop and nothing ever moved. Everything of value was down below.

Tossing the keys on a glass countertop that was so dusty the items within the casing could hardly be discernable, Jeff Hardwick checked his answering machine by dialing in another code for retrieval.

Nothing.

Jeff, nor his brother Stan, had heard from Grenier or Arruti in over a week, which was cause for concern knowing they had something going on in the Philippines with a high priority need for goods and wares.

Hanging up the phone that was specially built to encrypt all incoming calls and deflect all others not recognized by the computer, Jeff pulled out his cell phone and called his brother.

When Stan answered, he said one thing: "The vendor inquiring about the uniforms never called back."

And it was cryptically understood: The firm of Grenier and Arruti, for whatever reason, had put current purchases on hold.

Something wasn't right.

"*I see,*" he returned evenly. And without adding anything further, he hung up.

CHAPTER TWENTY-ONE

Vatican City

There is a chamber beneath the Basilica that is the nerve center of the *Servizio Informazione del Vaticano,* the SIV. It is encased behind walls of bomb-resistant glass, the room itself a marvel of engineering with the entire wall a massive screen TV that can be enabled to be a singular screen or divided up into multiple screens for multiple purposes. Computer consoles lined multi-tiered levels like a motion picture theater, the rear levels slightly elevated so that the patrons sitting in front can view the mega-screen without obstructing those behind them. The staff manning the consoles or pouring over data were uniformly dressed in black dress pants and tie, a white shirt, and a scarlet dress jacket bearing the emblem of the Vatican on the pocket; the crossed keys of Simon Peter—one silver, one gold—situated beneath the papal crown.

With diplomatic ties to more than ninety percent of the nations worldwide, the Vatican had a ringside seat.

As Cardinal Vessucci made his way down the winding stone staircase, hiking up the hem of his cassock while descending, his mind was stewing with many thoughts. He was about to lose his friend to cancer, leaving a vacancy upon the papal throne for which he, and two others, were considered the forerunners in a brewing campaign between conservative parties. Pius had already voiced his desire as to his successor. But the cardinal knew that every election was motivated by political machinations rather than the wishes of the incumbent.

When he reached the bottom stair, he could see the glass partition of the SIV Center. The video wall opposite the computer consoles gave a view to a collage of moving images, mostly of the Middle East, whereas others showed the hotspots of the Philippines and Brazil.

As he walked the length of the corridor, he came to a thick glass door, the framework of the glass panel bordered by titanium edging.

After giving a perceptible wave of his hand to the SIV agent on the other side, the man waved back in acknowledgment and began to type a series of numbers on a keypad. When the sequence was completed, the door opened, and a rush of cool air escaped the chamber. The moment he stepped inside; the glass door closed behind him with a whoosh that sounded like escaping steam. It was the sound of the chamber being sealed.

His other moving concern besides the impending death of his long-time friend was the welfare of his long-time brother in spirit, Kimball Hayden. After learning that the assassin could have killed Kimball, he was greatly disturbed.

He had never questioned the particular set of skills Kimball possessed. But now he had to wonder if the game had finally passed him by. *Was Kimball out of his league?*

This time—maybe.

Usually, the pressures of corporeal life were handled with the power of prayer and faith— the combination putting him at ease in the same manner of self-meditating. But his apprehension could not be mollified to any degree. And he knew it never would be until an assembled team of Knights could be sent to support him. Especially since Kimball's old team of highly skilled warriors were dropping in the clichéd term of proverbial flies.

Would the Vatican Knights fare any better?

The cardinal wasn't entirely confident since this assassin was unlike any other.

All he could do was pray and hope.

As the cardinal stood gazing up at the myriad pictures on the big-screen monitor, the assistant director of the SIV approached him.

"Afternoon, Cardinal Vessucci." The man was small and wispy looking, the collar of his jacket too wide for such a pencil-thin neck. And his face was as slender as the blade of a hatchet. But when he spoke his voice sounded as smooth as flowing honey. It was the voice of someone who could soothe the masses in the face of tragedy.

"My friend Carmello, how are you today?"

The assistant director looked at the video monitor and gestured with a sweep of his bony-thin hand towards the screen. "Busy," he said. "The world never sleeps."

"I see that."

"But as big as this planet is, nothing is impossible to find with today's technology."

"You found the Knights on sabbatical?" he stated this with a tone full of hope.

"Not all," said the assistant director. "But we did find Job."

"Where?"

The assistant director went to the nearest console with Vessucci at his heels. After typing in a set code, a portion of the screen in the northeast corner of the giant monitor began to take on the landscape images of a satellite feed. Mountains, valleys, and snow-capped peaks; rivers, lakes, and pools of blue water everywhere—the pristine image of Lake Lucerne, Switzerland.

"We were able to center in on the GPS coordinates of his cellphone after you provided us with his number. It's an amazingly simple tool. Based on the number, we were able to zero in almost immediately to his point."

"Have you found Joshua or Ezekiel?"

The assistant director shook his head. "We're still working on it," he said. "Neither seems to have a cellphone, laptop, or anything electronic that we could singularly set our sights on. It could be that they have yet to engage their devices."

"Or that they didn't bring any along. They are, after all, on sabbatical. Getting away from the real world is what sabbatical is all about—for prayer and meditation."

"We won't give up," he added. "If we found Job, then we can find the others. All it takes is determination and perseverance."

Vessucci smiled and clapped a hand on the diminutive man's shoulder. "That's true, my friend. But I need you to find them as quickly as you can. The situation is quite dire."

The cardinal looked back at the screen. It was uncanny, he thought, to look upon the earth with an almost omniscient point of view. And then: "Have you contacted Job yet?"

"Not yet. But we have agents on the way to inform him of his need here at the Vatican."

"Do you know where he is exactly?"

"Yes, Cardinal. By our coordinates, he's somewhere close to the Lion of Lucerne."

CHAPTER TWENTY-TWO

Lake Lucerne, Switzerland

The Lion of Lucerne is a sculpted monument of a mortally-wounded lion carved into the side of a stone face commemorating the Swiss Guards who were massacred in 1792 during the French Revolution when revolutionaries stormed the Tuileries Palace in Paris during the August Insurrection. When fighting broke out unexpectedly after the Royal Family had been escorted from the Palace to take refuge with the Legislative Assembly, the Swiss Guards ran low on ammunition and were soon overwhelmed by greater numbers with hundreds killed and many more massacred after their surrender. An estimated two hundred more died in prison of their wounds or were killed during the September Massacres that followed. So, in 1821, with the designing aid of Bertel Thorvaldsen, and the stone engraving completed by Lukas Ahorn, the sculpture had become a symbolic feature of the courage and the testament of the Swiss Guards.

And Job was proud to have served within their ranks before becoming a Vatican Knight.

Standing six one with 180 pounds of solid but sinewy muscle, Job was the only true Vatican Knight to hale from Switzerland, whereas others had come from other walks of life. At the age of ten his father, a judge in the Federal Court of Switzerland, sentenced a major figure in organized crime to life imprisonment for convictions ranging from racketeering to murder. As a result of his ruling, he was subsequently gunned down along with his wife and three children. Job, however, did not go without punishment as two of the assassin's bullets scored a double shot with two rounds to his back. But before he bled out, Job, or Johannes, was discovered by a nanny who quickly contacted the authorities.

And though he lived through the trauma, it was later determined to be in the best interest of the child that he falsely declared deceased by

105

the media to protect him from future vendettas.

Then, as an orphan, he was granted the opportunity to serve in the Vatican. At the age of eleven and less than five months after the death of his family, young Johannes began his three-year study to become an altar boy. But his studies were short-lived when he caught the eye of Cardinal Bonasero, who saw in him the proclivity to be someone possessing a very particular set of skills. After falling under the cardinal's auspices, he was then directed to follow the tutelage of Kimball Hayden and to serve in the glory of the Church as a Vatican Knight. But as Johannes became a young man and having been born in Switzerland, he found another calling to serve in the Swiss Guard. And he was granted that privilege, only to be incorporated into one of the most skilled fighting fraternities in the world once his calling as a guard concluded.

And fighting had become a constant way of life—sometimes protecting the Church and its citizenry to the point of bone weariness. So, as a measure against battle fatigue, a Vatican Knight was granted a short sabbatical to get away and commune with nature, with life, to explore his inner self through faith and God, and to find inner peace.

Right now, Johannes Eicher was in complete harmony as he sat beneath a cerulean blue sky on a bench facing the Lion of Lucerne, admiring the smooth contours and exceptional detail of the sculpture.

As he sat there a whisper of a breeze brushed against his skin like a sigh, a gentle massage.

And nothing could be better.

"Brother Job?"

Job started. To be called Job within the circles of the Church was one thing. To be called Job in his township when his true name was Johannes Eicher was another. The covert moniker of a Vatican Knight is always kept sacred and close to the vest.

Two men dressed in dark, matching trench coats approached him, their hands deep in their pockets. Both sported clean haircuts and faces so smoothly-shaven they appeared waxy. Around their necks, they wore the pristine white bands of the cleric's collar.

"I'm sorry," said Job. "Do I know you?"

The taller of the two feigned a smile and pulled his credentials from his pocket, a flipside wallet, and showed Job his ID card.

The *Servizio Informazione del Vaticano*, the SIV.

"I'm sorry to bother you, Brother Job," the man said, "I know you're on sabbatical, but the matter we bring you is of dire urgency."

"I was assured by the pope that my time alone would not be interrupted. I have another five days."

"But the message we bring you *is* from Pope Pius himself."

Job leaned forward with his hands clasped together in an attitude of prayer and eyed the Lion of Lucerne. "I know," he said, deeply saddened. "He's quite ill."

"His illness is not the urgency we speak of."

Job cocked his head. "Then why are you here?"

The smaller of the two took a step forward. "You know of us?" he asked. "About the SIV and what we do?"

"Of course, I do."

"Then you know we're held to a higher standard when it comes to keeping the secrets of the Vatican."

Job never took his eyes off the sculpture. "With all due respect . . ." He purposely let his words trail in a way to goad the SIV official to offer his name.

"Monsignor Gianicomo," he returned.

"With all due respect, Monsignor Gianicomo, what is it you're trying to tell me?" Job turned away from the lion and met the monsignor's eyes with a steely gaze. "Please."

"As agents of the *Servizio Informazione del Vaticano*, it is our sworn and noble duty to maintain all that is confidential and holy from the truth of the Shroud of Turin to the reality of the Third Secret. It is also our duty to know about the Vatican Knights and provide assistance when necessary."

Job was taken aback but refused to show it, his features unmoving. He was led to believe that the Vatican Knights were deeply entrenched as a black op group known only by the Society of Seven—a complement made up of the pope's six closest allegiances, with Pius serving as the seventh and supreme member.

But surprisingly enough, this wasn't the case.

The monsignor, however, could still decipher the warrior's thoughts. "We have always known about the Vatican Knights," he added. "Loyalty above all else, except Honor. It is also the creed of the SIV."

Job stood. And the man took a step back.

"You said the pope has asked for my services."

The man nodded. "He and Cardinal Vessucci have asked us to find you."

"And how did you find me?"

"We triangulated your position through the GPS in your cell phone," he said.

Job winced. *Of course!* It was such a simple method with today's technology.

And then with a calm but unmitigated authority in his voice, he said, "In the services of my pontiff, I gladly surrender my sabbatical."

The monsignor offered a smile, showing rolls of ruler-straight teeth. "Thank you, Job."

"Now tell me what it is that my services are needed for."

As they headed back to Job's hostel, Job was flanked by the clergy as they walked across the covered bridges that spanned the waterways, Monsignor Gianicomo gesticulated fervently as he waved his hands with a conductor's enthusiasm to affect his points.

He spoke of Kimball when he was a member of the Pieces of Eight with the American government, and whose members were now being killed off by someone who was levels above any assassin they had ever seen before.

—*Kimball can handle himself*—

—*Not this time. The assassin made it clear he could have killed him easily but chose to wait*—

Job listened intently, the features of his face going from stoic to concern; the way his brows above the bridge of his nose dipped sharply downward and the way he began to chew the inner side of his cheek—always a nervous habit.

But still:

—*Kimball is Kimball; a Vatican Elite*—

—*That may be so. But he may also be out of his league and needs your help*—

—*That goes without question. But Kimball Hayden is never out of his league*—

—*Let's hope so. Because right now he's all alone*—

They spoke further of Job's position to back Kimball up to better the odds, and how they were on the search for Ezekiel and Joshua to aid the supreme Knight in his hunt.

—*Kimball had to take this fight elsewhere before the assassin could bring his fight to the Vatican*—

—*Do we have an idea as to who he is?*—

—Nothing—

—With all your resources?—

—Whoever this man is, he's nothing less than a phantom—

A pause, and then in a tone of deference:

—So is Kimball—

The men continued onward toward the hostel, the once beautiful day no longer as severe cloud cover began to move in and threatened to open riotously.

CHAPTER TWENTY-THREE

The moment Kimball landed he rented a vehicle and, after purchasing a map, charted a course to the Hardwick brothers' store. After parking his rented car in a fenced-in lot that charged by the hour, Kimball grabbed the manila envelope on the seat beside him and made his way down streets lined with brick-row houses.

Trash filled the gutters as rogue curs lapped at the filthy stream of water meandering its way toward the sewage grates; and neighborhood toughs, all wearing colors unique to their gang affiliation, sat on the steps of residences shouting out in an undisciplined manner. But when Kimball walked by, they spoke not a word, their eyes focusing on the band of the cleric's collar. And then all of a sudden, they would slip into their second skin, becoming disciplined and quiet, as if the presence of the priest was deterrent enough for wayward behavior.

Kimball passed by poorly kept storefronts until he came across a building reminiscent of a warehouse, the cinderblock walls were laden with pictures of colorful urban murals. Above the door was a sign that was cheap in its design: HARDWICKS' ARMY & NAVY SUPPLIES.

Standing on the sidewalk across the way, Kimball drew the air with a long pull, filled his lungs with stale air, then released it with an equally long sigh.

The Hardwick Boys, he thought, were the last of a unique band of brothers.

Now, after all these years, he could only wonder how they would welcome him back into their fold believing he died so long ago when, in fact, he absconded from service.

Would they view him with the same disappointment as Hawk?

Stepping off the sidewalk, he was about to find out.

CHAPTER TWENTY-FOUR

When the Cessna landed the assassin stated to the pilot another monosyllable word: 'Thanks,' then collected his gear and melded with the crowd in the terminal, disappearing from the pilot's life hoping to be nothing more than a memory soon to be faded or forgotten.

After securing transport, he made a quick trip to Baltimore to challenge the Hardwick brothers and took vigil on an abandoned rooftop across the street from the surplus store. Earlier he had seen one of the Hardwick's entering the store, the man moving with all the pomp and circumstance of an aristocrat. The way he held his chin in a self-aggrandizing manner or the way he walked with a hitch in his gait, were gestures that *this* particular Hardwick thought he was well above everyone else on the urban jungle food chain.

It was also the 'Hardwick' myth that the assassin was willing to dispel with the aid of his pick.

As the day wore on, he took mental notes from the rooftop, as well as to draw the outlay of the streets. He noted entry and exit routes, vantage points from high and level surfaces, and charted a means of escape from several locations.

The assassin was planning well.

Within two hours of his arrival and approximately ninety minutes after Hardwick entered the store, the assassin caught the glimpse of a man walking with a purpose. The man was large and well built, and he wore a cleric's shirt with the pristine white band of the Roman Catholic collar. He also wore black fatigues with cargo pockets and high-ankle military footwear. On the pocket of his shirt was the emblem of a silver Pattée within a blue shield supported by lions: The symbol of the Vatican Knights.

Kimball Hayden!

The assassin watched from a safe distance surprised that 'the priest who is not a priest' was less aware of his surroundings, given the fact that he knew he was a targeted man. However, the assassin also knew that Kimball was untouchable until the Hardwick brothers were terminated.

For a long moment, he watched the Knight stand across the street from the surplus store, Hayden appearing lost in some type of self debate before stepping off the curb and making his way to the front of the mural-laden store. A manila envelope was in his hand.

No doubt the dossiers, the assassin considered.

Now the game would become harder, he thought, the competition much higher. But the odds of three to one deterred him little. He took out Hawk, The Ghost, with little effort, the old man's skills eroded over time. But the Hardwicks looked fit and ready to fight at the drop of a hat. And there was no doubt as to the skills of Kimball Hayden. Without reservation, the confrontation between these three just ratcheted up several notches to a much higher degree of difficulty.

This time Kimball would be waiting.

And so would the Hardwick brothers.

From his perch the assassin watched Kimball make his way across the street and to the establishment's front door. After another moment of hesitation, Kimball reached up and pushed the button.

Even from his position, the assassin could hear Kimball being buzzed in.

He was that close.

Jeff Hardwick could hardly believe his ears when the door buzzer sounded off. The army/navy surplus was widely known in the 'streets' to be a front and not truly an outlet for goods sold at all.

Curious!

Through the spycam, Hardwick could see the image of a large man. In his hand was a folder of some kind, perhaps an envelope. His first thought was a mail drop-off that had to be signed for. But with closer examination, he saw the cleric's collar. The man's face, however, remained obscured since he kept his eyes downward.

A priest?

When Hardwick reached beneath the counter, he did so for two reasons: one, to hit the buzzer to allow the man in; and two, to ready himself with a Glock, in case something wasn't quite copasetic.

He took the weapon and placed it within the waistband of his pants, covered it with the tail of his shirt, and buzzed the man in.

The man looked anything but cherubic, Jeff Hardwick thought. He had broad shoulders and a tapered waist, along with the angular and chiseled features of an athlete rather than a preacher. The edges of his eyes looked as hard as flint with the promise that a single spark could ignite something extremely volatile within. And when he walked, he did so with the type of authority neither of the Hardwick brothers could match, no matter how hard they tried.

This man moved like a seasoned warrior.

Hardwick slowly eased his hand behind him and found the familiar curve of the pistol's grip. "Something I can do for you?" he asked.

The large man moved closer. "Has it been that long that you don't even recognize me?"

Hardwick cocked his head to one side and closed his eyes into narrow slits, focusing. Like taking a splash of ice-cold water to his face his eyes suddenly flared with recognition, the whites the size of communion wafers. He slowly lowered his hand from behind and found a place on the countertop to steady him.

"Kimball?"

The Knight nodded. "It's been a long time, Jeff."

Hardwick stepped around the filthy glass casing, his eyes remaining fixed. "You're supposed to be dead—in Iraq. We held a ceremony for you."

"Can't believe everything you hear, right?"

"What happened?"

Kimball stared for a long moment before placing the manila envelope on top of the glass counter. "I ran," he said simply. "I couldn't do the job anymore."

The muscles in the back of Hardwick's jaw flexed. And Kimball could see something seething inside him.

"You ran." It was not a question, but a statement of aversion. "You of all people,' he said with contempt, "the biggest swinging dick in the unit, a coward?"

"It wasn't like that at all."

"You ran! Runners are cowards!"

"Jeff—"

"Kimball Hayden, the man without a conscience, the killing machine we all wanted to be, a coward."

113

Kimball sighed. This was not going to be easy.

"Why are you here? And what the hell is that around your neck? Now I know you didn't get all religious on me," he said. "God abandoned you as He did us for the choices we made as members of the Pieces of Eight. You think you're going to be absolved of your sins by masquerading as a priest?"

"I'm not a priest."

"Thanks for clearing that up," he said sarcastically. "To think you were a hypocrite as well as a coward."

"I didn't come here to ask you for acceptance."

"Then why are you here? And why are you wearing that damned collar if you're not a priest?"

Kimball raised a finger and brushed it lightly across the band. "I'm an emissary of the Church," he answered.

"An emissary? I'm afraid that's a ten-dollar word to me."

"It means agent or representative of the Vatican."

"The Vatican?" Hardwick couldn't help himself as he stared at the man, and then at the collar, noting the genuine cast of truth radiating from the man's blue eyes the same way a battery of heat shimmers off the desert floor. And then he noted the incongruous wear of black military pants and combat footwear. "From the waist up you're a priest," he said. "But from the waist down you're dressed as a soldier." Hardwick hesitated, and then: "What exactly do you do as an *emissary* from the Church?"

"Whatever needs to be done," he answered.

"Are you here to save my soul? Is that—like—a priority in the eyes of God or something?" His smile took on something mischievous and cruel, something maliciously twisted. "Are you here to save the Hardwick boys?"

He pushed the envelope across the glass surface of the countertop towards Hardwick. "In a way, I guess you can say that," he said. "But not in the way you think."

He opened the folder. Inside were a bundle of photos, black and white glossies. Lying on top was a photo of a legless Walker tied to a wooden table with the letter 'I' carved into his back.

"Let's start with this one, shall we?" said Kimball. "But first I think you'll need to contact your brother."

Hardwick's jaw began to fall, his features slowly descending into awe.

"Call your brother," Kimball stated firmly. "Now."

CHAPTER TWENTY-FIVE

Stanley Hardwick was just as amazed as his brother and filled with the same inbred disdain for any measure of cowardice, as he stared at Kimball from across the counter, his hardcore features twisted into a leer and his arms folded defensively across his chest. "I should kick your ass."

"You could try, but you wouldn't get too far."

"My brother tells me you're a priest of some kind."

"An emissary," he corrected. "Or is that a ten-dollar word to you as well?"

"I know what it means."

Stanley looked at the collar and gave off a chortle that sounded more like a single, snide bark of condescending amusement. "Here we are mourning your loss while you were sipping cognac in Italy." He shook his head. "You cowardly son of a bitch."

Jeff Hardwick pulled up next to his brother. They looked so much alike, Kimball thought. Not exactly twins, but close to it—same features and physiques with bully-like mindsets that were perhaps more of a learned trait rather than a genetic one.

"All right," said Jeff, "you're here, so now what?"

Stanley remained fixed with a hard stare as he remained unmoving behind the counter.

Sliding out the first photo, Kimball pointed out that Walker, the first of the Pieces of Eight to be targeted and killed by an unknown assassin, then continued with Arruti and Grenier in the posed sequence of the photo starting from the top row from left to right, then the bottom row, once again in the sequential order from left to right.

Stanley Hardwick seemed less hardened and soberer to the situation.

"We run an operation," he told Kimball, "of selling hard-to-find wares."

"You mean illegal weapons."

Stanley held his hands out as a gesture to emphasize the store in general. "You think we opened this place up to sell this crap? Of course not. Our profit comes from selling arms. We were Arruti's and Grenier's top suppliers."

Jeff Hardwick picked up the photos of Walker, Arruti, and Grenier, and held them in his hand like the splayed cards of a poker hand. "Now we know why they haven't contacted us," he said.

"How did you get these?" asked Stanley.

"Through contacts."

"I know that. Are you doing this through the Church?"

Kimball remained silent as Jeff put down the photos and picked up the glossy of Victor Hawk, AKA 'The Ghost,' lying face down in red clay. The letter 'R' was carved into his back. "There ain't anybody good enough on this planet to take out The Ghost," he said.

"Apparently, there is," Kimball returned. "He could have killed me too, but he didn't."

"That would have been no big loss," commented Stanley.

Kimball could almost feel the venom flowing from Stan Hardwick's lips.

"The Ghost was old, brother—lost his edge. That's what happens when you don't train consistently. You lose your edge."

"Really?" Jeff held up the photos of Arruti and Grenier. "Then what about these two?" he stated rhetorically. "We know they didn't lose their edge. They were still at the top of their game and we both know that."

Stan Hardwick refused to look at the photos. Instead, he kept his steely eyes on Kimball.

"This man, this assassin," began Kimball, "is targeting us for whatever reason. He killed five skilled soldiers in such a simple fashion it's hard to believe that it's just one man doing so."

"And you're sure it's just one man?",

"There was only one set of prints at Hawk's ranch."

"That only means to me that it took one guy to take out Hawk." Then: "Look, Hawk was nothing special. Not anymore. He let himself get fat and his skills suffered for it . . . He became nothing more than an old man living off the memories of a time long faded. A boy scout could have taken him out."

Kimball could hardly dispute the claim since one set of footprints could have meant that the assassin performed the mission solo. But assassin teams usually worked in unison with team concepts essential to the movement of completing the task successfully. Manpower was always critical to keep a *solitary* out of the crosshairs. If this assassin had backup, he found no evidence.

"Oh, no," he said. "I'm sure it's just one man. You know the rule: No one works rogue unless you are rogue."

"Then that begs a couple of questions, doesn't it?"

"Obviously."

"Like, who is this guy? And why is he doing this, to begin with?"

All three men stood stone-faced.

No one had an answer to either question.

CHAPTER TWENTY-SIX

Vatican City

For the first time since his diagnosis, Pope Pius was feeling uncomfortable. His chest felt heavy. And when he labored to do anything physical, he often struggled for breath.

Standing before a floor-to-ceiling window with a placating hand on his chest, Pope Pius afforded himself the moment to gaze upon St. Peters Square with an almost omniscient point of view, seeing everything.

From his vantage point, he could see the elliptical colonnade with two pairs of Doric columns forming its breadth, each bearing the Ionic entablatures of Baroque architecture. In the center of the colonnade stood the 83-foot-tall obelisk which was moved to its present location by Pope Sixtus V in 1585. The obelisk dated back to the BC period in Egypt and moved to Rome in the first century to stand in Nero's Circus. On top of the obelisk, it was rumored to hold a large bronze globe containing the ashes of Julius Caesar, which was removed when the obelisk was erected in St Peter's Square. The colonnade, the obelisk, the two exquisite fountains in the square, one by Maderno and the other by Bernini, were a fusion of other cultures. Perhaps a symbolic gesture to incorporate people from all walks of life, he considered. All people under the eyes of God, all with a defined culture, all blending to make a collective of One.

Soon it would be gone for the glory of His Light, he considered. And then the ailing Pius closed his eyes and smiled.

He had lived a glorious life.

Turning away from the window the pope made his way back to his desk with a hand over the burning irritation deep in his chest. His breathing became arduously difficult to maintain, his lungs demanding as his steps all of a sudden becoming too challenging to manage. When the pope finally reached his chair, he positioned himself over the cushioned seat and let his knees buckle, the pontiff falling onto the cushion.

In time, he found reserve with his breathing self-regulating to a normal rhythm.

And then he stabilized, his eyes remaining closed.

"Your Holy Eminence, are you all right?"

The pontiff did not hear the arrival of Cardinal Vessucci, who stood opposite him on the other side of the desk with his hands hidden beneath the wide sleeves of his garment.

Pius smiled. "It's getting worse, my friend. But yes, I'm fine."

"You look tired, Amerigo. Perhaps the physician—"

Pope Pius held up a halting hand. "Bonasero, nature will inevitably take its course. There will be times of discomfort. But in the end, I will end up in His glory and there will be no pain."

The cardinal nodded. "I only meant well," he said.

"I know, my dear friend. Your concern for me is uplifting." The pope slowly lowered his hand to the desktop. "So, what can I do for you, Bonasero?"

The cardinal took a seat. "There is talk within the College that Cardinal Marcello is garnering massive support to succeed you for the papal throne."

"There is always a storm before the calm, Bonasero. Politicking has always been the right of those in contention. You must do the same."

"I have, Your Eminence, but Cardinal Marcello appears to be pulling well ahead and might be the forerunner. I need your endorsement to members within the College."

"And you shall have them. But we still have time. It's best to listen to all sides to present enlightenment for all. People will always gravitate to those whom they believe will have the answer to resolve any solution."

"But Cardinal Marcello's voice is that of ultra-conservatism. I cannot compete with that in good conscience, knowing the necessity of the Vatican Knights. He, and others like him, would view them as an abomination against the principles of the Church rather than a necessity for the right of the Church to protect its sovereignty, its welfare, and its citizenry."

"And for that reason, you must make those within the College realize the world is forever changing in its philosophy. Then we, too, must change with it. If we don't, then the institution will eventually die." The pope let out a sigh. "You're well with words, my friend. Be patient and listen. Then let those weigh the options between tradition and necessity."

"Sometimes, Amerigo, traditionalist thinking is the most difficult obstacle to overcome. If I don't get that throne, the Vatican Knights will be no more—especially if Cardinal Marcello adorns the papal crown. And if that happens, then we will no longer be capable of protecting our citizenry abroad, or the interests and sovereignty of the Vatican." He paused for a brief moment, and then, "It's a different world, Amerigo."

"Not so different," he returned. "There have always been battles within and beyond the walls of the Vatican. There have been Crusades from every scale imaginable from the grand to the minuscule. Winning the recognition and ear of the College is just another crusade to be fought and won. And I'm confident the Vatican Knights will be around for quite some time."

"I pray that they will be, Your Eminence."

"Have you found those on sabbatical?"

Vessucci nodded. "We found Job."

"And Joshua and Ezekiel?"

"Nothing yet, I'm afraid. But their sabbatical is up in a few days."

"Let's hope it's not too late for Kimball, then."

"According to the SIV, Kimball contacted the brothers. So, there're three of them now. The odds are certainly in his favor."

"The odds were in his favor when he was with Mr. Hawk. And now, Mr. Hawk lies dead and Kimball's lucky to be alive." Pius began to nibble on his lower lip thoughtfully with his stare looking beyond the cardinal.

Never in his life had he questioned the skill set possessed by Kimball on whether or not it was enough to get him through any battle or skirmish. There was never a cause for true concern or worry or a possible misstep in his capabilities. His confidence in Kimball had always been as stout as the flying buttresses that supported the main structures of medieval churches. Such as they were the crutches that fortified architectural characteristics that were delicate, they became the hallmarks of strength the same way Kimball Hayden had become the pontiff's support that made him strong. He unknowingly allowed the Knight to become the basis of his pride, a dark vanity, and wondered if the Lord was now presenting a painful lesson by taking away that very source.

Is Kimball fighting a losing battle?

He hoped not.

The pope slowly closed his eyes. "I hope . . . I pray, that God Almighty is watching over Kimball's welfare," he finally said.

Please don't let him pay the price of an old man's vanity.

But for some underlying reason, he could sense the flying buttresses that supported him for so long begin to crumble.

CHAPTER TWENTY-SEVEN

Baltimore, Maryland.

The surplus store was locked down tight. A CLOSED sign attached the barred window of the front door.

Even with the buzz of the overhead fluorescents, the room held a sepulchral deadness to it. The light was feeble, at best, and the air was unmoving and hot.

They had moved the conversation to the cellar, which, at least to Kimball, appeared to be a warehouse of aged wartime goods and battle cutlery, such as bayonets and cavalry swords. The true cache, however, was hidden behind a false wall the brothers called 'The Vault.' Inside were weapons of every distinction from mobile turrets to RPGs to Gatlin miniguns, the bottom line translating to serious dollars.

Kimball moved about the weaponry, often tracing a finger over the weapon and feeling the sleekness of the RPGs or the multiple barrels of the minigun. "These are illegal?"

Stanley held up his hand, his thumb, and forefinger about an inch apart. "Just a little bit," he said.

"This—" Jeff held his arms out as if in homage "—is our cash cow," he said. "Grenier and Arruti purchased directly from us and supplied the rebels in the southern part of the Philippines."

Kimball cocked his head. "You mean they were supplying the same rebels they were fighting?"

"The very same," he stated. "The Philippine government hired them as—what they liked to be termed—a military security firm to stem the flow of terrorist groups to the north. But while the government paid them, they were also selling weapons to guerilla factions in the south to keep the conflict going. If there's no battle, then there's no payment. If there's no payment, then there's no profit."

"The rebel conflict could have gone on forever."

Jeff smiled. "As I said, it's a cash cow—a win-win situation for all of us. They get paid a fortune by the Philippine government to fight the same rebel faction while supplying them with our weapons on top of it. We were profiting from both sides and kept the fight going at the same time. The Philippine government had no idea."

"But we haven't heard from them in over a week," said Stanley. "Now we know why."

Kimball moved away from the weapons display area and made his way to a small table the Hardwick brothers were sitting at. Over the entire tabletop were the photos of what had been the reigning members of the Pieces of Eight, both before and after their deaths. He took a seat and began to shuffle through the pictures, noting the youthful poses when they were young and brash to the aged death postures with carvings in their flesh.

Walker was the first to go: the photo of a legless man tethered to the table, the letter 'I' carved in his back.

And then they spoke about Grenier and Arruti, not a simple tandem team to take down.

Ian McMullen wasn't much of a surprise, the man surrendering to the bottle long before the Pieces were disbanded. The consensus was that he resigned himself to the direction of his fate because alcohol was more of a kinship than his band of brothers—so much was the hold of his affliction.

Hawk, on the other hand, decided to rekindle with the spirits of his people and the Apache nation, rather than to profit with the Grenier's and Arruti's military security firm as a high-end operative.

When discussions finally turned to Kimball—well, he was something different altogether.

Jeff Hardwick continued to stare at him with a steely gaze, the fierceness in his dark eyes equal to the ferocity of whatever was left of his soul. "Now you know about us, so now we want to know about you—and about that." He pointed to Kimball's collar. "You used to be the big honcho of the unit," he said. "And now you tell us that you absconded for the salvation of the Church." He leaned closer to the Vatican Knight. "You think that after all the horrible things you did that God is going to forgive you? Forgive us?"

"I didn't come here to talk about me. What I've become, and for whatever reasons, is not on the table. I came here to save us from this." He swept his hand over the photos. "If we don't act now, if we don't come up with a game plan, then there'll be additional photos added to this group. And I'm talking about you." He points to Jeff. "And you." And then points to Stanley.

Jeff fell back in his chair, his gaze remaining hard on Kimball. "Do you really think I'm comfortable sitting here knowing what you did for a living, what you did to people, innocent or otherwise, and then have to stare at that collar you're wearing? When I work with people, I want to know who they are. And I don't know you, Kimball—not anymore. And if I don't know you, then I don't trust you. And if I don't trust you, then I don't work with you. It's that simple."

"You and your brother can't do this alone."

"Then I guess you better tell my brother and me who and what you've become." Jeff's features became as hard as his eyes, his manner deliberately adamant.

Kimball sighed, nodded, and then resigned himself. "All right . . . I'll bend."

Jeff Hardwick smiled with impish delight. "Please do."

The assassin watched and waited with the virtue of a pious man. From the rooftop of a building across the way of the surplus store, the assassin maintained a vigil watch. It had been more than three hours since Kimball Hayden entered the store. And all the killer could do was question what they were talking about—of the assumptions they were making at the moment and how to react.

Who was doing this?

Why were they doing it?

More so, how do we stop him?

These questions would be the natural course of inquiries, he considered, the questions of self-preservation. The questions of scared little men.

The assassin removed his backpack and rummaged through the rear pocket. Inside was a black-and-white photo of the Pieces of Eight; the men posing in machismo indifference for the camera in either a kneeling or standing position. Five of the team members had been crossed out; three remained. The next in line was Stanley Hardwick.

Tracing a finger gingerly over the image of Stanley H, the assassin decided that he would continue to adhere to the rule of engagement, no matter how difficult it was about to become. He would kill Stanley

125

first as the photo dictated, then Jeff, and then Kimball.

And the killer relished the thought but refused to betray any emotion with something as little as a preamble of a smile.

Replacing the photo to its rightful pocket, the assassin donned the backpack and stood at the building's edge, watching the store across the way.

The questions of scared little men, he thought.

The questions of scared little men.

CHAPTER TWENTY-EIGHT

Vatican City

If there was anyone with the look of a weasel it was Cardinal Giuseppe Angullo. His face was blade-thin, and his nose pointed outward like a snout above a weak chin. His eyes were constantly flared to the size of half-dollars that forever darted around his sockets. And when he spoke, he did so with a nasal twang. Yet in the eyes of his constituency, he was a man who could be king.

When he entered the pope's chamber he did so stooped at the shoulders. Not because he was physically infirm or twisted at the joints, but as a quasi-bow of respect. When he stood tall within the cast of the pope's shadow, he did so at six foot four.

"Your Holiness," he greeted.

Before taking the cardinal into his grasp he held up his blessed ring, which was dutifully kissed by Angullo, then pulled the cardinal into his embrace. "It's good to see you again, my old friend."

After accepting the embrace, Cardinal Angullo fell back and measured the pope with his hands still clutching the pontiff's shoulders. "You look well, Amerigo."

The pontiff waved a dismissive hand. "You lie," he said with a weary smile. "I'm losing weight, albeit weight I should have lost a long time ago, and I look as if I haven't slept when all I do is sleep." He motioned a hand toward a button-studded chair of Corinthian leather in front of his desk. "Please," he said. "Have a seat."

The cardinal took the chair, hiking up the tail of his priestly adornments as he did so, and looked upon the pope with those constantly flitting eyes. "You wanted to see me?' he asked.

The pope nodded and hesitated as though he was seeking the proper wordage. And then: "As life goes," he began, his words taking on a serious measure, "so eventually comes an end to that life. And as you know, Giuseppe, I am in the twilight of mine."

The cardinal repositioned himself in his chair with his eyes darting and flitting about, the signs of anxiety.

"You know why I've asked you to my chamber?"

The cardinal's voice warbled with nervous tension as he spoke. "I believe to see where I stand prior to the College's selection as to who will sit upon the papal throne."

The pope smiled warmly. "Very good."

"Your Eminence, considering the state of your condition, I must honestly say that I'm not comfortable discussing this matter with you."

"Giuseppe, politicking is a way of life. Without it, institutes would crumble. And we must see that the institute of the Church lives on. We must choose wisely so the Church will not be seeded with the misgivings of corruption, or the Church will inevitably fail. Now I know you covet the throne I sit upon—that's understandable—but the names of two others have surfaced more so than yours: That of the good cardinals Bonasero Vessucci and Constantine Marcello."

"With all due respect, Your Eminence, I, too, covet the throne. So, I think you're selling me short simply because you see me in the shadows of giants."

"No, Giuseppe, not at all. I'm merely posing theoretical points for the best possible rule of the Church. As you know, Cardinal Marcello maintains rigid, ultra-conservative viewpoints which may prove detrimental to the ever-evolving mindset of the Church's citizenry. If we don't bend with the changing of times, then history has shown that, by nature, man will ultimately seek a religion to conform to his needs rather than the needs of scripture. Although we must adhere to the conservatism that God seeks among His children, we must never lose sight that the free will of man must not be exorcised, either. We must find that happy medium."

"Are you asking me, if I should become the swing vote, to pressure my constituency to move to Cardinal Vessucci's camp?"

The pope leaned forward. "The Church holds many secrets, Giuseppe, things I cannot tell you at this moment—things not within the scope of Cardinal Marcello's acceptability, but an absolute necessity if the Church is to survive." The Vatican Knights were the first to come to the pontiff's mind.

"I hope, Your Holiness, that you're not talking about corrupt matters to justify the means."

"Of course not," he said. "All I'm saying, Giuseppe, is that there are matters that are not simply black and white. And sometimes situations in the gray area can be a difficult matter with tough decisions that do not always pan out. What I'm saying, my friend, is that we need a pontiff who is willing to bend in his thinking, someone willing to conform to times that are growing more difficult by the day."

"And you don't think Cardinal Marcello, or me, can maintain such a capability?"

"The good Cardinal Marcello does not, and you know that."

"And you don't believe my camp is strong enough to get to the coveted seat?"

The pope leaned forward. "Your camp is strong, Giuseppe. But it's not as powerful as the camps that follow Marcello or Vessucci. I'm afraid, by the will of God, that you may become the swing vote, as to who will succeed me."

"And, of course, you want me to endorse the man you favor: Cardinal Vessucci."

Pope Pius fell back into his seat. "He has been groomed for this position for a long time. He knows the secrets of the Church since he is the secretary of state."

"With all due respect, Your Holiness, being secretary of state of the Vatican is not an automatic succession to the papal throne."

"I know that, Giuseppe. But Cardinal Vessucci has had a huge hand in the matters of the Church over the years. The transition would be an easy one."

"Cardinal Marcello is a traditionalist, such as me. Why would I jump to a camp that is not of my viewpoint?"

"What you do, Giuseppe, you don't do for yourself. You do it for the sake of the Church. Politicking can be a particularly good measure if the welfare of its citizenry benefits from it greatly. And in my heart, I believe that the good Cardinal Vessucci is the man to hold the papal scepter."

The cardinal smiled. "You're also asking me to surrender my passion of obtaining the coveted seat by stepping aside so that another can take the throne?"

"I'm asking you to make a great sacrifice and to do what is right," he said imploringly. "I'm asking you to sacrifice your personal need over the needs of the Catholic citizenry."

The weasel-faced man sat back, his eyes darting about in

deliberation. "As you know, Your Holiness, I covet the throne as well as Vessucci and Marcello. Therefore, I will campaign as such since it is my right. But if I recognize that my camp is too weak, then I will consider your offer to endorse the good Cardinal Vessucci."

The pope smiled, nodded. "That's all I can ask for, my friend."

Cardinal Angullo got to his feet easily. The pontiff labored to his feet and held out his ring for the cardinal to kiss. The cardinal grasped the pontiff's birdlike hand and kissed the ring.

"But keep in mind, Your Holiness, that what we have spoken of here today has not been set in stone. In final, when it comes down to what I believe is right for the Church or the welfare of its people, will ultimately be my choice in the end. Whether it's Vessucci or Marcello, only God can direct me to that decision."

Pope Pius feigned a smile. "Then I'm sure He will shine His light upon you and such a decision will be obvious."

"Perhaps, Your Holiness."

In closing, the pontiff clapped a hand on the cardinal's shoulder and ushered him to the door. "And thank you for holding counsel with me in my chambers," he told him. "I expect the matters we spoke about today is between you and I and nobody else?"

"Such as the way of politicking," said the cardinal.

"Good. And it was good to see you again, Giuseppe."

"Same here, Your Holiness. And take care of yourself as much as you can, all right?"

The pope nodded. "I will, my friend. Thank you."

When he closed the chamber doors the room became a vacuum, the noise simply sucked out leaving nothing behind but dead silence. From his stooped position, he looked upon the door with a single thought: Politicking was an essential tool to secure a beneficial future. But he also realized that one man's ambitions often outweighed his sense of morality to do the right thing. And in the case of Cardinal Angullo, the pope considered that personal gain was foremost in the cardinal's passions rather than the welfare of the constituency.

Perhaps he was reading too much into it, he thought. And he prayed that he was wrong in his assessment.

But somehow, he could not completely grasp the concept that bringing Cardinal Angullo into close counsel was the right thing to do.

Turning away from the door and with a great deal of effort, he made his way to his desk where, once he was seated, gazed out the windows that overlooked St. Peter's Square.

Beautiful, he thought, glimpsing the Colonnade. *Simply . . . beautiful.*

And then he closed his eyes.

CHAPTER TWENTY-NINE

Baltimore, Maryland.

What was left of the Pieces of Eight sat in a small room in the sublevel of the surplus store. The old-time warriors were sitting beneath the feeble glow of a single bulb burning from the ceiling, the men holding counsel in a room whose walls were lined with every model and make of every firearm available for the black market.

Jeff and Stanley sat on one side of the table, Kimball on the other.

For the good part of an hour, Kimball explained his reason for absconding from service and the Pieces of Eight. He then went into detail about his solo mission to Iraq, the killing of the shepherd boys, and his subsequent epiphany. And then he discussed how he was given a chance of salvation through the Church. What he neglected to inform them of, however, was his lead role as the Master commando of the Vatican Knights.

"Dude, you didn't even know the words to 'The Lord's Prayer' back then," said Jeff. "You know the words now?"

Actually, he didn't. He was glad that Jeff proposed the question as rhetorical.

"And out of the goodness of their heart the Church, or the pope, just walked right up to you for no reason and offered you the chance of salvation for what reason?"

Kimball was starting to feel cornered. Unlike Stanley, who was unschooled, Jeff was a learned individual who had the capability to eye every possible angle, like a prosecuting attorney.

"They didn't come to me," he lied. "I went to them."

"So all of a sudden you have this epiphany—"

"What's an epiphany?" asked Stanley.

"Shut up. So, all of a sudden you have this epiphany, and the Church is willing to just open its arms in forgiveness to a killer like you." Jeff snapped his fingers. "Just like that, huh?"

"No, not just like that," said Kimball, grabbing his collar. "As you can see, I'm indebted to the Church for the rest of my life."

Jeff stared at the pristine white collar. "And if you walk away?"

"Then I'll end up like you," he told him. "I'll be damned."

Jeff finally fell back into his seat. "I can't argue with that," he said. "But I wouldn't hold my breath if I was you, Kimball. Your atrocities can never be forgiven, no matter how much you bow down to your new-found God."

Sadly, Kimball thought the man to be spot on with his assessment.

And then Jeff leaned forward once again and placed his elbow and forearm on the table. "You think you can push aside your conscience long enough to be one of us again? You think you can kill this guy?"

Kimball nodded. "Even the Church recognizes the right to defend itself," he said. *Hence, the Vatican Knights.*

Jeff stared at Kimball long and hard, deciphering whether or not the man could be trusted and brought into the Hardwick fold. Kimball could still be an asset given his very particular set of skills. "Have you kept up with your abilities?"

"I exercise."

Jeff sighed as if being taxed. "Have you kept up with your abilities?"

"I can hold my own," he countered.

"I don't need a liability, Kimball. I need assets."

"My skills have never wavered," he said firmly.

"Well, imagine that," Jeff said cuttingly. "A priest who can wield a knife like no other. I find that quite odd. Don't you?"

"Look. We can sit here and go in circles all you want about me and what I can or cannot do, or we can discuss how to set up a perimeter and protect ourselves against an assassin who is getting closer with every breath we take."

Jeff picked up the edginess in Kimball's voice. "All right. But let me say this. Once this mission is over, then you can run back to the Church and live out your life of hypocrisy. I don't ever want to see you again."

"I'm here to help all of us. I'm not here to win your approval. Just keep that in mind."

Jeff smiled sardonically. "Then let's start talking suspects, shall we?"

"Yeah . . . Let's."

CHAPTER THIRTY

Vatican City

The chamber of Cardinal Marcello's quarters was not opulent, but comfortable in its amenities. There was a recess in the wall large enough for a ceiling-to-floor bookcase that held religious tomes in hardbound. Against the east wall were two bullet-shaped windows, the top portions adorned with stained glass that gave a pristine view of the Gardens, and between them sat a single-sized bed bearing the colored comforter the same as his scarlet and gold dress.

As the sky was beginning to show the red bands of dusk, the cardinal closed the scalloped drapery and took a seat behind his desk. Before him stood Cardinal Angullo, his head, and neck protruding forward from his body like a vulture's.

"So, Pius is already lobbying on behalf of the secretary of the state." Cardinal Marcello tented his fingers and began to bounce the tips thoughtfully against his chin. "What he says is true, however. My camp of followers is equal to Vessucci's. And truth be told, my friend, you *are* the swing vote."

Cardinal Angullo began to pace the area before Cardinal Marcello's desk. "He spoke of your penchant of being far too conservative for the seat, too unyielding to bend with the masses."

"I believe that we must adhere to the scriptures as they were written. The will of the people must bend to the will of God. God must never bend to the will of the people," he said.

"He also spoke of secrets," he added. "Secrets that are known by a selected few."

"Secrets are made secret for a reason, Giuseppe? The subject matters involved often give rise to discussion and debate."

"I then asked the pontiff if the secrets held were corrupt. He says 'no.'"

"That's because it's easy to look at something and justify the action

135

if the means are achieved, morally or otherwise."

Cardinal Angullo stopped pacing, his neck craning forward. "You know as well as I do that, I also seek the seat you and Vessucci covet?"

"I do."

"I tell you this because I know where I stand, Constantine. My camp is small but powerful."

Cardinal Marcello stopped bouncing his fingertips off the base of his chin. "What is it you're proposing?"

The corners of the cardinal's lips edged upward. "A shared seat," he finally said.

"You know as well as I do that the papal throne cannot be shared."

"Not directly, no. But it can be shared, nonetheless. Like the throne is shared between the good Cardinal Bonasero Vessucci and Pope Pius."

"You want to sit at my side?"

"As an assistant, yes." The cardinal began to pace once again, back and forth, just in front of the cardinal's desk, this time looking ceilingward as he spoke and deliberated. "The seat of the secretary of state is appointed by the pope, yes?"

"It is."

Cardinal Angullo stopped pacing and leaned over the cardinal's table with his knuckles resting on the desktop. "If you promise to relieve Cardinal Vessucci of his duties as secretary of state and appoint me in his place, then I will lobby with my camp to support you in full. With my numbers converging with yours, then Vessucci will lose his bid for the papal throne."

"To be honest, Giuseppe, your proposal seems unethical in its own right."

Cardinal Angullo stood erect. "Politicking may seem that way. But as Pope Pius has stated, politicking is good if the masses as a whole benefit from it. If there are secrets untold, secrets in need of moral interpretation, then it is up to us to render corrections and make right what is wrong."

Cardinal Marcello began to mull over the offer.

Then: "I could also offer the same agreement to Vessucci, if, of course, my terms do not appease you."

Marcello took on an angered look, his brows dipping sharply over the bridge of his nose. "Are you giving me an ultimatum?"

"I'm merely politicking, which is never pretty by any means, but a necessity of survival. I come to you with this offer because I believe you to be the man deserving of this position besides myself, of course. But let's make something quite clear: I'm in a win-win position as the swing vote, to better my position within the Vatican. You would do so if you were in the same position, Constantine. We all covet the throne at one time or another. However, not everyone is handed the papal throne the way I'm handing it to you."

Constantine Marcello closed his eyes, the muscles in the back of his jaw working. The man was right, politically speaking. And then: "Fine. If your camp supports my endeavors and backs my camp, then the seat of secretary of state is yours. I'll reappoint the good Cardinal Vessucci to another esteemed position."

Angullo smiled. "Then I will begin to lobby in your behalf . . . Your Holiness."

Cardinal Marcello snapped a hard glare at Angullo. "I'm not the pontiff yet, Giuseppe. Do not address me as such as long as Pius lives. He's a good man who deserves our respect."

Angullo bowed his head. "I beg my forgiveness, good Cardinal. I meant no disrespect."

"Is there anything else?"

"No."

"Then have a good night."

Cardinal Angullo perpetuated a weasel-like smile, bowed, and then left the cardinal's chamber with his garment trailing behind him.

When the chamber door closed, the walls echoed resoundingly, just like the question that continued to bounce off his conscience: *Did I just nail my soul to the Devil's altar?*

For the sake of absolution, he promised himself with a soft sell that he would make things right with God by justifying his actions since the easiest thing man can do is justify anything as long as the measures achieve the means. And he was sure that God would truly forgive him for righting a terrible wrong.

Whatever dark and unholy secrets were currently being managed by the Vatican, God would surely see the cardinal as a champion of Light and a crusader against any transgressions within the Church.

Nevertheless, the good cardinal began to pray, hoping this to be God's divine plan rather than the selfish pining of human ambition.

CHAPTER THIRTY-ONE

Baltimore, Maryland

"Who stands to lose the most by our presence?" asked Jeff.

"After twenty years, who would care?" said Stan.

"Exactly."

Kimball remained silent, though he was musing.

Jeff watched him with a keen eye, then, "Any ideas, Kimball? Any ideas at all?"

Kimball leaned forward, his eyes focusing on an imaginary point on the opposite wall. "Let's begin with the obvious," he started. "We know that it has to be somebody involved with the knowledge of the Pieces of Eight, right?"

"OK."

"And those with knowledge of the Pieces of Eight were whom?"

Jeff nodded his head in agreement. "The highest political factions," he answered.

"And the Joint Chiefs," added Stan.

"True. But the role of the Joint Chiefs was strictly to inform us of our targets in foreign locales. The engagement was only approved by the political brass."

Jeff added, "So it wouldn't make sense for anybody from the JCOS to get involved in this. Their job was strictly to identify insurgent forces and assess whether or not such targets posed a threat to the sovereignty or safety of the United States."

"And how to act was the decision of the Commander in Chief," said Kimball.

"But why now?" asked Stan. "Why twenty years later?"

Kimball raised a finger for emphasis. "Now we get into the Who, What, Where, Why and How of things," he said. "We all know that the Ford administration banned the CIA to commit assassinations against foreign targets abroad. But that didn't stop ensuing presidents to engage in covert operations. Remember, people, espionage is espionage; it's not child's play. That's why they created the Force Elite and groups such as the Pieces of Eight. Guy's like us kept the world in check without the backlash from the court of public opinion, if things didn't go well."

"So, what you're saying," began Jeff, "if I'm reading you correctly, is that you believe George Herbert is involved in this?"

"All I'm saying is that Bush was the main player who signed off on every mission we performed, all of them. I'm simply trying to look at this from a logical point of view. But logic doesn't seem to be fitting in any of the scenarios I'm running through my head right now. But maybe if we come up with the 'why' of things, then maybe pieces will start to come together."

Now Stan piped in. "Yeah, but why not do this ten years ago? Fifteen years ago? Why now?"

"Good question. So, the new question would be: Why are we a threat now and not ten or fifteen years ago as Stan just stated? Why would George Herbert be afraid of us all of a sudden? What has he to lose, if anything, right now?"

"I think you're reaching," said Jeff. "George Herbert has nothing to fear from us."

"That's true," he said. "But there was one event he signed off on with extreme reluctance, do you remember?"

Jeff nodded, slowly at first, the memory coming to the fore. "A close ally of the president informed him that Senator Cartwright was blackmailing others within the Senate to argue points of his support against the president, or he would ruin their careers by making public information regarding unscrupulous backgrounds. Cartwright became a pariah who promised to take down leading people in the Bush administration including Bush himself with the material he gathered against certain alliances. Cartwright was strong-arming decisions that shouldn't have been made from those in the Senate due to his blackmailing techniques and was about to be investigated for inappropriate activity."

"But it would have opened up an entire can of worms, so to speak."

"That's right. And do you remember what happened next?"

Kimball nodded. It was all too clear. "Senator Shore proposed in closed quarters with the president that Senator Cartwright was too dangerous and needed to be taken out of the equation. You eliminate the source of the problem, and then the problem goes away. It has always been the solution since the beginning of time."

"True. However, it was the first proposition made by rulers of our government to take out a political giant within our own ruling body. Senator Shore spearheaded the motion to get it done, remember? Bush was dead set against it. And it's never been confirmed that he signed the paperwork to initiate the attack against Cartwright. He was CIA, so he had to weigh his options first until he could see no other way to rectify the situation. But he may not have had anything to do with it. If you remember, it was Senator Shore who sent us to rectify the situation. Not Bush. And nobody knows that better than you, Kimball, since you were the one to run the blade across Cartwright's throat on Shore's demand."

Kimball had an instant flash of recall, the driving of the blade across the old man's flesh, the way his lungs naturally coughed up the blood in gag reflex, and the way the senator slumped against his desk and died as the staccato flashes of lightning filled the room.

Yeah, I remember.

"Things like that happen in third-world countries, not in the United States," Jeff added. "If something like that ever resurfaced—"

"It would be emphatically denied," Kimball interrupted testily.

"Maybe not," said Stan. "The killer was never found. It makes for good fodder."

"You've forgotten one thing."

"Yeah. And what's that?"

"You brought it up yourself. Why now? Why not ten or fifteen years ago? Why not when it happened?"

Stan conceded.

"Because Bush has nothing to do with it," said Jeff. "And you're right, it would be great fodder. Bush has nothing to lose. But . . ." He let his words trail, the corners of his lips edging upward.

"OK?" Kimball said it in a way for Jeff to lead on.

"OK, but . . . Senator Shore has everything to lose. Think about it. I think those pieces are starting to come together, Kimball."

And he was right. The Senator had recently won the primaries and was positioning himself for a run at the White House seat. In fact, his ratings held a double-digit lead above the incumbent.

"The only thing that stands in his way is his past, which we are a part of. If the nation knew he was directly responsible for sanctioning a hit on a US senator, his career, if not a lot more, is gone."

"So now you think he's cleaning up the mess, just in case?"

"Think about it: Only a handful of men outside the JCOS knew we existed. But only one man fought hard for the eradication of Senator John Cartwright. Senator Shore lobbied and conspired to have that man murdered, a leading senator no less."

Kimball looked at a photo of the senator. Although Senator Shore had aged over the past twenty years he was still youthful in appearance, his once raven hair having gone silver gave him a distinguished appearance. But Jeff was right, the man conspired and led the charge for Cartwright's dispatching from the senatorial ranks and won. It was the only time that a US government official was assassinated by the hand of his political constituency.

"But Shore thinks I'm dead," said Kimball.

"Not anymore. Not if what you told me was true about the assassin having the chance to kill you at Ghost's ranch but didn't. Don't you think he alerted Shore by now?"

Kimball fell back in his chair, thinking. Sure, everything sounded plausible, but that was about it. Plausibility wasn't palpability. It was simply theory.

"You know what I think," said Stan. "I think we need to set the senator straight, see what's on his mind." His lips curled with impish amusement and Jeff followed like the second pea in the pod, his smile mirroring his brother's.

"You know something, kin, you might just be right."

Great! "You expect to walk right into a senator's residence and have a chat, is that it?" asked Kimball.

Jeff steadied a hard glare. "I'm sorry, but would you rather we wait here for his goon to walk in and put a bullet in our heads?"

"We're just speculating," he returned.

"Whatever we come up with is just speculation. We need to act and find out."

"I agree," said Stanley.

Kimball hesitated. How he wished the Vatican Knights were here, he thought. Working with the Hardwick brothers was always spontaneous and chaotic. You never knew what was going to happen, no matter how much you planned for the perfect outcome.

"Well?" asked Jeff.

"You know where he resides?"

"The guy lives in a half-million-dollar estate a few miles north of D.C."

"He'll most likely have security, you know."

"Of course, he will. That just makes it all that much more fun."

"And no killing."

Jeff clicked his tongue. "Jesus, Kimball, you take the fun out of everything, you know that? What's the matter? That collar getting to you?"

"Or maybe you lost your nads or something?" Stanley added.

But Kimball remained adamant. "I said . . . *no* . . . killing."

Jeff got up from his chair. "Yeah. Right. Whatever . . . Are you hitching with us or not?"

Kimball stood to his full height, towering over the Hardwick brothers. "Let's move," he said.

CHAPTER THIRTY-TWO

25 Miles North of Washington, D.C.

The ride to the D.C. suburb was a quiet one for the Hardwick brothers and Kimball Hayden. Hardly a word was exchanged between them as they drove in a muscle pickup truck. Kimball was sitting in the backseat of the crew cab, breaking down and reexamining his firearm, a .40 caliber Smith & Wesson with a suppressor that was as long as the weapon's barrel.

Like the Hardwick's, Kimball dressed in a black tactical jumpsuit with cargo pockets, a duty belt, and military-issue footwear. The cleric collar was missing. In the breast pocket of his shirt was a flat can of black shoe polish. Before they breached the site, it was determined that they would go in black face.

When they reached Senator Shore's estate, they parked the vehicle approximately 200 yards away. Not too close, but not too far, either. Just in case things didn't pan out.

Slowly, carefully, with their heads on a swivel, they used the shadows as camouflage as they made their way to Shore's property on the hill. From their point, they could see the six-foot-high perimeter wall with ornamental spiking running its length. The grounds were perfectly kept, and the shrubs neatly pruned. The house was a magnificent two-story Colonial featuring columns and decorative fascias. Capes of roses hung from trellises. And immovable shutters surrounded windows with bullet-shaped arches. The bedroom, they knew, would be in the rear overlooking the pool.

Mounting the wall had been easy, the height hardly a deterrent. And the row of privet bushes in the center of the grounds provided a wonderful cover as they hunkered down behind them, the target of Senator Shore within striking distance.

"There should be at least three security officials from Capitol Police acting as Shore's security detail," Kimball whispered. "They won't be easy targets. But we've been here before. So, I'll reiterate what I said before: no killing."

Jeff snickered, his lips drawing into a smirk. "We do what we do to achieve the means. These guys aren't exactly going to let us walk right into the senator's bedroom."

"They will if they don't see us."

"And if they do see us?"

When they were warriors of the Pieces of Eight there was only one answer: *Remove the opposition without prejudice, so as not to compromise the mission.* That had always been the rule of engagement. And some things just don't change.

"The members of the Pieces of Eight are never seen until the moment of contact with the primary target. We're never to be seen by secondary units and that's what we were always about, Jeff. Stealth. Are you telling me you lost your edge?"

Jeff appeared insulted, the muscles in the back of his jaw working. "I haven't lost a thing," he returned. "I'm just saying that sometimes the possibility of engagement can't be helped, even with secondary units."

"I'll tell you something right now," added Stan, silently drawing back the slide of his firearm and charging his weapon. "If Shore's detail gets in the way, then I will engage them in a manner I see fit to see that the mission succeeds. And that, Kimball, is the bottom line. It's all about the mission. Not about some moral crisis you happen to be going through." He held the Glock up, the suppressor giving the gun's barrel extraordinary length.

"We didn't come here to murder. We came here to gather information. We're not even sure he's behind any of this."

"Are you kidding?" said Stan. Then: "Tell me something? Weren't you just in the cab of my truck for the past half hour breaking down your weapon to make sure it was in working order?"

"Listen. I see my weapon as a last resort. You and your brother have always been in the mindset of kill first and ask questions later."

Jeff couldn't help the smile. "Now tell me, is there any better mechanism of defense other than to kill your enemy before they get a chance to kill you?"

"That's the point. They're not our enemies. They're people doing their job and earning a paycheck."

Jeff then fed a bullet into the chamber of his weapon by drawing the slide back. "Then they should have worked safer jobs."

"No . . . killing."

"What . . . ever."

They moved to the end of the privet hedges until they had a full view of the estate.

"I don't see anybody," whispered Stan.

"They're around . . . Somewhere."

Kimball moved forward. "Stay close to the hedges. I'll maintain point; Jeff, you watch the periphery; and, Stan, you keep an eye on the rear flank."

"Who in the hell died and made you boss?" queried Jeff.

Kimball turned on him with the same bearing and intensity he once held as a member of the Pieces of Eight—that look of murderous fortitude. "Look. I didn't come here to argue. So, do you want to take point? Or do you want the periphery position? I don't care."

Jeff noted the fire in the warrior's eyes. It was the same vicious ferocity Kimball held moments before making a kill. And Jeff realized that he was the current object of his focus. "No, you're good," he told him, his tone less brash, less cocky. "You can take lead."

Kimball met his eyes a little bit longer before breaking off. And then he moved toward the house with the Hardwick brothers in tow.

A plain-clothed Capitol police officer was making a round of the grounds. Cradled within his arms was a TAR-21 mini assault rifle with a holographic view and NV scope. The man, however, moved with all the ease of taking a stroll, a telltale sign of complacency. When the officer rounded the corner of the house, Kimball and company moved quickly and took position beneath a semi-round balcony that overlooked the swimming pool. To the sides of the balcony stood trellises covered with roses that were thick and lush and blood red. And the balcony doors stood open, allowing for a crisp, midnight breeze to circulate the air of the senator's bedroom.

Kimball raised a fisted hand in the air and then pointed a finger to the balcony's landing. The brothers acknowledged his gesture, holstered their weapons, and quietly climbed the trellises while Kimball maintained his position on a bended knee and kept watch, the point of his firearm held out in front of him, scanning.

When the brothers quietly hit the landing, they motioned for

Kimball to follow, with Stan watching his back by monitoring the grounds from above.

Quietly, Kimball scaled the trellis. His movements were silent, stealthy, the man bearing incredible athletic economy as he mounted the balcony rails and took footing.

The doors were open, the scrim-like drapes floating with the course of a slight breeze, the gossamer fabric moving with phantasmagoric grace. Inside, the room was dark.

For a brief moment, the men stood silhouetted in the balcony's doorway, the light of the pool serving as the backdrop.

And then, in unison, they moved into the room and became a part of the darkness.

They closed the doors softly behind them, all spreading out, the points of their weapons directed to the bed. Stan went to the left side, Jeff to the right, and Kimball stood at the foot of the bed.

Senator Shore lay beside his wife, both beneath a single blanket that was being worked into a wild tangle by their shifting legs.

The senator lay on the left side of the bed slack-jawed, his limbs contorted in such a way it seemed impossible to be a position of comfort.

Carefully, Stan hunkered over the senator, his lips inches away from the senator's ear. "Wake up, Sunshine," he whispered.

The senator didn't move.

"Come on, Sunshine, wakey-wakey." Stanley reached out with the tip of his middle finger and flicked the lobe of the senator's ear.

The senator snorted in surprise, his eyes fluttering, then opening, his jaw closing with the snap of a bear trap. And then his eyes began to adjust to the darkness, his brain registering certain shapes and forms of things that did not belong.

Looking down, Stan smiled with malicious amusement. "How're you doing, Sunshine?"

But before the senator could react or respond, Stanley Hardwick clamped a gloved hand over the senator's mouth.

"Now listen to me," he whispered. "And listen well. You make a noise, you're dead. Do anything stupid, you're dead. Understand?"

The senator nodded.

"And that goes for your wife, too."

The senator's wife, however, remained dead asleep.

"Now I'm going to take my hand away. And when I do, you will answer our questions accordingly. Is that understood?"

The senator's eyes moved in their sockets, scanning. A large man was standing by the foot of the bed and another standing over his wife, the point of his firearm aimed at her skull.

Then again, from Stanley, and in the same measured whisper: "Is that understood?"

The senator nodded once again, the gesture telling Stanley he did not doubt his mortality, should he disregard the intruder's wishes.

"Good boy." Stanley removed his hand while directing the mouth of the pistol's barrel at the senator's head with the other.

Defensively, the senator began to draw the blanket toward the point of his chin, a weak barrier against a bullet. "What do you want?" he asked.

The level of his voice caused his wife to stir. He was not whispering.

"We just want to ask a few questions," said Kimball, who stepped closer to the foot of the bed. "And then we'll be on our way."

From what the senator could see, the large man was not aiming or bearing a weapon like the other two. But there was something about his features, the angle of his jawline, the breadth and width of his shoulders, the tone of his voice. This particular man reminded him of an old-time warrior he once knew nearly two decades before—a man whose empty coffin was buried as an honorary gesture by the Pentagon brass at Arlington.

"Do you remember me?" asked the large man.

The senator searched his memory further. "Should I?"

Kimball leaned forward and into view, which no longer left any doubt in the senator's mind.

The senator's eyes detonated with the sudden realization. "But you're dead."

"People keep telling me that. But, apparently, I'm not."

The senator's wife began to raise her head, slowly, suddenly realizing the voice was not her husband's. When she looked up and saw Jeff proffering her a wink, she attempted to scream. But Jeff quickly nullified that by placing a hand over her mouth. In an act of self-preservation, she began to beat his arms with open hands. But when she saw him calmly raise his firearm and felt the tip of the suppressor planted against her forehead, she quickly stilled.

"Calm down," he told her. "Or I put your pretty little brains all over this expensive silk you're lying on."

"Remember what I said," reminded Kimball. *No killing.*

"Just get on with it."

The senator sat up so that his back was square against the headboard. "Kimball Hayden," he said, his voice sounded awed, the surprise genuine. "You were supposed to have been killed in Iraq."

"Only he ran away from the mission like a spineless coward," said Stanley. "Isn't that right, Kimball? Tell him how you ran away from the mission like a spineless coward."

Kimball refused to respond.

Jeff, however, snickered in amusement.

Suddenly a visual of stereotypical inbreds flashed in Kimball's mind: the brothers no doubt poster children as descendants from the backwoods. How much he hated them.

Kimball took a seat opposite the bed. The Hardwick brothers maintained their positions with guns in hand with the mouths of their suppressed weapons inches away from the temples of their quarry, that of the senator and his wife.

The senator looked into the mouth of the barrel and could feel the power of the weapon. And then he looked Stanley in the eye, once again recalling the man and the wickedness of his personality. "Jeffrey Hardwick," he said.

"Actually, I'm Stan. Jeff's the one holding the gun to your wife's head."

Jeff smiled and waved his weapon the same way a friend would greet a close associate because he was happy to see them. But the action was committed simply out of cruel enjoyment.

"Why are you here?" asked the senator. "Why are you doing this?"

"Why are you killing off the Pieces of Eight?" asked Jeff.

The senator gave him a questioning look.

"I'm not killing anyone," he stated. "You people are nothing but a dark part of my history that I just want to forget."

"Exactly," said Jeff. "And what better way to do this other than by assassination?"

"I have no idea what the hell you're talking about."

"Really?" Stan pulled out a folded photograph, a copy, from one of his cargo pockets and tossed it to the senator. "Open it," he said.

The senator's hands shook as he picked up the photo and peeled it open. It was a print of the old unit, the Pieces of Eight, posing when they were in their prime. There was Walker and Arruti, faces he never wanted to see again, Kimball and that crazy drunken Irishman. What was his name? And, of course, there was Grenier and Hawk and the Hardwicks. They were young and brash and full of the piss and vinegar of true warriors who romanced thoughts that they were the meanest bastards to ever walk the planet. The thing was, they were, and they knew it.

The senator examined the photo, the memories of when he was a part of the presidential circle flooding back. He could recall with cloudless detail the moments he conferred with the president regarding missions as to who was to live or die, or where to send them to kill for the good of all nations by preserving and justifying our nation's right to serve as the policeman of the world, but as the judge, jury, and executioner, as well. The Pieces of Eight had served them admirably.

Scrutinizing the photo with what could have been construed as scientific examination, the senator became aware of the faces circled in red marker and the letters within: I-S-C-A-R. And then he traced a finger over their images with a soft touch.

"That's right," said Stan. "They're all gone, you son of a bitch."

"You think I had something to do with this?"

"Who else?"

"For what possible reason?"

Jeff looked the senator square in the eyes, both firing off solid gazes of determination. "Several years ago, you supported the act to assassinate a U.S. senator, yes?"

Senator Shore quickly glanced at his wife, who managed a look of surprise.

Jeff pressed the point of his suppressor against the woman's temple, causing her to mewl. "The one thing I don't have, Senator, is patience. So, answer my question. Several years ago, you supported the act to assassinate a U.S. senator, yes?"

The senator looked over at his wife who lay there as a wide-eyed doe while waiting for his delayed response. Then finally: "Yes," he said. "I did."

She closed her tear-filled eyes and turned away from him.

"Senator, were you keeping deep, dark secrets from the old lady here? Not good." Jeff clicked his tongue in mock chastisement. "You naughty, naughty senator."

"For chrissakes, Hardwick, Senator Cartwright was a monster who didn't know his limitations. That man eventually got to the point where he thought he was more powerful than the president and was willing to bring the man down, along with anyone else who stood in the senator's way. The process of democracy meant nothing to the man. It was either follow him to the end or fall where you stand. The man ended careers through blackmail rather than tact political lobbying."

"Senator, I didn't ask you why you thought the action to be justified. I simply asked you if you were a factor in deciding whether or not the senator should have been assassinated. And the answer— justified or not—is yes. You conspired and sanctioned the assassination of a powerful political figure serving within the United States Senate."

To the senator's left, his wife began to sob uncontrollably.

"Honey?" When the senator reached for her, she shunned him, shrugging her shoulder away from his touch. "I'm sorry." And then he confronted Jeff with a firm tone. "Get to the point."

"It's a simple equation, Senator, and not a very hard trail to follow."

"Your . . . point?"

"I'm getting there," he said. And then: "Right now you're the leading candidate in the polls to succeed President Burroughs as the new Commander-in-Chief, yes?"

"If you say so."

"I don't say so. The polls say so. You have a double-digit lead over your next opponent and the leader of the opposing party is very weak."

"So."

Stanley snatched the photo from the senator's hand. "So, the skeleton inside your closet about you conspiring against Senator Cartwright and sanctioning his assassination would doom your run as the next president of the United States."

"Nuts like you come out of the woodwork every day," he said. "People like you—those within the Pieces—never had a background or even existed per se. You'd just be cast aside as doomsayers and idiots. No one would believe you."

"That doesn't detract from the fact that we're still a threat, yes?"

"So, you think to cover up my past oversights that I need to destroy the source, is that it?"

"Bingo." Stan tossed the photo back at the senator. "And there's the source: the Pieces of Eight. The group you sent to murder a United States senator."

Shore examined the photo. "And what are the letters all about?"

"You tell us," said Jeff. "It's your game. Apparently, you're spelling the name Iscariot."

"I have no idea what you're talking about," said the senator, and then tossed the photo toward the foot of the bed.

"Iscariot," said Stan. "The betrayer of Christ."

"I know who Iscariot is. I just don't understand the concept of the lettering in the photo."

"Neither do we, but apparently, you're not going to tell us why, are you?"

"There's nothing to give up. I have nothing to do with anybody within the Pieces of Eight getting killed."

Kimball rubbed his chin thoughtfully. During the interrogation, he studied the senator with close examination and noted the man's responses through micro-facial expressions. So far, he could not find a crack in the senator's argument for his defense and believed him to be telling the truth.

"As long as we exist, Senator," said Jeff, "then we will remain a threat to your candidacy as long as we remain alive. Therefore, it makes sense to eliminate that threat, yes?"

"Again, you guys never existed in the eyes of the proper governing body. Even to this day, only a few know of your existence—"

"Which certainly narrows down the field of suspects greatly, don't you agree?"

"But you're the only one who stands to lose should this hit the media," added Stan. "And you know how much the media loves fodder."

"Do I have to say this again? Something like this would be immediately disavowed by Bush and me, should it come to light."

"Nevertheless, Senator, you know as well as I do that negative press—no matter its insinuations—would be a candidacy killer for you, especially when your opponents cry out for an investigation . . . Don't you agree?" asked Jeff. "As popular as you are, even you could not carry on through the backlash of negative press and survive."

"Seriously, after all these years, you think you're a threat to me out of the blue? If that were the case, I would have acted against you long ago."

Neither of the Hardwick brothers could argue that point. It was strong, solid, and viable. The man had grown to be a supreme statesman and now stood at the threshold of the presidency.

"Still," Stan finally said, "we pose a threat to no one but you, Senator."

"Apparently you're wrong."

"No, Senator, we're not." Stan turned to his brother and met his gaze. And Kimball could almost see the symbiotic connection between the two brothers like arcing synapses from one point to the other, the communication between them unmistakable, the agreement of what they had to do quite clear.

In unison the brothers simply nodded to one another and stood back, both aiming their weapons at the senator and his wife. It was time to take measures.

With the slowness of a bad dream, Kimball could not move fast enough as he reached out with a hand, not sure what he was going to do, and cried out. "*No!*"

The brothers were oblivious to Kimball as they fired their weapons in rapid succession, the room lighting up with muzzle flashes as the bullets penetrated their targets, the senator and his wife taking the shots and jittering with multiple impacts, the opulent backboard and wall becoming a canvas of blood and gore.

When it was over and the targets stilled, the room smelling like cordite, silence reigned.

Kimball stood in disbelief not knowing why he was surprised at the outcome since the Hardwicks were involved. When he told them there was to be no killing, they evidently accepted it as a suggestion, rather than a command.

"I said no killing."

"Yeah, well, welcome to the food chain," said Jeff. "Did you really expect that he would just let us walk away without retaliating in some form? What we did had to be done. You know that. And stop trying to be something you're not, Kimball. You're no priest. You're going to Hell just like the rest of us."

Kimball stood immobilized and stared at the bodies. The senator and his wife had been efficiently riddled with bullets, the sounds of the weapons silenced by suppressors no louder than spits, and no cries of pain from either victim. Yet Kimball knew he had compromised their position by yelling out in gut reflex. He turned to Jeff who was glaring at him with fury.

"Nice going," Jeff told him. "Now we're gonna have to fight our way out of here."

CHAPTER THIRTY-THREE

The assassin had followed Kimball and the Hardwick brothers from Baltimore. He had placed a simple GPS device to the bottom of their truck, the system sending an image of the pickup to the screen of his monitor, which was secured to the dash of his rented vehicle. From a distance of three miles, he could safely follow without being seen. And when the vehicle finally came to a stop close to Senator Shore's residence, he couldn't have been more elated.

The Iscariot Agenda was going well.

Parking the vehicle approximately a block away from where the Hardwick brothers parked their beefy pickup, the assassin found a vantage point on the slightly canted rooftop of a 24-karat home that had been foreclosed apparently for some time, at least by the appearance of the dead lawn and unkempt shrubbery. From his position, he had a perfect view of the pickup. And through the scope of the CheyTac M200, he appropriated from Hawk; the vehicle seemed within a stone's throw away.

With precise handling he removed the additional pieces of the rifle from his backpack and began to assemble them, carefully snapping the sections together. Once completed, the assassin mounted the scope and checked the landscape through the lens, the world becoming a phosphorous green with objects becoming clear and incredibly detailed.

After securing a suppressor to the rifle's barrel, the assassin found the wide trunk of an oak tree and sighted the weapon to its center. Maintaining a shallow and steady breath, drawing the crosshairs of the scope to the center of the tree's trunk, the assassin pulled the trigger, the gun barely sounding off.

When splinters of wood exploded to the left of his intended target, he recalibrated the scope and tried again, this time hitting his target dead on.

Closing his eyes, the assassin took a deep breath and released it with a long sigh. Once he felt a meditating calm sweep over him, he removed a photo from the side pocket of his backpack and examined it. It was a Photostat copy of the Pieces of Eight, the photo marked with circles surrounding the faces of those now dead.

Looking at the pickup truck, then back at the photo, and with Kimball and the Hardwick brothers currently engaged with the senator, the assassin knew he had more than enough time to set the stage for the next scene.

"No!"

There was no doubt in the minds of the two Capitol police officers that they heard the same thing. The cry was loud and crisp and clear.

From the first level, they quickly galvanized into action and grabbed their MP5's, the officers racking their weapons and heading for the semi-spiral staircase with the points of their weapons directed to kill.

Jeff, Stanley, and Kimball heard the footfalls of the officers climbing the stairway. Having no choice, Kimball removed his firearm and racked the weapon, chambering a bullet. Jeff and Stanley moved quickly to the hallway, the stairway to their left—the officers getting closer. To the left of the stairwell was a recess whose inner wall bore the artwork of something avant-garde.

"I got this," Stan whispered.

Stan went to the recess and hid behind the wall at the top of the stairwell. The Glock was in his right hand.

When the forward officer crested the top step, Stanley surprised him by darting out from the recess and came across with his left hand in a sweeping arc, the blow from the blade of his hand catching the officer in the throat, the clothesline strike causing the officer's feet to go out from under him as the force sent the man hard to the floor.

In fluid motion his gun hand came up and centered on the second officer, the man's eyes going wide with the quick realization that his life was about to end as Stanley fired off three shots in quick succession, the bullets impacting his center of body mass with the force driving the man down the stairwell. When the body came to a stop at the bottom step, the man's face was contorted and his body a broken ruin.

In a sweeping motion, Stan came around with the weapon and centered it on the man lying on the floor, gagging, his lungs fighting for breath as his hands clutched his throat where he was struck with a chopping blow. Without hesitation Stanley fired off two additional rounds, the bullets striking the officer in the forehead, two hard punches, his blood fanning out beneath him like a halo.

And just like that, it was over.

Both men had been killed within three seconds.

"Now that was a work of art," commented Jeff.

"We're not done yet," he said. "Don't forget the guy with the MP5 outside."

Jeff held up his weapon, waved it, and smiled. "I haven't forgotten."

Stan reciprocated with a smile of his. "Then let's go get him."

Kimball was beside himself. The Hardwicks were caught up in their blood lust. The killing was as much as an addictive drug with the brothers finding their fix with the pull of a trigger. This wasn't how it was supposed to go down, he thought. In and out with no one killed— the mission simply to determine who the assassin was behind the killings of the Pieces of Eight.

In Kimball's estimate, the senator had nothing to do with commissioning their demise. He was sure of it.

The Hardwicks, however, concluded something differently.

"Let's just walk away from this," he told them. "There's no need to take out the guard."

Jeff faced him with a disconcerting look. "What the hell happened to you?" he asked him. "That white collar you normally wear choking off the blood to your brain or something? You're turning into a pussy, Kimball. Keep with protocol and erase all elements of the opposition."

"The guard won't even know until we're gone."

"If he sees the bodies, then he'll call in reinforcements. We need time to draw distance between us and them."

Kimball knew he was right. That had always been the rule of thumb: Engage, destroy, and retreat. There was no platform he could truly debate from to quash the situation. Killing had always been their forte.

156

Conceding to the will of the brothers, Kimball had no choice but to follow, his position as team leader having been usurped by the Hardwicks.

The killing would go on.

The remaining officer who covered the grounds received a command through his earpiece. It was a call for backup, the voice frantic. When he responded through his lip mike he did not receive a reply in return, the frequency going silent.

The officer held his MP5 high, the weapon an extension of himself as he moved his head in a swivel, his world seen through the lens of the assault weapon.

From behind came a noise; barely perceptible, but still there.

He pivoted.

Through the lens, he saw nothing but the Italian cypresses swaying gracefully with the course of a light wind.

Then more noise, this time from the right, no doubt the snap of a twig.

Something was moving within the shadows.

The officer pivoted, then with slow efficiency made his way toward the source of the sound.

There it was, in the shadows, the silhouette of a man standing as still as a mannequin, waiting silently within a copse of trees.

"You! Move forward with your hands on your head! Now!"

The shape did not move.

"I said now!"

From behind, whispered words were spoken mere inches from the officer's ears. "Maybe he doesn't want to," the voice said.

The officer never heard the assassin sneak up beside him. The man's focus squarely on what was in front of him rather than keeping a peripheral awareness.

The officer quickly pivoted, the point of the gun swinging around.

Too late.

His opponent quickly knocked the MP5 out of his hands and came across with the blade of a KA-BAR combat knife, cutting through the man's neck with all the ease of slicing through a hot cake of butter.

The man's eyes widened, his neck becoming a second horrible mouth as he quickly bled out. Falling to his knees with his mortality slipping away, his head, although far from being severed, fell back like the cap of a Pez dispenser, the wide gash showing the plumbing of internal gore before falling back dead.

Jeff sheathed the knife and beckoned his brother from the shadows. "Nice job, man."

Stanley smiled as he made his way forward. "I never had a doubt."

"What are you talking about? You were nervous he was gonna pull the trigger, weren't you?"

"As I said, I never had a doubt. You were moving up on this guy like a cat."

After the two fist-bumped each other, they turned to the body. The wound glistened in the darkness like black tar.

"Kinda like old times, isn't it?" asked Stan.

"It certainly does get the blood going. I almost forgot what it was like."

Kimball came forward. He purposely remained far from the scene but kept a keen eye to see how it would play out. "I hope you two animals are happy with yourselves."

Jeff turned to him. "You know what I like about you, Hayden?"

"No. What?"

"Absolutely nothing." He squared off with Kimball, the six-inch height difference between them evident. "Your holier-than-thou attitude is getting on my nerves." Then: "You're not the same man, Kimball. One time you would have been bathing in this guy's blood after you gutted him . . . What happened to you?"

Kimball remained silent. But his mind answered for him. *It's all about salvation.*

After a short lapse of time, Stan stepped forward, grabbed his brother's arm, and began to escort him away. "We gotta get out of here," he said.

Jeff allowed himself to be led and Kimball followed, the men picking their pace up into a jog, then to a sprint, and made their way back to the truck leaving five people dead in their wake.

CHAPTER THIRTY-FOUR

Vatican City

Job was dressed in faded jeans that blossomed over the high ankle edges of military-issued boots, a black cleric shirt, and a Roman Catholic collar. His hair was set in a buzz cut and his sunglasses held an amber-colored tint to the lenses. In his hand was his duffel bag. Embroidered across the fabric was the emblem of the Vatican Knights, a coat of arms of a Silver Cross Pattée set against a blue background. The colors were significant in which the silver represented peace and sincerity, and blue the traits of truth and loyalty. Standing alongside the coat of arms were two heraldic lions rising from their hind legs with their forepaws against the shield, stabilizing it. The implication of the lions was a symbolic representation of bravery, strength, ferocity, and valor. It was also the symbol worn on their battle attire.

When Job exited the terminal, Cardinal Bonasero Vessucci was waiting for him by the loading curb beside the papal limousine wearing a conservative-style robe that was black with red buttons and scarlet piping. On his head sat a red zucchetto.

When the men saw each other, they gave off genuine smiles and, after Job dropped his bag, fell into each other's embrace.

"It's good to have you back, Job," said the cardinal, drawing back. "I'm so sorry that you had to be called back from sabbatical so soon."

"That's quite all right," he said, and then he picked up his bag and rounded the vehicle to the open trunk. The limo driver was standing there with his hands held behind the small of his back, a slight smile on his face, then stood back as he allowed Job to toss his duffel bag into the cargo bay. When the driver closed the trunk, Job and the cardinal found their rightful seats and settled in.

The car pulled away from the curb, the ride as smooth as sliding over the surface of glass, as the limo made its way to the main artery.

Job leaned forward, still wearing his sunglasses. "You said Kimball was in trouble?"

The cardinal nodded. "You know where Kimball comes from, don't you? You know of his background?"

He nodded. "He was an assassin," he said straightforwardly.

"Apparently, his old team is being terminated by an assassin and we have no idea who he is at this time. The SIV has no information as to who this killer is or why he's doing what he's doing. The only thing we do know is that whoever is doing this is going down the list and killing them in order. On the backs of each victim, he carves a single letter, spelling the name Iscariot."

"The betrayer of Christ. But why?"

The cardinal shrugged. "We think—Kimball thinks—that U.S. political factions may be involved in this to cover up past digressions. But the *Servizio Informazione del Vaticano* cannot find anything to support this."

"Their government is very good at keeping secrets close to the vest."

The cardinal nodded. And then: "A majority of his team is dead, all of them killed off by this assassin. And Kimball is running out of options. I need you to prepare yourself, Job. Ezekiel and Joshua will be ending their sabbaticals and returning shortly. If Kimball can get through the next few days, then I want you three to back him up."

"How's he holding up?"

The cardinal shook his head and managed a look of concern. "Besides him," he began, "he's working alongside two brothers who are as ruthless as Kimball is with his skilled techniques. Nevertheless, I would feel much better knowing that he had the backup of the Vatican Knights, instead."

The cardinal fell back into his seat and stared out the window, his eyes staring at nothing in particular, the world passing by in a blur. It was possible that Kimball could have neutralized the situation, he considered. But if he couldn't, then Kimball would have to return to the safety of the papal confines.

And if this should happen, then he would most likely bring his war to the Vatican.

Fighting for calm to quell the mounting anxiety, Cardinal Vessucci closed his eyes and began to pray.

CHAPTER THIRTY-FIVE

While the sun had risen in Rome, it was still early morning in Washington D.C. as Kimball and the Hardwick brothers ran down the street toward the pickup. Their pace was quick and silent as a feline that moved with predatory grace. And whenever possible they moved within shadows, using the darkness as their ally.

When they reached the truck, they quickly surveyed their surroundings, sighting nothing.

The night was still.

Kimball stood by the cab; his eyes filled with subdued rage. He knew he had to be careful because if he took on one Hardwick, then he would eventually be taking on two Hardwicks, a battle he might not be able to win.

Kimball lashed out; his tone was evenly measured, but it held a hint of resentment. "It wasn't supposed to go down like this."

"And how was it supposed to go?" said Stan. "Were we supposed to walk in, question the dude, then walk away? We're operators, Kimball. That's all we ever were. We move in, make a statement, and get out."

"And killing Senator Shore," added Jeff, "is a message to whoever is out there taking out the Pieces of Eight that we know who's involved, and that all actions are to cease and desist."

"We know nothing," Kimball shot back. "When he saw me, he was genuinely surprised. Don't you think the assassin would have told him that I was still alive?"

"Politicians are born actors. Of course, he knew you were alive."

"He had no idea."

Jeff placed his hand on the truck's handle. "You're wrong, Kimball. Shore was behind everything because he's the only one—the only one—who has any reason to fear the Pieces of Eight unless, of course, you have someone else in mind. If you do, then my brother and I will be more than happy to listen to whatever it is you have to say. So, tell us, do you have someone else in mind, someone who wants us dead?"

Kimball had to admit that he didn't. But Senator Shore surely fit the bill as a candidate who had everything to lose by the existence of the surviving members and what they knew. But there was nothing about him—his body language, the facial tics, or the way he spoke—that served as telltale signs that he knew anything at all.

"What's the matter, Kimball?" asked Stan. "You got no answer?"

"He's got no answer," said Jeff. "Because he knows we're right. Ain't that right, Kimball?"

Kimball ground his teeth, causing the muscles in the back of his jaw to work.

Jeff smiled. "I thought so."

When Jeff popped the door open of the pickup Kimball observed something wedged beneath the windshield wiper of something that looked like a flyer. "Wait a minute," he said. He removed the item except it wasn't a flyer at all, but a photograph. It was a print of the Pieces of Eight. However, this one had been amended. Unlike the other photos this one held an additional circle, another victim, the face circled in red with the letter "I" in it.

It was the face of Stanley Hardwick.

And then everything clicked.

They were not alone.

Kimball wheeled around immediately, motioning his hand for Stan to drop to the ground.

Too late.

Nobody heard the shot or saw the muzzle flash.

Stan went rigid, his back arching slightly as he balled his fists against the impact to the center of his forehead. His eyes darted momentarily, as if taking in the final moments of his life, then fell backward as stiffly as a plank of wood.

Jeff and Kimball took to the ground, searching.

Nothing.

"So much for your concept of the assassin ceasing and desisting once the senator was taken out," said Kimball. "Nice call."

"Shut up." Jeff quickly crawled to his brother who laid there looking skyward, a bloodless hole in the middle of his forehead, the pared-back flesh a blooming rose petal of pulp and gore as a thin ribbon of smoke rose upward from the opening.

"In the truck," ordered Kimball harshly. "Now."

Jeff looked at him, then back at his brother, then at the row of houses, growing angrier with each passing moment. He then cradled his brother's head within his arms, feeling a sudden and total loss of separation he never knew existed. It was like the complete severance of a body part, something that could never be replaced or made whole.

Stan Hardwick was gone forever.

"Get . . . in . . . the . . . truck," demanded Kimball.

Jeff looked at him with a lost look, a sad look, then lowered his brother's head, caressed his brother's cheek with the tips of his fingers, and quickly got into the cab, keeping his head down.

Kimball got into the driver's side with his head lowered, drove the key home, and turned the ignition, the truck roaring to life. In a fluid motion, he shifted into gear and stepped on the gas, the truck's wheels spinning, the rear end fishtailing as he pulled away from the curb and away from the area, the truck sliding into the turns as he went.

In the rearview mirror, Jeff saw the reflection of his brother lying in the street until the truck slid into its first turn.

And then he was gone.

"How did he know where we were?" screamed Jeff, raking his fingers constantly through his hair. "How did he know? We weren't followed! I made sure of that. There was no one behind us."

"You don't have to see someone to follow them," Kimball said.

And Jeff understood. "GPS," he said. "The son of a bitch placed a GPS somewhere on the truck."

"Bingo."

It would be the last word between them until they reached Baltimore.

When Kimball pulled into the alleyway behind the surplus store, he turned off the ignition and both men sat quietly.

After a lapse of silence, Kimball finally broke the ice. "I'm sorry about your brother," he said.

"You ain't sorry about Jack," he returned. "You hated him as much as he hated you."

Kimball sighed. "It'll take authorities a while to determine who he is because he has no history or listed identity. Most likely someone will recognize a photo and trace him back here . . . Maybe."

"Does it matter? The guy's dead."

"Look, Jeff—"

"Save it, Kimball. I ain't listening."

Jeff opened the door, got out, and slammed it shut behind him, shaking the truck. He then went to a steel door giving entrance to the shop, opened a metal box located next to the door with an ace key, tapped numbers on a keypad, and looked into the eye scanner. When he was done, the titanium bars went into motion and retracted, thereby unlocking the door. Grabbing the handle, Jeff swung the door wide and entered the premises, leaving the door open for Kimball to follow.

Unlike Jeff, Kimball exited the vehicle quietly and closed the door softly behind him. He stood there alone, examining his surroundings, the night silent despite the neighborhood, and wondered how long it would take for the assassin to make his presence known.

Probably not long at all, he considered. And then he took up Jeff on his invite and entered the store.

CHAPTER THIRTY-SIX

Vatican City

"Job has returned to us," said Cardinal Vessucci, as he made his way across the papal chamber.

Pope Pius looked drawn and pale, his features hanging more than usual. With a beckoning hand, he called the cardinal over to a vacant chair next to his, a couple of snifters of cognac on the table between them. "How are you, my good friend?"

Vessucci knew that the pontiff was dying by the inches; therefore, he refused to comment on the appearance of his physical state. Nevertheless, he couldn't help feeling the pang of sorrow for his close friend. "I'm well, Amerigo. Thank you." He took the seat next to the pope, a snifter of cognac already poured for him.

"Thank you for coming," said Pius, lifting the small glass. "Please, enjoy with me."

The cardinal lifted the glass, motioned it forward in salutation, and sipped from it before gingerly placing the glass back on the table. "We've yet to find Joshua and Ezekiel," he told him. "And most likely we'll simply have to wait until they return in a few days. So, I'm sorry to say that Kimball will have to make do with what he has."

"Any news on his front?"

The cardinal nodded. "Just that he's working in collusion with the Hardwick brothers." Neither man commented on the savage characters of the Hardwicks after reading their dossiers proffered to them by the SIV. But most likely they were thinking the same thing: Kimball Hayden was not in a good place. The Hardwick brothers were as cruel and vile as the assassin who was hunting them. And both men had to wonder if Kimball would fall back into the mold of what he used to be or grow into the man they wished him to be. "He'll be fine," the cardinal added without conviction.

But the pope could see right through his friend with incredible insight and noted that the cardinal's concern was equally as grave as his. The pope feigned a smile. "I know," he said, his conviction just as weak.

"But I am concerned about one thing," he added.

The pope waited.

"If Kimball does not conclude this matter in the States, then he'll most likely bring this private war of his to the Vatican."

"Then we will be prepared," said the pope. "If Kimball fails in his mission to neutralize the situation, then consider it a blessing that he can return to us at all."

"Still, a war is a war." The cardinal reached for his cognac. "And there is another matter of concern, I'm afraid."

"You would be talking about the good cardinals Marcello and Angullo, yes?"

Vessucci nodded, sipped from his glass. Then: "There are statements from very reliable sources that the good Cardinal Angullo is campaigning on behalf of Marcello in return for some kind of recompense, should Marcello be elected to the papal throne."

"Campaigning for the throne is one thing, Bonasero. Politicking for favors to obtain something on a personal level is something altogether different. Cardinal Marcello is well aware of this and will not fall into dark ambitions."

The cardinal leaned forward in his chair. "Good men are often blinded by ambition, Your Eminence. You know that. Now I'm not saying that Cardinal Marcello is corrupt—not at all. What I am saying, however, is that any man who wants something bad enough will *justify* anything to accomplish his goal. And that includes setting aside morals for what he believes to be the better good for all."

"I've known Cardinal Marcello for many years," he said. "As ambitious as he is, I truly believe that he would never devalue himself in any way."

"Devalue or not, that is why men are men; they make mistakes. And if the rumblings are true, if Angullo is truly persuading his camp to follow Marcello's for the sake of personal enrichment, then the Vatican Knights will be no more should he be elected to the post."

Pius looked toward the windows and mulled this over. "Are you sure of your sources?"

"Some are from Angullo's camp; people with concerns."

"Then perhaps I should speak with Cardinal Marcello about his misplaced ambitions if this is the case." The pontiff then laid his glass down on the tabletop and labored to his feet, then in a shuffling gait made his way toward the windows that overlooked St. Peter's Square. "None of us can afford to lose our way," he finally said, watching the masses moving along the Colonnade. "The Vatican Knights are a valued component to the safety of our citizenry abroad. Without the Knights, without Kimball, I wouldn't be here myself, especially after what happened in the States and aboard Shepherd One. They are essential to the needs of the Church."

"But Marcello will not see it that way. And if he is elected to the throne . . ." He let his words trail.

The pontiff nodded. "Send word that I want to see Cardinal Marcello immediately," he said.

Vessucci got to his feet, clasped his hands together in an attitude of prayer, then bowed his head. "I will do so immediately, Your Holiness."

And then he was gone.

CHAPTER THIRTY-SEVEN

Baltimore, Maryland.

Kimball and Jeff Hardwick were in the sub-basement inside the Vault, the room well lit, the walls were pristine white and lined with rows of all kinds of weaponry. On the table in the room's center was an olive-green duffel bag. Jeff was stuffing items inside, gearing himself for an immediate evacuation. He had packed minimal clothing items, toiletries, but his main goods were the weapons he had in storage. In the bag he placed a Desert Eagle, suppressors, plenty of ammunition, combat knives, throwing stars, and two other handguns, a Glock and a Smith and Wesson. Most importantly, he tossed in about a half dozen fake passports.

Against the far wall was a safe that was not concealed. After playing with the dial and opening the door, Jeff pulled six bundles of cash that Kimball assumed to be $10,000 packs, for a total of $60,000.

"What about all this?" Kimball said, waving his hand to indicate the multitude of weapons adorning the walls. "Are you just gonna leave them here?"

Jeff didn't answer him, at least not right away. The man stopped packing and stood idle, his face growing incredibly long over the past few hours. With mechanical slowness, he leaned over the table and placed his knuckles on the top for support. His eyes were staring at nothing in particular. But Kimball could tell that his mind was active.

"Stan wasn't too bright," Jeff began. "Instead, he was all guts and glory, always willing to take that first step when no one else was willing to do so, including me." His face began to crack, a slight quiver of the chin. "When we were kids in school there was this kid who was huge for his age. I mean really big, you know." His voice began to crack. "And one day he tried to hit me up for money. When I was reaching into my pocket for change Stan would have none of it. I mean, here was my brother, a guy much smaller than me, and he took this kid on. Well, Stan ended up getting smashed down to paste, and the kid ended up with my money anyway. But I never saw my brother the same way again—at least, not as my little brother." He turned to Kimball whose eyes were glassy with the sting of tears. "Day after day this kid came after me for money, and day after day Stan stood up for me and took the beatings instead. So, here we were, me and my little brother, who was much smaller than me, showing off guts I wished I had."

Jeff drew away from the table and began to pace the room in a grid. "Then one day," he went on, "my little brother took me to this tiny hole-in-the-wall shop. But what he took me to was much more than that. It was a martial arts studio. But it was the beginning of us as brothers working as a team not to be fooled with. So, we grew together, became inseparable. Then one day when this kid came at me for my money, I knew I was ready and stood my ground with my brother at my side, all guts and glory Stan was. Needless to say, my brother and I beat this kid so bloody because we wanted to make a statement. And a statement we made. Nobody ever messed with us again. And you know what? We loved that feeling of toughness, that feeling of invincibility. So, we became the very thing that we abhorred most. We became bullies who were no different from the kid we destroyed that day on the playground. And because of him, we became something else. And then one day, when we were ready, we went back to destroy our creator."

Kimball stepped forward. "I'm sorry for your loss, Jeff. I am."

Jeff's face suddenly became hardened, the muscles in his jaw working. "Don't you dare feel sorry for me, you son of a bitch. Don't . . . you . . . dare." Jeff galvanized himself into action and placed more essentials in the duffel bag.

And then, at the top of his lungs and driven by rage, "DON'T YOU DARE!" And then he broke, sobbing like that bullied little boy he once was on that playground.

CHAPTER THIRTY-EIGHT

Vatican City

Cardinal Marcello lightly knocked on the pontiff's door. He was wearing a black cassock with scarlet buttons, piping, and fascia. On top of his head sat a scarlet zucchetto.

"Come in." The pope's voice, like always, was warm and comforting, a genuine smile on his face.

When Cardinal Marcello stepped inside the papal office, he saw the pontiff sitting at his desk with his hand pointing to one of the two empty seats in front of him. "Please," he said.

Marcello sat down.

Then, from Pius: "And how are you today, Constantine? Good, I hope?"

The cardinal nodded and smiled. "I'm fine, Your Eminence. Yourself?"

"Considering the circumstances, I guess I'm as well as can be expected." The pontiff leaned forward, clasped his hands together into a fisted joining of prayer, and gently placed them on the desktop. His smile never wavered as his demeanor remained consistently warm and inviting.

"Something on your mind, Your Holiness?"

Pope Pius bowed his head, the single act of nodding sufficing as an affirmation to the cardinal's query. "There are rumblings within the Church," he finally told him, "that Cardinal Angullo's camp may be uniting with your own to secure your position as the next pope."

"Your Eminence, with all due respect and barring the state of your condition, it is my right as cardinal to seek out the coveted position that will be left vacant by your passing."

The pope raised his hand. "Don't get me wrong, Constantine. You have every right to politick for my role—as does anyone else. Without ambition, there can never be progress."

"Then I'm afraid I don't understand."

"To follow your ambitions is a wonderful thing," he continued. "It promotes us all to be better. But how you pursue those ambitions and what you leave in your wake is an altogether different matter."

The brow above the cardinal's left eye arced questioningly. "I'm still not following."

The pontiff leaned back into his seat, his smile washing away. "There're rumblings," he said evenly, "coming from the camps that if you were to secure your role as pontiff, then you would be willing to offer a recompense of some sort. Tell me this is not the case?"

Cardinal Marcello betrayed nothing with so much as a facial tic, or the raising or lowering of an octave in his voice as he spoke. "Your Eminence, politicking does not come without making allies through whatever means that are readily available."

"Then it's true? Instead of winning the seat by the merits of your past actions as a cleric, you've decided to take it by pure ambition by compensating others for the favor of their vote?"

"It's politicking," he returned.

"What you politick, Constantine, is your skills. You bring to the table what you have done in the past and show what it is that you can do in the future to better the Church, not yourself. It's always been about the Church."

"And there lie my ambitions," he countered. "I seek to better the Church."

For a moment they stared at each other. There was no animosity or underlying subterfuge by either man. They were simply coming square with one another regarding their philosophies.

The cardinal then settled back into his chair and tented his hands so that his fingertips pointed ceilingward. "May I be candid," he asked, "since we're talking about rumblings?"

"Of course."

"It's said that you have spoken about the Church holding secrets only the pope can know about. So, my question is: Is this true?"

"Then it's obvious to me that you have spoken to Cardinal Angullo."

"Then it is true. The Church does hold secrets."

"If you become pope, then you will learn that secrets are sometimes better left untold."

"The reason for secrets—with all due respect, Your Eminence—is that there is usually a certain degree of immorality tied to them."

"Or perhaps they can cause controversies that often lead to division rather than unity."

"Semantics," he quickly responded.

"Semantics or not, we all know that God does not favor acts of immorality. If you begin your term as pontiff with an immoral act of obtaining a position by recompense rather than merit, then you will continue to commit and justify immoral acts and cast them off as a necessity for the sake of the Church. And this cannot be, Constantine."

"However, Your Eminence, you sit here and say that it's quite all right for you to justify the secrets of the Church, even though they may bear a certain degree of immorality to them. If that's the case, then I guess one man's morality is another man's immorality."

The pontiff's face had slowly gravitated to that of a puppy-dog hang. The conversation had grown to a bitter display of counteroffensives of one man's vision against the other, which he wanted to avoid. And his lobbying efforts had failed miserably. If anything, his action of calling the cardinal to his chamber adversely affected Vessucci's chances of securing the highest seat in the land. He suddenly realized this with grave regret.

"This secret," began the cardinal, "are you willing to tell me?"

The pope sat silent and studied the man in front of him. Should he become pope, then he would have to know about the Vatican Knights. "No," he finally said. "Perhaps someday you will understand the necessity for such secrets."

"Not if they hold something immoral to them."

"There is nothing immoral to the secret I bear. Just controversy."

"I see." The cardinal got to his feet. "Unless there is anything more, Your Eminence, I have matters to attend to."

The pontiff stood and held out his ring finger, proffering the Fisherman's Ring. The cardinal dutifully kissed it, bowed in honor of Pius, and exited the chamber.

Pope Pius slid slowly down into his chair, truly concerned about the fate of the Vatican Knights.

CHAPTER THIRTY-NINE

Baltimore, Maryland

When Jeff finished packing the duffel bag and with Kimball standing idly by, the former assassin hoisted the duffel over his shoulder and stood before his former teammate, their eyes locking on to each other not so much as macho posturing, but in knowing that this would be the last time they saw each other as the last of a dying breed.

"I know it didn't seem like it, but it was kinda good to see you again," he told Kimball. "You stirred up old memories. Good memories. And I'm not talking about the killing, either. I'm talking about the times we all hung out together as a family since we didn't have anyone besides ourselves. You, me, my brother, Hawk—everyone." The corners of his lips rounded upward into a marginal smile. "Even that crazy Irishman," he added. And then the smile was gone.

Kimball took a step forward and undid the arms he had crossed around his chest. "Where will you go?" he asked.

Jeff headed quickly out of the Vault and made his way to the stairwell. Kimball followed close behind.

"I have accounts all over the world, which is to say that I'm set for the rest of my life. So, I'll probably go somewhere nice. Somewhere tropical where the women don't have to wear their bikini tops because the weather's too nice and it's not against the law." And then, with far more seriousness in the tone of his voice: "Somewhere where *he* can't get to me."

Kimball knew he was referring to the assassin. "Stay safe."

"Trust me. I plan to."

When they reached the top level of the shop Jeff placed the duffel bag on the floor and went to the keypad next to the security door. With lightning strikes of his fingers, he tapped in a code against the numeric keys and the bars retracted from the door, unlocking it.

As the door automatically opened with mechanical slowness behind him, he surveyed the shop one last moment, absorbing the moments he and his brother shared here. It was dirty. It was dingy. But it was theirs and it was home.

Without turning to Kimball, he said, "And what about you? Are you going back to the Church?"

"Yes."

"Are you happy there?"

"I am."

Jeff closed his eyes, the download of this memory complete. Then: "I'm glad for you," he finally told him.

As Jeff stood in the doorway facing the truck and with his back to Kimball, he said, "We don't stand a chance, do we?"

"There's always a chance."

Even though Kimball could not see it from where he stood, Jeff feigned a smile. "Well, at least these guns in my duffel will double my chances against him, don't you think?"

Kimball didn't answer.

So Jeff answered for him. "Yeah, I didn't think you'd agree with that," he said.

Jeff went into the alleyway, unlocked and opened the door to his pickup, tossed his duffel bag into the rear of the truck, got inside, situated himself, and then rolled the window down. For a long moment, he sat there and stared straight ahead, saying nothing. But before too long he faced Kimball with his hard-lined features bearing no sense of emotion—good, bad, or indifferent. "One thing's for absolute certain," he finally said. "No matter what you're doing with the Church or how long you wear the collar, I'll see you again, Kimball. Only I'll see you in Hell. And that's a fact."

With that, Jeff toggled the button and the electric window rolled up between them.

After the assassin fired the shot that killed Stanley Hardwick, he calmly broke down the rifle with quick efficiency, then headed for his vehicle and engaged the GPS monitoring system just in case Kimball and Jeff Hardwick decided to alter their return course, which they didn't.

Without a doubt, he knew they had killed the senator, an added plus to the entire agenda. And then he followed them right to their Baltimore door with them most likely realizing that there was a GPS frequency module attached to the vehicle.

But that wasn't the only thing attached.

From his vantage point on a wrought-iron landing of a fire escape less than a half a block away, the assassin had a clear view of the pickup.

In his hand was a metal box, silver, about the size of a cigarette pack. When he saw Jeff leave the store and head for the truck, the assassin raised the four-inch aerial, lifted the protective plastic covering the button, and placed the pad of his thumb on the button.

With the patience of a saint, he waited.

As the window of the pickup rolled up, Kimball stepped closer to the doorway, closer to the alley, their eyes locking for the last time.

Standing at the threshold, Kimball's mind toiled with the thought of seeing Jeffrey Hardwick in Hell. And he had to wonder: Was the man right in assessing Kimball's mission for deliverance something unattainable? Had he already secured his fate by the actions of his past? Certainly, this was what Jeff was alluding to. But Kimball had come to realize long ago that for every two steps taken toward redemption, there will always be someone there to knock him back. But that was all right since success did not come without struggle. His reaction to Jeff's statement was to simply smile back.

When the window rolled up to its full extent, Jeff reached forward to place the key into the ignition. Attached to the dash, however, by tape, was a scroll. Jeff peeled it away and began to unfurl the material. As he did, he saw that it was a photo of his old unit, the faces circled in red, the letters visible. In the red circle surrounding his face was the letter 'O.'

The assassin was here—inside the cab!

Oh, no!

Jeff tossed the photo aside and immediately rushed to panic as he tried to disengage the seatbelt to exit the vehicle, the one-time elite commando whimpering like an abandoned puppy.

His hands moved quickly, the thumb pressing the latch.

Nothing.

He then pulled at the belt, slapped the button, tugged at the strap. And then his heart began to race and thump, his blood coursing with speed induced by adrenaline. The roar of blood-rushing thunder now reached his ears, causing him to grow deaf to anything beyond the center of his world. Panic was setting in, his sight going red at the periphery and closing in.

The latch was jammed.

And he saw the reason why.

There was a piece of metal jamming the mechanism. It was rigged that once the belt was clipped in, then it was nearly impossible to undo.

And then he remembered.

His knife!

But the moment his fingers touched the hilt he heard an audible click—and then the whine of something gearing up. It was a sound he heard many times before with explosive devices.

Now it had become the sound of his life coming to a quick and bloody end.

Taking his fingers off the hilt of his knife, Jeffrey Hardwick turned and looked out the window one last time. The last image he would ever take in would be that of Kimball Hayden standing in the doorway of the surplus store. And oddly enough a single thought came to his mind: *The priest who is not a priest.*

With that his world became a white-hot flash as flames poured into the truck from the ventilation systems, engulfing him, the incredible heat quickly building to the point that the pickup's tempered glass exploded outward in all directions. And then the enormous explosion— the yellow mass of hot flame boiling upward into a fireball, the vehicle then taking flight and performing a fiery cartwheel before coming down as scorched metal, the flames continuing to fan outward from the charred debris.

From the sky a flaming photo seesawed back to Earth, the edges burning inward. When it landed on the ground the flames consumed its entirety until there was nothing left but ashes that would eventually be cast aside by the wind.

If it had remained, anyone would have seen the red circle surrounding the face of the last man in the photo.

Time can be measured in milliseconds and perhaps even quicker—and sometimes much too fast for the human mind to react, even in self-preservation.

As Kimball stood in the doorway mulling over Jeff's parting comment, he observed the former assassin pick something up inside the vehicle's cab—a piece of paper by the looks of it—and examined it. Suddenly he galvanized himself by moving with a sudden quickness, his hands searching for the release of the belt, then pounding the assemblage—once, twice, three times.

And then he stopped.

He turned to Kimball, his face and eyes bearing the telltale signs of what Kimball thought he would never see on the face of a Hardwick brother. It was the look of a man realizing that his life was about to end and there was nothing in his power to grant him a reprieve. All that was left was undeniable fear.

Their eyes met briefly.

And then the cacophony of the white-hot explosion immediately followed by force of the concussion. The energy had driven Kimball off his feet and projected him through the air until he collided with the wall, the impact of the collision leaving an indented impression of his backside in the drywall. Getting to his feet, and with the wind knocked out of him and his world a blur of double vision, Kimball looked as if he had risen from ashes that were the color of moon dust as he stood there not truly cognizant of where he was or what just happened. As his surroundings became a little more balanced, with the taste of blood and copper in his mouth, Kimball made his way to the door the same way a man fights his way through a desert sandstorm—with his hands before him while marching laboriously forward against buffeting winds.

He then grabbed the edges of the doorway and used them as a crutch, the sensation of incredible heat suddenly striking him and forcing him to retreat. From his point, he could hear the loud crackle of flames as the truck burned. Behind the wheel sat the blackened remains of Jeffrey Hardwick, his skin consumed to the point where the formation of bones was already beginning to appear.

Kimball stumbled deeper into the store with his stomach rolling into a slick fist as a wave of nausea from the trauma of striking the wall overtook him. Taking deep breaths with his hand over his abdomen, the feeling began to subside.

Removing his cell phone from his cargo pants, he dialed a quick-dial number and waited until he received an answer.

It was Cardinal Vessucci.

"They're all gone," said Kimball.

To the cardinal, even over a long distance, could tell that Kimball appeared out of breath. *"Are you all right?"*

"They're all gone," he repeated. "He got them all, Bonasero. I'm the last one. I'm all that's left."

"Are you all right?"

"I'm fine . . . Just . . . a little winded, that's all."

Outside, the flames continued to crackle loudly.

"What's that?"

"Just a little bonfire, which Jeffrey Hardwick happens to be a participant of."

"Oh, no."

"He's still out there, Bonasero. He's still coming."

"Then come home, Kimball."

"If I do that, then I won't be coming back alone. He'll follow me and we'll bring this war to the Vatican, which I'm not willing to do."

"We found Job. He's here. Joshua and Ezekiel will be back shortly from their sabbatical. By the time you get here, you'll have their backing. One assassin against four Vatican Knights favors you greatly."

"I don't want anyone else hurt," he said. "I've never seen anything like this guy. He's as lethal as anyone I have ever seen."

"Kimball . . . Come home."

"I'm not sure I want to do that."

In the distance was the sound of sirens, the authorities getting closer. Kimball, with the phone still to his ear, forced his way past the heat and onto the street.

"Kimball, come home. Although Amerigo won't admit it, he's getting worse by the day. You need to see him."

"How long does he have?"

"The doctor said months—three, maybe four at the most. But who knows? At this rate . . ."

"Even with chemo and radiation?"

"He's rejecting all forms of treatment. He simply wants to expire as God intended him to."

Kimball sounded agitated. "Did it ever occur to him that maybe doctors were placed here by God to help him live longer?"

"I know you're angry, Kimball. But what kind of a life would he lead only to suffer the last few moments of his life bedridden and sedated to the point that he was no longer aware of his surroundings?"

When the sirens and lights from police and ambulatory vehicles rounded the bend, Kimball fell back into the shadows until the vehicles passed him by.

And then: *"He wants to go to his Heavenly Father on His terms, not his."*

Kimball had to forcibly choke back the sting of tears. Besides Cardinal Vessucci and a few others, Pope Pius XIII had become his most unfaltering supporter believing that the Light was well within Kimball's reach, should he decide to follow its path. He had forgiven Kimball for his indiscretions and loved him like a son. And Kimball had loved him deeply like a father. Having one of the most significant men in the world believe in you when you did not believe in yourself spoke volumes. And Kimball was crushed.

"I didn't mean to snap," he finally said.

"It's understandable. We all love him, and he will be missed."

Kimball stood looking at the glow rising from behind the building like a halo. "I'm coming home," he said distantly.

"He'll be happy to see you."

And that was the breaking point for Kimball as he could no longer hold back the tears. And for a second time within days, tears began to flow, although they did so without him breaking into racking sobs.

"Kimball?"

He closed his eyes to blink back the rest of the tears. "I'm here," he said, his voice managing to stay even. "But, I'm most likely bringing the war back with me."

"Then we'll be waiting."

After the explosion set the vehicle in flight in spectacular motion, he lowered the aerial and let the plastic cap fall over the button. From his perch he watched the fires burn, thinking there was something quite hypnotic about them, a certain graceful quality about the way the flames danced with a life of their own. Nevertheless, he reveled in the fact that he formerly introduced Jeffrey Hardwick to a short dose of what was waiting for him in Hell.

This he was sure of.

When the sirens began to sound off in the background, just as he was about to take flight, he saw Kimball Hayden exit the building and take flight on his. The man looked disheveled and completely disoriented, his gait more like a man in a drunken stupor. Within a few moments, however, he seemed to have gathered himself and appeared unharmed, the large man rushing for the shadows.

That's good, the assassin thought. Kimball Hayden survived the blast after all. Now with Kimball as the last man standing, and after watching those around him fall, which no doubt cast an air of his infallibility, the assassin wondered if he was breaking him down mentally, as well. Killing Kimball Hayden had now become optimum.

Taking in a deep breath, with the smell of fire and ash heavy in the air, the assassin watched Kimball as he disappeared into the shadows. *No matter what,* he told himself, *I will follow you to the very stretches of your run and finalize my crusade by driving a knife across your throat. And when I stand over you and watch you bleed out, then, and only then, will I smile the moment the spark of your life finally fades away.*

And true to his word, the assassin gave chase.

CHAPTER FORTY

Vatican City

"There are secrets within the Vatican," Cardinal Marcello confirmed as he and Cardinal Angullo walked along the path the divided the Old Gardens. "The pontiff called me into his chamber and questioned me regarding whether or not I was offering recompense for your support in my pursuit of the papal throne."

"And what did you tell him?"

"The truth," he said. "I told him I was doing what was necessary to make allies. He, on the other hand, believes that I should proffer my past merits as a cardinal to the College, rather than to bolster camps with promised incentives."

"And what about the secrets?"

"The pontiff was candid," he said. "He claims the secrets are not being withheld from the constituency because they bear any sense of immorality . . . but are more of a source of unwanted controversy."

"Controversy, my dear Cardinal, is normally derived from prospects considered at the very least, amoral."

"My sentiments precisely," he said. "And as I told the dear pontiff, one man's morality is another man's immorality. Should any subject bear the weight of causing controversy, then it has no place in the Church. Morality and controversy cannot exist cohesively together."

"And did he entrust you with any secrets?"

"No. He told me nothing."

"Then perhaps I can enlighten you with something my sources informed me of while lobbying them on your behalf."

"Go ahead."

"Have you heard of the Society of Seven?" he asked.

"No."

"Allegedly, they're a most powerful council made up of the pope, Cardinal Vessucci, and five of the most trusted cardinals within the

College who are closest to the pope," he said. "They are the sole keepers of the Vatican's secrets."

Cardinal Marcello stopped in his tracks, as did Cardinal Angullo, the men staring at each other as they were surrounded by a riot of floral colors of the garden.

"Allegedly?"

Angullo shook his head. "Allegedly, yes. But I'm trying to verify this as we speak."

Both men turned and commenced their walk along the pathway.

"Such a secret in itself can be held very close to the vest," said Marcello. "To prove something of such caliber may be impossible to do."

"This is true. And perhaps the truth will never be discovered on whether or not they truly exist, or if they truly bear the secrets of the Vatican. But if it is true, then Cardinal Vessucci is in league with enormously powerful people."

Cardinal Marcello nodded. "Vessucci confers with few besides the pope, so determining who they are can be easily assumed if this is the case."

"And if this is the case, proven or not, then we must—or you must, as pontiff—take action to purge any clandestine factions within the Vatican."

"I would hate to prosecute anyone without confirmation?"

"The pope has already acknowledged the fact that the Vatican holds secrets, which he is unwilling to unveil to you because he feels that he can't entrust you with them. That is why he called me into his chamber prior to your meeting. It was an obvious lobbying effort on his part to coerce me by having my camp support Cardinal Vessucci so that the secrets can be maintained."

Cardinal Marcello nodded his head in agreement. "It's always been obvious that he wants the good cardinal to succeed him."

"But I have promised you the support of my camp ensuring you the papacy in return for the seat of secretary of state. Now I ask you for a second favor that will guarantee you that seat."

Cardinal Marcello stopped in his tracks. "I thought the seat was already guaranteed the moment I offered you the appointment of secretary of state, upon my commission of the throne."

Angullo raised his forefinger. "All I ask is but one thing," he said. "The thing I ask will serve to protect you and the throne, should the

Society of Seven exists."

"Go on."

"The Vatican has diplomatic ties with ninety percent of the countries worldwide. What I ask of you is this: Once you have secured the title as pope, then you'll need to appoint Cardinal Vessucci and his allies to archdioceses across the globe to weaken his ranks."

Cardinal Marcello stood idle. The man was a seasoned cleric much older than Angullo. He also saw the subterfuge of every man's rhetoric and the mind games they played to better position themselves for something esteemed. And Marcello saw this. "Now it's clear," he finally said. "What you say you do for me you also do for yourself. I am thirty years your senior, and by the laws of nature, I should pass before you. But you only lobby on my behalf because it will do two things: You obtain the second most powerful seat in the Vatican. And by usurping the position held by Cardinal Vessucci, you will then be the second most powerful man in the Vatican. Secondly, by appointing the good cardinal to an archdiocese elsewhere, I break up his constituency which leaves you with the most powerful camp in the Vatican upon my passing. What you're doing is setting yourself up for the papal seat in the future."

"What I do I do for the good of the Church," he said. "I won't deny that my ambitions are the same as yours, Constantine. But I do believe if Cardinal Vessucci bears secrets that may be amoral, even though he is a good man, he can be a threat to the welfare of the Church—albeit unknowingly—since the road to Hell is truly paved with good intentions. Is that something you can afford to turn a blind eye to?"

Cardinal Marcello mulled this over carefully, digesting the cardinal's every word. "I'm not convinced that what you tell me is *all* for the good of the Church," he said. "I also believe that you're positioning yourself by eliminating Cardinal Vessucci, who seems to be more of a threat to you than he is to the Vatican. But I also find your reasoning sound. So, I'll grant you your second request. But if you come to me with a third, then I will seek the papacy without the service of your following. Is that clear?"

The cardinal parted his thin lips into a smile that flashed more like a grimace. "Totally," he said.

CHAPTER FORTY-ONE

"Again!"

From the wings of the training center located in an uncharted building situated between St. Martha's Chapel and the Ethiopian College about 200 meters west of the Basilica, Kimball watched from the shadows as Joshua, Job, and Ezekiel partook in mock combat using wooden katanas.

Brass torches lining the walls were lit, the flames dancing, the shadows against the walls moving in macabre fashion.

In the center of the chamber, Ezekiel served as the object of the attack as Joshua and Job flanked him, their katanas held forward with the blunted points aimed at their target. Slowly, and with practiced prudence, they circled the young Knight looking for the proper moment to strike.

Ezekiel held his ground, the point of his wooden blade before him as he kept his faux enemies at bay deciphering what defensive techniques to use upon the moment of attack. By now he knew his instincts should have been honed to the point of natural reaction, striking out with skilled movement independent of the mind—a reaction against action. But Ezekiel knew he wasn't there yet, the man still deciding between intellectual decision over instinctive reaction. But he was close, and he knew it. And so did Kimball.

Joshua and Job circled him, anticipating, the tips of their katanas rising; telltale signs to Ezekiel that they were getting ready to strike.

So, he ground the balls of his feet against the floor, readying himself to pivot and defend from all points.

And here they came.

Job and Joshua struck from opposite sides, the blades of their swords cutting, slashing, and slicing, the air divided with a series of whooshing sounds.

And then the sound of contact, wood against wood, blade against blade, the young men joining together as action-reaction, the blades of the swords becoming blurs as Ezekiel skillfully defended his position.

From one side to the other Ezekiel brought his blade up, over, and across with blinding speed deflecting blows proffered by Joshua and Job. His movements were skilled and fluid, his actions now driven more by instinct than thought. And then he came across and struck Joshua's sword above the hilt, the faux weapon breaking, the wooden blade skating across the floor and into the shadows.

Joshua exited from the battle—now considered a kill by the rules.

Now Ezekiel was one on one with Job, a truly skilled warrior, both hands on their hilts as they clashed with subdued fury. Blow after blow, strike after strike, Job drew Ezekiel to the far side of the arena. And then Ezekiel countered with a primal scream, only to find an inner reserve and struck back with unbridled force.

Up and over and across he countered with lightning-quick strikes, the energy of his muscles driving his counterpart backward, Job becoming the defender, his eyes flaring, blades clashing. And then Job ducked and drove his blade across the tissue above Ezekiel's knee, a debilitating stroke that ended the contest.

Job had become the victor.

Disappointed, Ezekiel dropped his weapon.

"Very good," stated Kimball, emerging from the shadows. "Going up against two of the best is never an easy task."

"But I still lost," he returned.

"I would have been surprised if you won. To defeat a couple of Vatican Knights is no small feat, Ezekiel. You should be proud of yourself. You nearly pulled it off."

Job laid his sword aside and stood next to Ezekiel, as did Joshua. They stood side by side as brothers not by nature, but by camaraderie. They had grown together—spiritually, mentally, and physically.

And Kimball had watched them grow from adolescents to teens to young men. Each one developing a strong constitution where knowledge became power and power became knowledge. They had become learned and skilled and devoured anything books could offer. But even more so, they had developed the fortitude to live their lives by the proverb that loyalty was above all else, except honor. Kimball Hayden was proud of them.

And now, in his time of need, they will serve him and become his shield.

Several hours later, Kimball's plane began its final descent into Fiumicino Airport in Rome. Job, Joshua, and Ezekiel continued to remain within his thoughts as the jumbo jet touched down on the runway.

After a forty-five-minute wait for his bag at the carousel, Kimball grabbed it and left for Passenger Pickup. Parked next to the curb was the papal limo, the driver holding the door open for Kimball. Inside, Cardinal Vessucci sat waiting, smiling the biggest smile Kimball had ever seen.

It was good to be home, he thought.

"It's good to see you again," said Cardinal Vessucci.

"Yeah, well, unfortunately, my mission was a huge failure. I'm totally lost, Bonasero. Whoever is doing this remains faceless. I'm no closer to solving this than when I was the day I left."

"It was believed to be a political faction."

"There was only one person who had anything to lose by the knowledge that the Pieces of Eight held. But I honestly don't believe he had anything to do with any of this. The man was genuinely surprised to see that I was alive, whereas the assassin *knows* I am. You would think that type of information would have gotten back to the senator."

"And this political factor?"

"Dead," Kimball quickly said.

"By your hand?"

"No. I had no intentions of killing him. But the Hardwick brothers saw differently, I'm afraid."

"I see."

"When will Ezekiel and Joshua return?"

"Soon," he said. The moment he answered, the limo hit a groove in the road, which caused the vehicle to buck hard before rolling back to a smooth journey.

And then: "I'll need them, Bonasero. I can't do this alone."

"I know. And believe me, Kimball, the pontiff and I feel much better with the security of the Knights behind you. We'll get through this together."

Kimball turned and viewed the landscape whipping past, noting the full greenery of the trees and the true aesthetic beauty of Rome.

Without turning back to the cardinal, he asked, "How is the pontiff?"

"He's well."

Kimball faced him, his features firm. "How is he really?"

Vessucci took in a long breath. "He has cancer, Kimball. And he's dying. Mentally and spiritually he's the same man. Physically, however, he's breaking down every day and it tears my heart out to see this slow degradation of a great man. But as Amerigo always does with a smile on his face, he reminds me that it's a way of life."

"I'll miss him."

The cardinal looked out the window. "The world will miss him."

They drove on in silence—the men looking out the window acknowledging the scenery of Rome's historical heritage of aged columns and marbled structures.

All of a sudden it seemed that life was too short to let things pass by without an appreciative eye.

CHAPTER FORTY-TWO

It's said that if you do not view everything daily but return after a long gap of interaction with someone, then the changes are evident. But if you see someone daily, then the changes are not as clear. Such was the case of Pope Pius XIII.

When Kimball saw the man, he seemed to have aged dramatically over the past few days. He was pale. And his face was beginning to drop as his jowls became more pronounced. But the old man's smile was remarkably genuine as the pontiff raised himself from his seat to greet Kimball as he walked through the chamber doors.

The men fell into each other's embrace, and suddenly Kimball felt a terrible pang of impending loss and did not release the man after a long moment.

"I'm glad you're well," said the pontiff, drawing away.

"Your condition . . ." Kimball let his words fall away.

"It's all right, Kimball. I'm fully prepared. And that makes all the difference in the world. Now please," he said, gesturing to the chairs in front of his desk. "I want you and the cardinal to have a seat. We have much to discuss."

Kimball was dressed as a Vatican Knight—the black cleric shirt and Roman collar, which was incongruous to the black fatigues and boots. Cardinal Vessucci wore his typical black cloak and scarlet zucchetto.

"What's going to happen to me is inevitable," began the pope. "What may also be inevitable, if Cardinal Vessucci does not ascend to the papacy, is the continuance of the Vatican Knights."

Kimball turned to Vessucci, then back at the pope. "Bonasero has a strong camp," he said. "And he's the secretary of state. He's well-positioned."

Pope Pius nodded. "He is. But it has come to my attention that Cardinal Angullo's camp is going to merge with Cardinal Marcello's."

"Has this been confirmed?"

"I've been told by those who are neutral that the camps are merging."

"What does that mean?" asked Kimball.

"It means," started Cardinal Vessucci, "that my camp has been severely weakened."

"The world is becoming secular but Cardinal Marcello is unwilling to bend, even in small measures. And the traditionalists within the rank and file see this as a moment to fill the papacy with a staunch conservative, which Bonasero is not."

Kimball leaned forward. "Are you saying that if Cardinal Marcello wins the papal throne, then he'll disband the Vatican Knights?"

"Cardinal Marcello will not see the Vatican Knights as saviors of the citizenry of the Church. He will see them as a military force and equate them with warfare and brutality."

"But that's not what we're about."

"I know that. And Cardinal Vessucci knows that. And so do those within the Society of Seven. But certain constituencies within this Church will never align themselves with those who agree with the existence of the Vatican Knights for the reason I just proposed to you."

"Then we'll enlighten them," said Kimball.

"To inform the constituencies of the Vatican Knights will cause controversy and most likely division within the Church, which we cannot afford. The pope is the bearer of Vatican secrets and must hold them close to keep the Church from dividing. However, all secrets must be delivered to the pope in a way that the mantle is passed, and he must become the Bearer. And as the Bearer, he has the right to choose what to do with those secrets accordingly. Knowing that Cardinal Marcello is conservative by nature, he will most assuredly disband the Knights, which is something I would believe to be in grave error."

"So, what do we do?"

"In the time I have left, the good cardinal and I must campaign with due diligence. I still have some pull with those who are traditionalists. And Bonasero has a good report with those in the College, who have remained neutral. I believe together we can develop a constituency that will exceed Cardinal Marcello's. But it will take work."

"Do you think this can be done?" asked the cardinal.

"It has to be done," he returned.

"Why don't we just operate under the guidance of Bonasero and the members of the Society of Seven?" asked Kimball.

"No matter what, my friend, we cannot and will not hold secrets from the reigning pope. If we begin to do that, then structure within the Church begins to break down. The pope is the figurehead of Catholicism and must sit upon the papal throne in full control. If he is not, then the institution will ultimately fail from corruption within. What the pope knows, what the pope has to know, is optimum."

Kimball fell back into his seat. Things weren't looking up.

The pope then addressed Kimball. "But what is even more important, my friend is to protect you from whoever it is that is out there trying to kill you. Without you, then there can be no Vatican Knights."

"Not true," he said. He instantly realized the adulation. "Isaiah and Leviticus can easily lead the teams. A Vatican Knight is a Vatican Knight."

"But none as unique as you are. And that, my friend, was not meant to be flattery."

Kimball bowed his head with humility. He truly respected this man who saw in him what he did not see in himself: underlying goodness. "Thank you."

"With the grace of God," said Pius, "then we will be able to win on both fronts."

"And if we don't?" asked Kimball.

"Then the Church will come under the power of a Traditionalist. And the Vatican Knights will be no more . . . And if you do not survive the war that is sure to follow you, then we will all lose."

CHAPTER FORTY-THREE

Vatican City. Three Days Later

"He's out there. He's deadly . . . And he's coming our way."

As required, Joshua and Ezekiel returned from their sabbatical. Along with Kimball and Cardinal Vessucci, they gathered inside an uncharted building that served as a barracks that was situated between the St. Martha's Chapel and the Ethiopian College, about 200 meters west of the Basilica. The building itself was simple and nondescript, its purpose to draw little attention other than it being a housing relic created of fieldstone and cement mortar.

The interior was an antiquated throwback where everything was constructed of stone and rock shingle the color of desert sand. Along the walls were ornamental sconces—the natural light came in through stained glass windows that chronicled the Stations of the Cross. In the center was the Circular Chamber, a huge rotunda that separated the building into two separate wings. It was the room of ceremony where a man either became a knight of the Vatican or as an assembly area where viewings were held for knights who had fallen in combat.

The Chamber's floor was a mosaic masterpiece of art majestically cobbled together to form the emblem of the Vatican Knights. Centered within the coat of arms was a Silver Cross Pattée set against a blue background.

And not only did the crest serve the Vatican Knights as a symbol of positive fortitude, but also as a constant reminder of what they were as the emblem appeared everywhere throughout this house of divinity. The coat of arms was depicted in stained glass images and served as the titled insignia on their uniforms and berets. It was also acid-etched into the stone wall above the door of their living quarters.

Standing on the outskirts of the mosaic emblem with their hands clasped together behind the small of their backs, with their feet slightly parted in the at-ease position, Kimball paced back and forth briefing his team of what was to come. Yet his tone was steady and his features stoic.

"You all know what I was before I became a Knight and what I did," he said. "My past is no secret to anybody in this room. And now it appears that it has come back to haunt me. And I mean literally." He stopped pacing and took a spot in the center of the mosaic coat of arms. "Whoever is hunting me is doing so with a skill that rivals the Vatican Knights," he added. "He's stealthy, he's deadly, and he's methodical. In fact, he took out an entire team of seasoned vets who were once considered to be the best the world had to offer in the field of wetwork assassinations. And that's saying something."

"Is there anything—anything at all—that we can go on?" asked Job. "Is there anything that can give us an edge?"

Kimball nodded. "Nothing," he said. "This guy's without a face."

"And a Shadowman is usually impossible to beat," added Ezekiel. "If we don't know our target, then how are we supposed to neutralize the situation?"

"We have to draw him in," said Kimball. "And wait for him to make a mistake."

"But that can come at a cost," said Joshua.

And Joshua was right, he considered. Costs often came with the loss of life the moment the assassin revealed himself while making his targeted kill. Perhaps the flash of a muzzle or the victim's dying moan. Anything that would draw attention to those acute enough to realize that something was out there whetting its desire to kill.

But this time they'd all be watching for those little imperfections.

Cardinal Vessucci crossed the floor wearing his traditional cloak and scarlet zucchetto and stood next to Kimball, who served as a physical antithesis to the much smaller man. He then asked the Knights to bow their heads in prayer, and then he spoke softly in Latin, only to finalize the prayer with the signature mark of the Cross. "And may God be with you," he said.

Kimball crossed the chamber floor, his footfalls echoing off the stone walls. "This is personal and none of you have to get involved in this," he told them forwardly.

"Yes, we do," said Ezekiel. "Vatican protocol states we must protect our citizenry. Are you not a part of that?"

Kimball conceded with a marginal smile. Ezekiel's message was clear. And he could see upon the faces of Job and Joshua that the sentiment was jointly shared. What it came down to was a single proverb signifying the mindset of a Vatican Knight: *Loyalty above all else, except Honor.*

"Thank you," he said.

Job broke from the ranks. "What are we waiting for?" he said. "We have a war to prepare for."

And that was the problem as Kimball turned to Cardinal Vessucci, their gazes meeting in such a way that words weren't necessary. The worrisome look on Kimball's face said it all: He was not comfortable bringing his war within Vatican jurisdiction. But Vessucci's expression was quite detailed with his features a well-scripted arrangement that indicated that the Vatican was not about to abandon Kimball after what he had done for the Church. And like many others in need, the Church would give him sanctuary.

Then to Vessucci in a voice that was soft and low, "Thank you."

The cardinal smiled, bowed his head, and placed a closed fist over his heart. It was the salute of the Vatican Knights. And in Latin, he said, "Loyalty above all else, except Honor."

Kimball reciprocated with a salute of his, with a closed fist over his heart.

Vatican City is the smallest country in the world, yet to Kimball, it was the most pristine.

Not much larger than a golf course and with a population of just over 700 people, none of them permanent residents, the city served as the spiritual hub presiding over a billion Catholics.

Kimball walked leisurely along the paths of the Papal Garden. The sky was as blue as Jamaican waters and a mild breeze grazed against his skin. Flowers bloomed in colorful riots from all around. But the surrounding magnificence seemed to have little or no interest to Kimball as his mind worked anxiously trying to determine the identity of the assassin.

He was certain that Senator Shore had nothing to do with the entire matter. But because the senator was the only person of interest who came to mind, the accusing finger automatically pointed in his direction. Now the senator lay dead along with four others who had no reason to be. If political factions were behind this, then the killings no doubt grabbed their attention, and a message was sent as the Hardwick brothers intended. But the killings continued as the brothers had fallen victim within hours of the senator's assassination. So, if the message was received in the form of a dead senator, then it had no effect. The killer was marching forward. And Kimball was now the designated target.

He was the last of a dying breed.

Passing clerics with a smile and a nod, Kimball racked his brain further. The consensus was that the common denominator stemmed from a single incident more than two decades ago: the sanctioned killing of a United States senator by other reigning political factions serving at the time. But the senior authority during that legislature either passed or retired into obscurity. There was no doubt in his mind that Senator Shore had the candidacy on the line with enough skeletons to fill a walk-in closet. And if anyone had reasons to cover up a past that had demonized a democratic government through decisions of iniquity at that time, then the senator seemed the likely candidate to sanitize anyone that could bring him down.

The only one, he thought.

But something else told him differently—that instinctive gut feeling a soldier develops in the field after numerous battles, that sensation that the threat remains, and the predator is still on the hunt.

But why?

The answer eluded him.

After more than two hours of contemplation, Kimball slowly wended his way along the paths back to the housing of the Vatican Knights. When he entered, the residence was tomblike and unnervingly quiet. Job, Ezekiel, and Joshua were most likely in the armory, he considered, and then he walked across the chamber floor, his footfalls echoing with hollow cadence as he traversed the mosaic design of the Vatican Knights. It was also the chamber where fallen Knights were waked after losing their lives in battle. And then he wondered if he would be viewed like those who had fallen before him, as he was being buried in the grottos beneath the Basilica.

He stood upon the mosaic crest, upon the silver Pattée, and appreciated his surroundings. In the moment of final tribute, the Vatican Knights would stand at the fringes of the area wearing the compliment of full dress, as the pontiff and those within the Society of Seven presided over the fallen while saying his eulogy. Once the ceremony was over, the assigned pallbearers would carry the coffin to a marble tomb within the grottos beneath the Basilica.

It was a cold place, he thought; sepulchral and earthy. But it was hallowed ground.

Moving along the corridors that lead to the residential quarters, he noted the acid-etched crest of the Vatican Knight's above each door.

Entering his chamber and closing the door behind him, he found himself within a small room, the dimensions not much larger than a prison cell. But here he was always at peace, even though it was far from opulent in any sense of the meaning.

Against the left wall was a single-sized bed with an accompanying nightstand and dresser. Opposite that against the right wall stood a small dais with a Bible upon it that had gone unread, a votive rack with candles that had hardly been lit, and a kneeling rail meant for prayer. On the wall centered between these two opposing sides was a stained-glass window with pieces of leaded glass forming the colorful image of the Virgin Mother reaching out her outstretched arms in invitation.

Here, was tranquility.

He sat on the edge of his bed, the mattress bowing beneath his weight. Above him, the Virgin Mary's arms were glowing with the light of the mid-day sun as they seemingly reached out to him. Standing, he traced his fingers lightly over the image, the warmth radiating through the glass, the Virgin Mary all but real.

He sat back down and closed his eyes. There was nothing but silence.

Opening his eyes, he looked across the room and noted that the Bible was in an awkward position with its cover open and the book placed upside down on the dais. Rarely had he opened the book to reveal the pages—but even more so to leave the book in such a way.

Somebody was here, he concluded.

Getting to his feet he crossed the room in a couple of steps.

The book was open and upside down on the podium. However, the ribbon bookmarker marked a different page of the biblical text. After leafing through the pages to the bookmarked spot, it was there that he found a Photostat copy of the Pieces of Eight.

Within the split moment it takes for a heart to misfire, Kimball could swear that his heart did so in the form of a swift punch to his chest.

All the faces of the team were circled with a red marker, including his. But this photo was different. Within the red circle surrounding his face was the letter 'T.' The word 'Iscariot' now complete.

In seconds, his emotions went from shock to rage to confusion, and then to rationalization after factoring in the impossibility of the moment. But in a calm measure, he realized that the truth of the matter had now become a certainty.

The assassin was here.

CHAPTER FORTY-FOUR

Vatican City

By growing up together and learning how to battle in the arenas had made them as close as brothers could be without the blood ties.

They had been orphaned at an early age at the expense of assassinated family members and brought to the Vatican for a resurgence. What they got was a chance to be the crusaders of a modern world—where unity, faith, and devotion had become ingrained within their character.

But as children of tragedy, it had taken them longer to conform to new surroundings in a new land.

As teens, they had grown and studied together, and then they learned to fight with faux knives and wooden katanas. They had become exceptionally learned, studying the tomes and eclectic philosophies from such men as Aristotle, Epicurus, and Thomas Aquinas. Masterful pieces of art also had their place in the teachings with certain works serving to develop insight by those who could point out and interpret the artistic subtleties of Da Vinci and Michelangelo. For a Vatican Knight, it was believed that the development of the mind was equally as important as the body, the two coalescing into a combination that fashioned men of impervious will, staunch character, and the mindset that loyalty was above all else, with the exception of honor.

After classes they were given time to grow as children do and given time to play and, at least to a degree, granted moments of mischievous deeds, which were met with punitive actions. The cardinal saw this as an important element of growth. The punishments meted out as a tool to show them which deeds were acceptable, and which were not: The difference between right and wrong.

In times of play, they often found an affinity for playing with the pinball machines in the sacristy above St. Peter's, which were mostly used by the altar boys in training with the Vatican. And as teens they experimented with wine, discovering the worlds of intoxication and hangover, which Bonasero Vessucci thought was punishment enough.

Everything had become a formula for learning and discovering the world within, as well as the world without. And no three people could have learned to become closer in bond than Job, Joshua, and Ezekiel.

They had become inseparable.

In a room that was 100 meters south of the chamber where the Society of Seven often met to determine missions of the Vatican Knights, there was a small armory where the Knights often gathered to choose the best weapon to fit the needs of the assignment. The room was windowless and walled with granite, mortar, and limestone. Above them hung bright reservoirs of fluorescent lighting and an ancient door that was thick and wooden and held together with black iron bands and rivets, which led to a larger room bearing a cache of weapons.

"This is different," said Job, racking the barrel of a Glock for smooth action and release. "We never fought a phantom before. There was always a face or a name or something to go by."

"True," said Ezekiel, "but isn't that what a Vatican Knight is all about? To be tested?" He held a KA-BAR in his hand and began to spin it with the same ease and skill as a majorette twirling a baton, the knife spinning in blinding revolutions before he finally placed it on the table.

Job smiled. "Show off."

Ezekiel gave off a small chuckle and went for an assault weapon. "Being tested is what makes us better," he added. "There's always something new to learn. If we don't, then we stagnate." He held the point of the weapon ceilingward and pulled the slide. The noise of the action rebounded off the walls in emphasis.

"Still," said Joshua, "tested or not, I like to know who we're up against."

"Ditto," said Job.

"As do I," returned Ezekiel. "But that's not the case here, is it?"

"No. I guess not."

They examined the weapons, breaking them down to the minimal piece and putting them back together. Gearing up was optimum and a weapon going defunct in the middle of battle was often fatal. So, they made sure their weapons were always primed.

When Job placed his readied combat rifle aside, he suddenly caught the spangled glitter of something beneath the flare of the fluorescent lighting. It flashed like a diamond, the sparkle just enough to draw his attention away from his duties.

Inside a canvas bag to the right of the table, lying partially beneath a folded camouflaged boonie cap, was something that held a mirror polish to it. Looking over his shoulder he noted that Joshua and Ezekiel continued with their prepping.

Reaching into the bag he moved the cap aside and traced his fingers over the smoothness of the metal cylinder.

What's this?

Removing it from the bag he held it aloft, turning the item from side to side to examine it. It was silver and polished, and he could see his reflected image in a funhouse sort of way, warped and disfigured. And it was cold to the touch.

There was a red button on the cylinder, a perfect placement should it be depressed by the thumb.

With curiosity a large part of Job's nature, he pressed the button.

From the head of the cylinder, a pick shot up so quickly that he almost did not perceive the action of the pick extend at all. The tip was wickedly sharp and keen, the point capable of boring through most surfaces with the right force applied behind it, especially the human skull.

"Well, well, well—what do we have here?"

Footsteps, from behind, the approach of someone coming closer for examination, and then silence.

"Can I see that?"

"Sure." Pressing the button, the pick fell back into the cylinder with the same lightning speed. And then as if passing the baton in a relay race, he handed the Knight the cylinder. "Be careful," he said. "That thing can do some damage."

The cylinder was taken away.

"I bet it does," said the receiving Knight.

And then he ejected the pick.

Kimball's world was that of thin corridors and stone walls the color of desert sand. As he raced down the hallways his mind reeled, the photo in his hand crushed due to tension. The assassin had walked right through the front door, past security, and directly into his chamber. This man was a ghost, he considered—something that was becoming truly unstoppable.

The halls were for the most part vacant as he hastened his way toward the armory, once in a while passing a bishop who gave him an inquisitive look as he rushed past them.

Passing through darkened corridors that led to the chamber where the Society of Seven often congregated, passing medieval doors and numerous ancient torches that lined the flat rock walls, Kimball found his way to the armory, a small room approximately thirty feet beyond an arched entryway.

The Knights were here, no doubt. And he would quickly galvanize them into action. But when he opened the door to the area, the smell of blood and copper hit him with such impact that he knew that he had arrived too late.

Two teammates were downed, crimson pools of blood as thick as oil, spread evenly across the floor as the smell of blood hung cloyingly thick in the air like a pall.

For a dizzying moment Kimball stood over the bodies without expression, his mind quite desensitized as the scene took on something surreal, something that was dark and dreamlike and hanging on the fringes of the macabre.

But when he slowly craned his head to a marking on the wall made with cold sweeps of a bloodied hand, he noted a single word written on the stone.

ISCARIOT

Suddenly Kimball felt the pang of reality strike him, that dreamlike quality of the surreal suddenly gone like a wisp of smoke cast apart by a wind that left nothing behind but the truth: His team was gone.

Slowly, Kimball closed his eyes, the word ISCARIOT burning like an afterimage beneath his lids.

The assassin had made his statement.

Cardinal Bonasero Vessucci was weighing his candidacy heavily as he made his way through the corridors beneath the Basilica. Often, when he was not walking the Old Gardens, he would stroll through the corridors that led to the Necropolis. Here it was quiet and undisturbed. The world, at least for the moment, was strictly his.

200

Word coming from the camps was that Cardinal Marcello was amassing a huge following with the aid of Cardinal Angullo, leaving Vessucci's chances, at best, to acquire the papal throne with a marginal chance, even with the sponsorship of Pope Pius. Should he lose the bid, then as secretary of state he is duty-bound to divulge all confidential information regarding the Vatican, beginning with the Third Secret, and ending with the Vatican Knights.

His chief concern was the continuance of Kimball and his team. Without the support of Marcello, then the Vatican Knights would become obsolete, this much he knew. The complexion of the Vatican would change almost immediately. The sovereignty of the Church in foreign lands would be at grave risks, as well as the welfare of its citizenry if no source of defense could ever be implemented. They would be left open to opposing forces, which were growing numerous by the day in an oft-changing world where fanaticism was becoming the norm.

And there was no doubt in his mind that as pope, Marcello would simply turn a blind eye to worldwide atrocities.

The cardinal continued to mull over the situation, as well as ways to politick to dissuade those in Angullo's and Marcello's camp to join his. But nothing was coming.

In the tunnels where there was no natural lighting, the cardinal shuffled along with his head down and his mind working. Around him, the shimmy of flames from gas-lit torches cast ghoulish shadows along the walls.

It took several moments, however, for him to realize that the dancing shadows were not his.

Somebody was here with him.

He raised his head. "Hello?"

About twenty feet away stood a shape that was blacker than black. Whoever it was stood unmoving. Even the light of nearby flames could not illuminate his features for identity.

"Who is that?"

No answer.

"Is something wrong? Is there something I can help you with?"

The Shape took a step forward into the feeble lighting, the brim of his camouflage boonie cap covering a majority of his features. In the marginal glow of light, the cardinal could make out enough of the man's features to identify him.

The man smiled, showing ruler-straight teeth. "Good day, Cardinal."

Vessucci returned the smile. "Well, well, well, what's brings you down here?"

The man's smile faded. "Things," he said.

"Things?" There was something about the man's voice that didn't seem quite right to the cardinal. The man's tone held an edge to it. "What do you mean by things?" he asked carefully.

"Just . . . things."

The man stepped closer. But this time there was something menacing about him.

Vessucci took a step back. "Is everything all right?"

"Everything's just fine," he said. In the delicate cast of lighting, the man held something in his hand that held a mirror polish to it. It reflected the color of the torches' flames, the colors of red and yellow, and orange. So, when he held up the metal cylinder it appeared to blaze within his grasp. "Everything's just fine," he said. And then a pick shot up from the cylinder, a spangle of light gleaming from its tip. "Just do as I tell you, Cardinal. That's all I ask."

Reality hit Kimball like a two-by-four, the man now on his knees. The two men that lie dead were more than just soldiers for the Church. They were his friends and to a lesser degree, they had become, in a sense, surrogate children. Cardinal Vessucci had entrusted them into his care when they were on the cusp of being teenagers. He nurtured them with character development, taught them the ways of righteousness as the Church would want him to. And he watched over them like a parent. For years they were his, their coalescing forming a bond much greater than that of mentor and student.

They had become family.

For a man with staunch will and reserve, he refused to shed additional tears. He had been a soldier for too long, his state of mind unwilling to bend to his feelings knowing that a breach of emotion often signaled a weakness that prohibited him to continue on with his role as a warrior. Yet there was something underlying he could not reject or face. But it existed all the same. It was that raw emotion that made him human trying to surface. It was the feeling of loss and sadness, and above all else, the condition of grieving.

Softly, while cradling the head of one of the fallen Knights, he ran his fingers delicately through the young warrior's hair while keeping his eyes fixed on the other Vatican Knight, who lay supine less than five feet away, his eyes at half-mast, showing nothing but slivers of white.

Slowly, Kimball's eyes worked upward to the writing on the wall. The word ISCARIOT had dried with a Knight's blood; however, blood runnels continued to drip from the letters.

And then rage consumed him.

Clenching his jaw firmly, he carefully lowered the head of the Vatican Knight and got to his feet.

He immediately went to the armory table and hefted his favorite weapon, a KA-BAR knife, and toyed with it the same way a gunslinger twirls his firearm before holstering it. The knife felt good in his hand, excellent balance, and good weight. And then he strapped on a pair of sheaths, one for each leg, two knives; the man was getting ready to go to town.

On his hip, he holstered a Smith & Wesson .40 caliber, his favorite for precision shooting. And then he recalled the monsignor and the sessions they held about killing. He recalled the monsignor defining Kimball's actions as the before and after scenario, from when he was an assassin with the American government to that of a Vatican Knight. The differences were that he killed because he *wanted* to and not because he *had* to. And that was where the differences lie: from what he used to be to what he had become. As an assassin for the United States government, he killed because he wanted to and did so without impunity. But as a Vatican Knight, he killed as a measure of defense after exhausting all other means to protect himself or the welfare of others.

But looking at the word ISCARIOT emblazoned on the stone wall, he realized deep down he would never change. He was what he was: a killer. After making wonderful strides, he now concluded that he *wanted* to kill, and not because he had to.

Salvation would have to wait another day.

As he was leaving the armory, he noted the sketch on the wall one last time, ISCARIOT, and then gazed upon the Vatican Knights lying on the floor in blood pools that had glazed to the color of tar. There were three in the armory, this he knew. And a single question emerged: *Where is he?*

CHAPTER FORTY-FIVE

Beneath Vatican City, The Necropolis

The Vatican Necropolis, also known as the Scavi, is virtually a city that lies five to twelve meters beneath the Basilica. Between the years 1940 to 1957, the Vatican supported archeological digs which uncovered parts of the city dating back to Imperial rule when pagan beliefs flourished. In 2003, during the construction of a parking lot, more of the city was revealed where chambers of preserved frescoes and mosaics of Christian traditions were discovered rather than the previously discovered tombs of pagan castes.

South of St Peter's Basilica is a marker allocating the place where the obelisk once stood in the circus of Nero. Today, this obelisk sits in the middle of St Peter's Square. It was here that Saint Peter was rumored to have been crucified and buried in a simple rock tomb that extended north along the via Cornelia. To the right of the Sacristy, beneath another archway, lay the entrance to the Necropolis.

The assassin had made his way to the Tomb of the Egyptians with Cardinal Vessucci and sequestered the man inside the mausoleum.

Painted in the center of the north wall is the Egyptian god Horus, the God of the Dead. Surrounding them sarcophagi filled the room with carved bacchanal settings bearing mythical scenes, which gave the tomb its name.

"Why are you doing this?" Vessucci asked. He sounded more perturbed than frightened.

The assassin ignored him.

"You are a Vatican Knight."

"I know," said the assassin. "Loyalty above all else, except Honor."

"That's right. And where is the honor in this?"

The assassin leaned forward and cocked his head. "In war, Cardinal, the only consistent thing is that both sides believe they are right. And these opposing sides are bound by a code of honor that is different from their opponent. It's a code of honor that is diverse from his enemy—yet a code, nonetheless. Your honor is not my honor. I have a different set of rules, a different agenda."

The assassin looked away and lifted the cylinder. While in play with his device, he pressed the button over and over again. The pointed stem shot in and out, in and out, and he repeated this process of retracting and activating the pick over and over again.

. . . *Chick* . . .

. . . *Chook* . . .

. . . *Chick* . . .

. . . *Chook* . . .

Time seemed endless for the cardinal.

"And what is your agenda? To destroy Kimball?"

The assassin stopped pressing the button and stared at the cardinal for a long moment. "My agenda, Cardinal, is to deny the man his salvation and send him to Hell where he belongs."

"And you do this by killing off his team?'

"What I did, I did for a reason. I didn't do it for the sake of 'just because.' Those men got exactly what they deserved."

Cardinal Vessucci nodded his head in disbelief, his face taking on the semblance of a man about to break because of overwhelming regret. "There's no need for this," he told him. "Kimball has fought very hard to turn away from his past."

"Sometimes, Cardinal, a man can never truly turn away from what he really is. And that's about to be tested."

The assassin continued to work the cylinder, the pick shooting upward and then inward in measured repetition until the walls of the Egyptian Tomb echoed with the sound of the weapon's play.

. . . *Chick* . . .

. . . *Chook* . . .

. . . *Chick* . . .

. . . *Chook* . . .

There are seven stages of grieving with anger third on the list. Kimball was already there, leapfrogging the first two stages with lightning speed as he made his way toward the cardinals' quarters of the *Domus Sanctæ Marthæ*, the residence named after St. Martha, which lies on the edge of Vatican City but adjacent to St. Peter's

Basilica.

His eyes were focused and determined, his features hard and dogged as he quickened his pace. Although he wore his required cleric's shirt and Roman Catholic collar, he also wore his martial pants and military boots. To cover up the weaponry, he wore a coat long enough to cover the KA-BARs sheathed to his thighs and the firearm holstered to his hip. When a marginal wind blew, however, the tails of the coat rose and billowed behind him, giving someone who may have been looking for the chance to spy the armaments he was carrying.

In a hastened manner, he crossed the square to the *Domus Sanctæ Marthæ*, the hotel-like residential dormitory of the cardinals, and ventured inside. Kimball took the steps two at a time until he reached the third floor, then walked down the corridor toward Vessucci's quarters. After knocking on the door and receiving no answer, he quickly entered the residence and summarily shut the door behind him.

Although far from spacious, the quarters were quasi-luxurious with scarlet décor, gold-fringe hem work at the base of the scalloped drapery, polished brass accouterments, and carved moldings of cherubs and angels across the ceiling. The cardinal's room was immaculate. The bed made with military precision; at least enough to bounce a quarter off, thought Kimball; and the wooden blinds were wide open, giving a sweeping view of the Basilica that was no less than two hundred meters away.

Kimball went from room to room calling out the cardinal's name.

A cool wind came in through the window—enough to raise the tail of his coat as he stood in the center of the room, the coat's tail flagging enough to pull back and reveal his KA-BARs and firearm.

As soon as the wind died away the flap of his coat fell to his sides, hiding everything. The jacket, it appeared, served nothing more than a façade hiding all that was true underneath.

As Kimball was about to exit, he noticed a cell phone lying next to a crystal trinket by the door. It was something he missed earlier, something with a note attached to it.

After grabbing the phone and giving it a quick perusal, he then read the attached letter: DIAL #8, IF YOU WISH TO SEE THE GOOD CARDINAL AGAIN.

Kimball examined the phone for a brief moment before dialing the button and waited.

And there was no mistaking the voice.

"I see that you found the phone," the assassin said.

"Why didn't you just leave it in the armory along with your other message?"

"And risk having security find it instead of you so that they can track my phone down through GPS? No thanks. That would have been the first thing the SIV would have done at a murder scene once they got a hold of it."

"Why are you doing this?" Kimball's voice sounded pained.

"I think it's quite obvious, don't you?"

"Bonasero was like a father to you."

"Like you tried to be a father to me?"

"Look. Your war is not with him. It's with me."

"Oh, you're right about that. I have no intentions of hurting the good cardinal. He's just the honey to draw the fly to the trap. And it's time, Kimball. This has been a long time coming."

"Where are you?"

"We're inside the Tomb of the Egyptians," he told him, "in Necropolis. And come alone. If you bring security with you, I'm afraid Cardinal Vessucci will follow the same fate as the Knights who lie dead on the armory floor. Is that clear? Is there any question as to what I want from you? I want it understood that this battle is between you and me."

"You have nothing to worry about," he said with an edge. "I'm coming alone. And when I get through with you, you son of a bitch, it won't be pretty."

"Yeah, well—we'll see."

The assassin hung up.

Kimball stared at the phone for a long moment before placing it gingerly on the nightstand. Slowly, as his face began to drop with regret, he made his way across the room and stood before the window. Straight ahead stood the Basilica—such a magnificent structure, he thought, less than two hundred meters away and located above the city of the dead.

Closing his eyes, he took in a deep breath and released it with an equally long sigh. And in the flash of a moment regret consumed him, the sting of tears welling. And from the corner of his eye, he let one slide and course along his cheek to the base of his chin.

Why did it have to be you?

CHAPTER FORTY-SIX

During his time with the Vatican, Kimball had trained many. But training Joshua, Job, and Ezekiel had been his favorites, almost remolding and reshaping arts of work into classics. Only he did so without the use of his hands, but by influencing them with psychology and schoolings, and with paternal direction encompassing body, mind, and soul.

As children, he recognized the fact that as children they had to engage in recreation. Often, he would take them to the fields to play fútbol, only to top it off with a trip into Rome for gelato. They had always been high-spirited youths, happy. Joshua had always been the biggest and held the highest degree of machismo, always asserting himself with posturing to be first and foremost. Of the three Job was the most gregarious, always quick with a joke. But in the arena, there was no question that he was the most competitive who possessed the need to win at all costs, even if that cost was his sacrifice. Ezekiel was the workhorse who trained hours on end to be better, stronger, and faster than the rest. Slow to develop, Kimball spent numerous hours with him so that the future Knight could exceed his expectations. With indefatigable effort, Ezekiel fell and rose to every occasion, learning that success always came after a struggle.

And now it had all come down as a horrible and final curtain call, Kimball thought. Two lives were gone and a third was about to be snuffed out if he had his way.

On occasion, tours are offered into the depths of Necropolis. On this day, however, the 'City of the Dead' was quiet.

Kimball took the steps quietly, the Smith & Wesson firmly within his grasp.

Above him incandescent bulbs glowed feebly, making his intrusion less than stealthy.

At the bottom of the steps sat the Tomb of the Egyptians.

Kimball stopped and listened.

Nothing.

Another step downward, closer to the tomb, the point of his weapon directed to kill. Within meters, he knew the assassin lay in wait.

And then he realized that he was the 'T' in Iscariot.

Within his vision, he saw one of many sarcophaguses within the tomb. And then he saw the cardinal sitting beneath the ancient portrait of Horus, God of the Dead.

The Vatican Knight reestablished his grip on his firearm.

The owl-eyed cardinal remained still but was not bound or gagged.

Kimball finally hit the landing to the Tomb of Egyptians.

And then from his left a Chinese star flew silently through the air with amazing precision and struck Kimball's weapon, the firearm knocked from his hand and to the floor. In reaction, he reached for the pistol.

"Don't," ordered a voice.

Kimball froze, knowing the lethal accuracy of the assassin's ability.

"Well, well, well. Leave it to you to come to a knife fight with a gun," the assassin said.

He stepped forward, from Kimball's left, a Chinese star within his hand.

Kimball turned with his face a mask of controlled rage and watched the assassin place the star within a secured pocket.

"You are, and will be, the 'T' in Iscariot," he told him.

Kimball squared off with the assassin and clenched his fists at his sides. "I cared for you like a son," he said.

Ezekiel made his way toward the cardinal with a feigned smile, his eyes cautiously fixed on Kimball. "The truth, Kimball, is that you only cared for yourself," he stated evenly. "The only reason why I was chosen to be a Vatican Knight was so that you could pacify your feelings of guilt. Isn't that so?"

"I gave you a chance!"

"At what? To serve you after you murdered my grandfather?"

"I gave you a chance!"

Ezekiel halted and stood his ground. His eyes focused on Kimball with a steely gaze. Then in a manner that was calmly forced, he said, "You murdered my grandfather and left me without family."

"Your grandfather went too far against forces he should not have opposed. He was becoming a threat to democracy."

Ezekiel cocked his head. "A threat to democracy? My grandfather *was* democracy!"

Now it was Kimball's turn to force calm. "Senator Cartwright became a wayward politician whose power grew too much for him to handle. He threatened senators and congressmen in both Houses with career-ending blackmail if they did not support his agendas deemed critically dangerous to the sovereignty of the United States."

Ezekiel couldn't help the surfacing smile. "And here you are," he began, "standing before me as a Vatican Knight justifying the act of murder."

"I was under orders by my superiors at the time to eliminate a valid threat."

"So that makes it all right?"

Kimball hesitated. And then: "No . . . No, it doesn't."

Ezekiel began to pace once again, never turning his back on Kimball. "I was only six," he said. "And I remember quite vividly when you entered the estate and killed my grandfather. I was hiding inside a cupboard, remember? And then I heard my grandfather say that he created you . . . and that the monster had finally returned to kill its creator. It was the last thing I heard my grandfather say before you opened the door to the cupboard. And it was then that I saw him lying against the desk with his throat cut. I'm sure you remember that moment, don't you?"

Kimball did not answer, believing the question to be rhetorical.

"Instead of following through with protocol by eliminating me, you allowed me to live. And with some semblance of humanity, you caressed my cheek as if to say that the murder of my grandfather would somehow pass into obscurity and that all would be forgiven and forgotten."

"You were just a child."

"And as all children do, they grow to become men." Then in a manner that resonated like an admonishment, he said, "You should have killed me along with my grandfather, as you were ordered to do. Now your past has caught up with you, Kimball. And in your case, it has . . . *I* am now the monster who has returned to kill *its* creator. Just as you have betrayed my grandfather, I have now come back to betray you . . . I am your Judas Iscariot. And I will destroy you."

Kimball began to pace with agitation and grace. "You can try," he said.

Ezekiel matched Kimball's actions, the men pacing in concert like mirror images.

"By failing to follow protocol and allowing me to live, it will cost you your life."

"Ezekiel, maybe I failed you, granted. But I tried to give you what your grandfather couldn't give you, which was a good life."

"And there we have it," he said. "I was nothing more to you than a pet project to help appease whatever guilt you were feeling at the time."

Kimball took on a quizzical look.

"Don't look at me like that," said Ezekiel. "I'm not stupid. I know about the two boys you killed in Iraq during an operation, and how that moment became an epiphany for you to seek salvation."

Their pace quickened, each matching the other's actions by moving like caged animals whose tensions were mounting with every pass.

"I recognized you immediately the moment you entered the boy's home. I never forgot your face. In fact, I thought you came back to finish the job until I saw the cardinal."

"I wanted to help you," he said.

"You wanted to save me because you were ridden with guilt! You didn't want to help me! You wanted to *save* me because you couldn't save those boys. And by saving me you were saving yourself! I was nothing more to you than someone who could fill that gaping hole in your life that was crammed full of despair and regret. *I* became your act of redemption! *I* became the child who could save *you*! Admit it!"

Kimball sighed. "Perhaps in the beginning, yes, I agree. But over time you became so much more, Ezekiel. Of the three, I became closer to you than I did with Job or Joshua."

"You're getting me all misty-eyed."

"Look. I don't expect you to forgive me, not after what I've done. But what you've done has exceeded any chance of salvation in my eyes and the eyes of the Church. You killed your two best friends."

"Job and Joshua were nothing but an extension of you," he stated sourly. "Do you have any idea how much I truly hated them? I hated everything that revolved around you, anything you had anything to do with. My passion for you and everything you were about became my hatred. And my hatred became my passion and crusade. Job and Joshua were a part of you like the Pieces of Eight. And I wanted you to watch everyone close to you die. But unlike you, I had no intention to reach out to you with any sense of humanity once they were gone."

"You could have killed me at Hawk's ranch."

"Sure, I could have. But my agenda was quite clear. I wanted to destroy everything that was about you. I wanted your legacy to die by the proverbial pieces. And I wanted you to watch everyone who had been a part of your life disappear until you had nothing left to draw from. I wanted you to see your life minimized to nothing before the moment of your death."

Kimball couldn't help feeling a hurtful pang: such hatred. And then he removed his long coat and draped it over a sarcophagus.

Ezekiel quickly noted the knives sheathed to the warrior's thighs but expected no less since they were Kimball's weapons of choice.

"There's no turning back," said Kimball. "Not now. Not after what you've done."

"What I've done was no different than what you've done. So, perhaps you're right. Perhaps there is no turning back after what we've both done. No salvation, no true hope of ever achieving redemption . . . Now you can stand there all day if you want and tell me how sorry you feel for all the horrible things you did and why you did them. But let's face it; confession doesn't always save the soul."

Kimball nodded. "And that's why I'm going to kill you with the feeling that I *want* to. Not because I *have* to."

Kimball took a quick and worried glance at the cardinal.

"Don't worry about him," said Ezekiel. "I'll keep my word regarding his welfare. Even though he's a major part of your life, he's still a clergyman. My war is with you. And besides, perhaps on the Day of Judgment, this moment of letting him live will give me a pass into White Eternity."

"You really believe that?"

Ezekiel nodded. "No more than you are believing that your salvation is within reach."

Without comment Kimball slowly reached down and undid the snap of the first KA-BAR sheath with his right hand, then followed up by undoing the second snap with his left. Grabbing the hilts of the knives, he retracted them slowly from their holds, the sound of the slide between leather and metal minimal.

Ezekiel also approached the situation with the same sense of caution by never taking his eyes off Kimball and readied up. Reaching up and over his shoulder, he grabbed the handle of a katana and slid it free from its scabbard that festooned his backside.

"I see you have your toy," said Kimball.

"One of many. But unlike the wooden one you trained me with, I promise you this one is very real, very sharp, and very deadly."

"I appear to be at a disadvantage."

"I always said mine was bigger than yours."

Kimball held up his KA-BARs. "But two is always better than one."

"We'll see."

The men slowly converged on one another with Ezekiel holding the polished blade of the katana in front of him with both hands, while Kimball gripped the knives tightly within his.

In trained combat fashion they sized each other up, the men looking for gaps, creases, and moments of weakness.

The warriors were closing in, circling, seeking.

And then came an opportune moment.

Ezekiel came across in a horizontal flash of the katana's polished blade and struck Kimball's knife, the attack easily deflected with such casual ease on Kimball's part that it slightly unnerved Ezekiel.

"Is that all you've got?"

Ezekiel reflected a cautionary smile. "I haven't even started." As the last word left his lips, Ezekiel pivoted on the balls of his feet and attacked Kimball with a flurry of blows. The blade came downward, then across, followed by jabs and strikes, all neatly deflected by Kimball as sparks flew, danced, and died. The momentum of the fight carried them across the chamber, close to a sarcophagus, Kimball running out of space.

The katana struck in rapid succession, the arcing sweeps of the blade moving too fast for the cardinal to see anything other than brief flashes of light from the blade's luster.

Kimball countered defensively, his arms and hands moving with incredible speed, more by intuition than thought, the KA-BARs matching the same lightning speed as Ezekiel's, strike, jab, defend.

Numerous sparks began to fly, the pace of the men gathering impetus as the blades struck repeatedly against one another, metal against metal, sparks flying everywhere as if the weapons were forged from flint rather than steel.

Kimball moved backward, losing ground, the stress beginning to weigh on him as his face began to contort with the strain of effort. His arms moved in blinding motions, up, down, across, deflecting the blade of the katana time and again.

Ezekiel appeared to pick up his effort, sensing a kill, the arcing strikes fluid, poetic, the speed of the blows wearing down his opponent.

Blow after blow Kimball was forced into a slow retreat, his back against the sarcophagus with less than a meter to spare.

And then in a vertical blow, Ezekiel brought the blade down as if to divide the man in half. But Kimball crossed his knives so that the blades made a perfect X and caught the blade within the upper-V portion of the X.

For a long moment, time stood still with the men eyeing each other while their chests heaved and pitched for oxygen, the instant a welcome respite from the activity with the blades locked.

"You're getting old," said Ezekiel, his breathing labored.

"Yeah, well, for someone half my age you shouldn't be sucking wind the way you do. I should have trained you better."

Ezekiel smiled with malicious amusement. "I will admit . . . you are good."

"And I'm about to get better."

"Really?"

"Yeah . . . Really."

On that note, Kimball went on the offensive. He cast aside the katana's blade and went after Ezekiel with a series of blows and moves that were so poetically smooth that it seemed like a choreographed ballet to Cardinal Vessucci. Kimball's arms moved with such incredible speed that it seemed impossible to defend against. But Ezekiel did so, marginally, his face taking on the look of someone who had misjudged his opponent and was quickly losing confidence.

His mentor was now in his element, striking blow after blow, steel against steel.

And Ezekiel began to look choppy, his motions uneven as he desperately deflected wave after wave of Kimball's attack, the continuous barrage driving him backward as Kimball gained ground, the momentum now his as his confidence waxed, the blows becoming quicker, stronger, the intent to kill Ezekiel set by the determination of his squared jaw flexing.

After casting aside the blade of Ezekiel's katana, Kimball came across with his KA-BAR and sliced Ezekiel across the abdomen, tearing the flesh but not gutting him like he intended to. Ezekiel stumbled backward and confused, with the tip of the katana lowering toward the floor, and slowly, his defenses gone.

And then he fell to his knees, a hand over the wound as blood seeped steadily through the cracks of his clenching fingers. "You killed me."

"Not yet. But I intend to."

When Kimball stepped forward to finalize the action with a quick thrust of his KA-BAR, Ezekiel's hand flew outward with incredible speed, a Chinese star taking flight.

Kimball reacted spontaneously, lifting a forearm just enough to catch the star, which was aimed for the throat. While Ezekiel knelt with a hand over his gash, he was also reaching for his three-pronged weapon. It was a sophomoric mistake on Kimball's part to allow him to do so, and he chastised himself the moment the star imbedded within his flesh.

The razor-sharp prong bit deep, snapping one of the twin bones in his forearm, rendering the arm useless. And a KA-BAR fell to the floor, leaving him with one.

Ezekiel got to his feet, slowly, his face blanching to the color of the underbelly of a fish. The katana was still in his hand. But he held it in such a way that his body English said that there was little power, if any, to proffer a killing blow.

Nevertheless, he tried.

Wincing, his gut burning with white-hot pain, he struggled to lift the point of the katana at Kimball. "I'm tired of this game," he managed. "Let's get this over with."

With surprising willpower Kimball didn't think Ezekiel was capable of in his condition, the rogue warrior brought the blade up and across in an arc, the blows coming in slow succession with one hand managing the blade while the other covered his wound.

Even with one arm out of commission, Kimball easily deflected the katana, the volleys coming without effort.

And Kimball finalized the event with a sweeping arc of his, the blade of his knife cutting Ezekiel deep across the shoulder, the katana finally dropping to the floor of the chamber.

Stumbling backward with the look of a man totally lost, Ezekiel reached blindly into one of his many hidden pockets for a Chinese star. But there were none, his pockets empty.

Kimball reestablished a firm grip on his KA-BAR until he was white-knuckled.

And then he ventured forward with obvious bloodlust, raising the blade for the final cut.

"Kimball!" Cardinal Vessucci voice was loud and firm, like a father admonishing a child before a wrongful act can be concluded. "He's lost."

Kimball stopped, his eyes still focusing on Ezekiel who looked like a man about to fall. "He killed Joshua and Job," he said. "Good people who didn't deserve to die. He murdered my team, the Pieces of Eight."

"Then he shall be judged by God when his time comes. Don't fall back to what you used to be, Kimball. I beg you."

Ezekiel chortled. "As I told you, Cardinal, a man can never truly turn away from what he truly is. And Kimball failed the test."

"You're still alive, aren't you?"

"Only because the cardinal stopped you," he returned. "The truth is you don't have the will to stop yourself."

Kimball sighed and lowered the knife.

Ezekiel leaned against the wall, blood all over him.

And Kimball made his second mistake. The moment he went to aid the cardinal to his feet he heard a snicker from behind.

It was the pick shooting up from a cylinder.

"Kimball, look out!"

But the warning came too late.

The cylinder flew across the chamber, the pick finding its mark on Kimball's upper chest below the right clavicle. Suddenly his world lit up with pinprick stars of light flashing within his field of vision, which was turning purple around the edges. He could see Ezekiel moving with a surreal slowness toward the katana; saw the cylinder emerging from his chest, the pick wedged deep. There was no pain, at least not yet. And the cardinal's voice sounded distant and deep, like a tape being played on its lowest setting, whatever he was saying much too slow to comprehend.

The gun, lying on the ground to his right, was situated near the base of the sarcophagus.

Just as Ezekiel was wrapping his hand around the hilt of the katana, Kimball grabbed the firearm and held it weakly aloft, then aimed it at Ezekiel. The purple edges were closing to a mote of vision, his sight pinching toward darkness. And then he pulled the trigger.

Shots dotted the wall surrounding Ezekiel, causing him to duck.

. . . Pow . . . Pow . . . Pow . . .

The bullets missed their target, pocking a wall that was priceless with the history of antiquity, with chips flying everywhere.

Ezekiel dropped the katana, placed a bloodied hand over his head, and ran out of the chamber.

Kimball's hand fell weakly to his side, the Smith & Wesson falling from grasp but not too far from his hand.

Cardinal Vessucci then aided Kimball by cradling his head within his lap. He could tell that Kimball was fading, his pupils contracting and his sight becoming detached from his reality. "You'll be fine," he whispered to him.

And then he faced the exit where Ezekiel had escaped.

All was incredibly quiet.

And then to himself, he said, "I never thought I'd live to see the day when a Vatican Knight went rogue."

The old man sighed.

CHAPTER FORTY-SEVEN

Vatican City. Three Months Later

Almost three months to the day Pope Pius XIII was diagnosed with cancer, he passed peacefully away in his sleep.

At the moment of the pontiff's death the Cardinal Camerlengo, the title held by Cardinal Dominico Graziani, stood at the pontiff's bedside and ritualistically called the pope's name three times without response. After he completed the aged tradition, the medical staff then determined the pontiff's death and authorized a death certificate. The Camerlengo then sealed off the pope's private apartments and made the event public by notifying the Cardinal Vicar of the Diocese of Rome. Once he alerted the Vicar, Cardinal Graziani then prepared for the Papal funeral rites and the nine days of mourning, known as the *novemdieles.*

During the interregnum, the period of an interim government, Cardinal Graziani became the leader of the Church and summarily directed the election of a new pope with the support of three cardinals, who were elected by the College of Cardinals, and began the tradition of the Conclave.

On the day of the election, the cardinals took seats around the wall of the Sistine Chapel, took a paper ballot, then wrote a name on the ballet. One by one, with Cardinal Vessucci at the head of the procession, the cardinals proceeded to the altar where a chalice stood with a paten on it. After holding their election slips high to show the Conclave they had voted, they then placed the ballots on the paten and slid them into the chalice.

When the cardinals took their respective seats, Cardinal Marcello and Vessucci gazed upon each other and gave nods of support. The word was that some in Angullo's camp were vacillating with their decisions and determined that Vessucci was the proper candidate. But going into the Conclave the numbers weren't yet determined as to whose camp was strongest, the cardinals keeping their votes close to the vest.

Rising to the altar, the Cardinal Camerlengo, along with three aids, counted the votes and read the names out loud so that they could be written on the tally sheet. And Vessucci bowed his head in defeat. As they read off the names it appeared that the tally was not in his favor since all that was needed was the majority vote, which was half the Conclave plus one.

After the last name was tallied, an assistant ran a needle and thread through the center of each ballot and bound them together. He then burned the ballots using chemicals that would give off white smoke.

From the chimney, the emerging smoke was as white as the billowy clouds that served as the backdrop against a bright blue sky. And the bells of St. Peter's Basilica began to toll.

A new pontiff had been chosen.

Cardinal Constantine Marcello had been selected to fill the vacancy of the Apostolic See under the name of Pope Gregory XVII. And Cardinal Vessucci was suddenly rendered impotent. There was no doubt in his mind that the disbanding of the Vatican Knights would be inevitable under the occupancy of Pope Gregory.

And there was nothing he could do about it.

CHAPTER FORTY-EIGHT

Paris, France
One Day After the Election of Pope Gregory XVII

Ezekiel sat at an outdoor eatery with a small cup of latte before him. In his hands was the *Le Parisien*, a Parisian newspaper.

After escaping Necropolis all bloodied and fatigued, he found his way to a hack doctor who healed his wounds for a nominal fee, along with an additional charge upfront to keep him quiet. But when the doctor hinted that he would renege out of the deal unless Ezekiel came up with more of the required sum originally agreed upon, Ezekiel grabbed a scalpel and threw it across the room, impaling a cockroach that was scaling the wall.

Point made!

After that, the doctor said nothing more and aided the assassin with his healing.

Once Ezekiel was able to travel, he made his way to France and kept a low profile.

Now, almost three months to the day after the battle inside Necropolis and sitting beneath a uniform blue sky with the Eiffel Tower serving as the backdrop, with pigeons cooing and pecking at the flakes of his croissant lying about his feet, Ezekiel's heart grew heavy inside his chest.

On the front page of *Le Parisien* was a glorified obituary regarding the death of Amerigo Anzalone, Pope Pius XIII. It covered the man's life, his rise to the papal throne, and the final days of his life as a servant to Christians around the world.

How I must have disappointed him in the end, he thought. And he was deeply saddened. Although the man had gone rogue, he respected the pontiff and wished deep down that Pope Pius had forgiven him on so many levels. For some reason, this was important to Ezekiel as he sat there musing over the times he stood within the glory of this man.

Please forgive me.

Slowly, he lowered the newspaper to the white-clothed tabletop and watched the pigeons gather at his feet without fear—the birds pecking, eating, and cooing while life, as usual, moved on.

It was a beautiful day, yet a sad one as well.

And then the birds took flight, their wings beating everywhere in sudden panic, nothing but a wall of feathers. And then they were gone.

In their place stood a well-built man with fair complexion, raven hair, and a wedge of pink scarring beneath his chin from a horrible accident. "Disgusting creatures, don't you think?"

Ezekiel said nothing. He just stared at the man.

The man with the scar pointed to an empty chair at the table opposite Ezekiel. "May I?"

"Do I know you?"

Without waiting for Ezekiel's invite the man took the seat. "In a way, I believe you do," the man said.

Ezekiel waited.

When a waiter came forward the man waved him off, crossed his legs in leisure, and cupped his hands over a knee. "We've never met face to face, but I'm sure you've heard of me," he told him. "In your circle, you would know me as Abraham Obadiah."

As stoic as Ezekiel was, his eyes started as he reached for a weapon.

The man quickly raised his hand. "Don't," he said. "Do you really think I would sit at this table without the proper resources backing me up?"

"I'd kill you before they had time to react."

"I hardly doubt it," he returned. "Look at your chest."

Ezekiel did, finding three red spots from laser sightings directed over his heart. However, he could not spot the assassins in hiding.

Ezekiel could feel his anger bubbling. A few years ago, this man sitting before him was responsible for the kidnapping of Pope Pius and the executions of bishops within the Holy See. Of this man's entire team, he was the only one to escape after Kimball and his team of Vatican Knights waged war against Obadiah's military elitists and defeated them.

"Why are you here?"

Obadiah stared at him briefly before digging a photo out of his pocket and placing it on top of the open pages of *Le Parisien*. The

222

photo was aged, but still in excellent condition, not grainy. It was a photo of a much younger Cardinal Bonasero Vessucci. The man beside him wearing the black fatigue pants, military beret, boots, and a cleric's shirt with a Roman Catholic collar, was Kimball Hayden.

"When the blood relative of a superior American senator is taken in by the State of the Vatican, it draws attention." He tapped the photo. "This was taken a day after papers were filed for your release into their custody with no questions asked by state agencies. The people I work for always take notice of such things like that."

"What's your point?"

He pointed to Kimball. "This man," he said. "Who is he?"

"Why?"

The man's tapping became more adamant. "Who . . . is . . . he?"

The men squared off against one another with hardened gazes. And then, with measured calm, Ezekiel said, "His name is Kimball Hayden."

Obadiah fell back into his seat. "Kimball Hayden," he uttered distantly, his eyes growing detached. He now had a name. "And what does Kimball Hayden do?"

"Why do you want to know?" Ezekiel asked harshly.

Obadiah leaned forward. "Let's just say that my team keeps an eye on things globally for the welfare of humankind."

Ezekiel smirked. "Espionage," he said. "Word at the time of the pope's kidnapping was that you worked for Mossad."

"You can believe whatever you want," he returned. "If that was the word, then that was the word." The man leaned further forward, as if in close counsel. "Now tell me, who is this Kimball Hayden? And what was his interest for the only surviving relative of a powerful American senator?"

Ezekiel did not draw close to Obadiah. Instead, he closed his hands together in an attitude of prayer and placed them over the photo. "He is a Vatican Knight," he told him. "As I was."

Obadiah fell back once again. "A Vatican Knight?"

He nodded. "The Vatican has its team of elite commandos," he returned. "It was the Vatican Knights you clashed with on the day the pontiff was freed from captivity . . . And it was Kimball Hayden who led the team."

Obadiah nodded. "I know," he said, raising his arm and showing off a ragged scar. "He did this to me."

"He should have killed you."

"But he didn't." A pause, then: "And why you?"

Ezekiel took in a breath and let out a sigh. "To become a Vatican Knight, you must be without family, someone who is orphaned. From a young age, you are trained to be learned and skilled in combat."

"Fascinating," he murmured. "Taking pages directly from a Spartan legacy by rearing a child to become an elite soldier. But why you?"

"Kimball murdered my grandfather," he said.

"While working under the auspices of the Church?"

"No. At that time he was an assassin for the United States government."

Obadiah was blown away. This was incredibly damaging intel his League did not have; the murder of an all-powerful political figure sanctioned by figures within the White House. "And your role?"

"I was chosen by Hayden because of personal reasons."

Obadiah smiled. "For salvation," he said. "He raised you for his salvation."

"You're very perceptive."

"The man has a conscience that cannot be placated, so he serves the Vatican to achieve redemption. But for him to do that, he believed that saving you after he destroyed your life was a way to make amends."

"Touché."

"Then you were nothing more to him than his puppet?"

Ezekiel looked away. "He tried to save me."

"Sure he did." Obadiah removed several photos from his jacket pocket and spread them over the tabletop. They were postmortem shots of the members from the Pieces of Eight. "I'm impressed with your handiwork," he told him. "Our intelligence knew about the Pieces of Eight, but we could not determine who these people were or what their role was. But when we were informed that they were being terminated, our sources had to find out why ex-GI officials were being eradicated, whether the reason was political or otherwise." He tossed another picture on top of the others, this one taken through the lens with NG capability. It was a photo of Ezekiel leaving the ranch house moments after he killed Hawk. And then another photo was laid down by Obadiah, this one showing Ezekiel on the rooftop with a sniper rifle moments before he shot one of the Hardwick brothers with pinpoint accuracy.

"And then we realized that this had no political implication behind it at all—that this was nothing more than a personal vendetta." Obadiah tossed the third photo down, this one of Kimball Hayden from a distance. "And it was this man you wanted dead, isn't it?"

Ezekiel stared at the photo, said nothing.

"When I saw this photo, I recognized this man right away. I knew it was the man at the depository who freed the pontiff and took out my team. I never thought I'd ever see him again." Obadiah picked up the photo and examined it. "Kimball Hayden was a member of the Pieces of Eight, and now a warrior for the Church. Talk about extremes."

"What do you want, Obadiah?"

"My redemption," he quickly told him. "When I saw this photo as the man targeted by the grandson of a powerful senator now bearing very particular skills that rival my own, I saw the opportunity for my salvation. So, I waited, hoping that you would fulfill your goal of terminating this man from our lives." He laid the photo down and sighed. "But you failed in your quest."

"I have not forfeited my goals," he said. "Kimball Hayden is one of the best in the world at what he does."

Obadiah rubbed at the scar on his arm. No one knew better regarding that statement than he did.

"Now he'll be waiting for me, which makes my agenda all the more difficult to achieve."

Obadiah stopped rubbing the scar. "And that is why I am here," he stated. "It appears that Kimball Hayden has become our white whale. So, I offer you a proposal."

"A proposal?"

"Work with my group," he offered. "Kimball Hayden may become a liability in future ventures. Therefore, he must be taken out of the equation. Against one of us, the odds are even; but against two, then the odds are skewed in our favor."

"Why would I want to join with a man who tried to assassinate the pope?"

"What I did was purely business with political aspirations behind the motive. But in the end, when I realized the mission was over, I was the one who cut the bonds of the pontiff's chains and set him free. I may be a fanatic in my duties to my organization, but I also recognize the fact that if the journey is over, then it's over. There was no point in killing the pope."

"But your team tried."

"And they suffered the ultimate cost at the hands of Kimball Hayden and the Vatican Knights." He held up his arm, the scar was still ugly and purple. "Including myself."

"Looks like a small price to pay considering that the others paid with their lives."

"True. But he hampered my skills somewhat. Nevertheless, I'm still skilled."

The men measured each other carefully from across the table for a long moment.

And then, from Obadiah, "Do we have an alliance, Mr. Cartwright?"

"I go by Ezekiel."

Obadiah smiled, and then lifted his hand as an offering. "Fine," he said. "Then do we have an alliance, Ezekiel? Shall we hunt the white whale together?"

Ezekiel looked at the proffered hand, then at Obadiah, noting stoicism on his face.

The former Knight lifted his hand and joined it with Obadiah's. "Are you Mossad?" he asked.

Obadiah smiled. "Perhaps," he said. And then with a wave of his free hand, the three red dots disappeared from the center of Ezekiel's chest.

And a new alliance was born.

CHAPTER FORTY-NINE

Vatican City

Pope Gregory stood inside the papal chamber when a knock sounded at his door. Standing alongside him with his hands clasped together was Cardinal Angullo. They had been in discussion on many levels. Now it was time to implement new changes.

Pope Gregory rounded his desk and took a seat. "Come in."

Cardinal Vessucci entered, leaving the door open for Cardinal Angullo who headed out of the chamber. When he passed Cardinal Vessucci, he stopped and bowed his head with Vessucci reciprocating—with no doubt a certain tension between them existing—then moved on. The cardinal closed the door softly behind him to leave Vessucci alone with the newly-elected.

"Please," said the pontiff, gesturing to an empty chair before his desk. "We've much to discuss."

Vessucci took the chair. "Congratulations, Constantine. The position has been well selected by the College."

"My understanding is that it was close. It appears that many in Cardinal Angullo's camp amended their votes, making it closer than it was. But that is something we will never know for sure. But the fact, Bonasero, is that I am the newly-elected pontiff."

Bonasero Vessucci bowed his head in homage.

"And there are things to discuss," the pope added. "Things that need to be clarified."

"Of course, Your Eminence."

"But first let me say that I'm sorry for the loss of Pope Pius. I know he was a close friend of yours. He was a good man."

"He was a *great* man."

Pope Gregory nodded. "I can't argue with that," he said. The pope fell back into his chair in leisure, studying the cardinal before him. And then: "A few months ago I sat in that same chair talking to

227

Amerigo, who lobbied on your behalf. And we ended speaking about secrets should the Apostolic See become mine."

"There are secrets, yes."

"I know. And I informed him that secrets were kept because it was my opinion that there was something immoral attached to them. But as I found out about The Third Secret, that is not always the case. The Third Secret must be kept because of the nature of the calamity should the secret prove true."

"I understand."

"But there are other secrets, aren't there? Secrets you're privy to."

"There will always be secrets," he returned.

"Pius told me so. He also told me that if I should sit upon the throne of the Apostolic See, then you are obligated to tell me the secrets held by the Vatican."

"He told me the same."

Pope Gregory leaned forward. "It has come to my attention that you are a member of—what they call—the Society of Seven. Does such a group exist?"

The cardinal hesitated. The group had been covert for years. Their name had never been whispered to anyone outside the legislative body. But it had.

"Does such a group exist?" he repeated.

And then: "It does."

"And you are a reigning member?"

"I'm a member, yes."

"Was Amerigo a member?"

"He was."

"And who else is involved?"

"Besides me, there are five others. Pope Pius served as the group administrator, as did Pope John Paul the Second, and many popes before him."

"John Paul—how long has this group been around?"

"Since World War Two when the Nazis began to occupy surrounding territories."

Pope Gregory appeared stunned, his jaw-dropping slowly. "I see." Then: "And what exactly is the purpose of this group?"

"To protect the Vatican on all fronts," he said. "We make sure that the sovereignty of the Vatican, its interests, and the welfare of the citizenry is protected throughout the world."

"And the seven of you do this alone? This . . . Society of Seven?"

"No. We delegate a force to troubled spots around the globe."

"A force? You mean members of the Swiss Guard?"

Vessucci nodded. "No," he said. "I'm talking about a very special force with very special people."

Gregory waited patiently.

"As you know, Your Holiness, the Vatican has diplomatic ties with over ninety percent of the countries worldwide. And in a good number of them, a skirmish will arise from time to time with members of Catholic citizenry getting caught in the middle."

"So, you dispatch this force?"

"Yes."

The pontiff began to roll his fingertips across his desktop as he sat there mulling over the dialogue. "Not the Swiss Guard?"

"No, Your Holiness."

"And is this group one of the secrets Pius was alluding to?"

"That's possible. I wasn't here during your discussion. So, I can't inform you as to how much he let their existence be known to you."

"Then why don't you enlighten me," he said. The pope stopped drumming his fingers, the room growing absolutely quiet.

"They are known as the Vatican Knights," he said. "They're an elite group of commandos sent on missions as directed by those within the Society of Seven. Their duty is to go into hotspots and salvage a situation before the situation is completely lost."

"Are you talking militants?"

"I'm talking soldiers—"

"You're talking militants who go into battle situations under the waving banner of the Vatican?"

"I am."

Pope Gregory leaned forward. "This isn't the Middle Ages where we spread Christianity with the point of a sword."

"It is not their intent to spread Christianity," he said. "They are sent into situations to save lives. And like I said, it is our duty to protect the sovereignty, the interests—"

"And the welfare of the citizenry," he completed. "And the duty is not for us to save. Fate is the governing hand of God. Not a militant group!" The pontiff fell back into his seat, keeping a steady eye on the cardinal. And then more calmly, "Have these Knights ever killed anybody?"

"They have."

The pontiff nodded. "Since when did murder become an agenda of the Vatican?"

"They don't murder," he retaliated, perhaps louder than he wanted. "They do whatever is necessary to achieve the means."

"There will be no mercenaries under my watch," he told him firmly.

"They are not mercenaries. They are protectors of the faith."

"The word of God is the protector of Faith."

"The word of God alone will not protect the Vatican or its interests or its people of what is about to come. It's a different world out there and Catholicism is becoming a target for fanatics. Even past popes saw the right to protect the Vatican and its interests. And the Vatican Knights have been that way for over sixty years."

"I will not support or sanction militants under the banner of God," he returned adamantly. "If the citizenry should fall victim by the sword, then let those who fall by the sword be accepted into God's grace while those who yield it fall into God's fury. We are not a military unit!"

"Your Eminence, it was the Vatican Knights who saved Pope Pius in the United States when he was kidnapped by militant factions, and it was Kimball Hayden who saved the pope's life aboard Shepherd One when the plane was hijacked."

"Kimball Hayden?"

"He's the team leader."

Pope Gregory seemed to reflect on this for a moment. "And where is this unit housed?"

"In a building next to the Old Gardens," he answered.

"On Vatican grounds?"

"Yes, Your Holiness."

Pope Gregory nodded. "This is a new regime, Bonasero, you know that, yes?"

He nodded.

"I will not have a military faction of any type existing under my campaign as pope of the Vatican, is that understood?"

"Your Eminence, I plead you; their importance to the salvation of what's coming makes them a necessity. They are the shield that protects the Vatican beyond city limits. To disband them would surely leave us wide open to assaults across the world."

"You have to have faith, Bonasero, to believe that the world is not

230

this Hell you make it out to be. The word of God is strong enough to penetrate all hearts."

"That is true. But some people see and hear God differently. And sometimes what they hear is not always the words of kind rhetoric."

"Faith," was all that the pope countered with.

Cardinal Vessucci closed his eyes. He was not surprised given the nature of Marcello's mindset, which was widely known within the College of Cardinals.

"You will disband this unit immediately," he told the cardinal. "And I mean today. They will not spend another night on holy ground and defile everything Catholicism stands for. Is that understood?"

"Your Holiness—"

"I said, is that understood?"

The cardinal nodded. "It's understood."

"And you will say nothing to anybody about these . . . Vatican Knights. Is that also understood?"

"Yes, Your Holiness."

The pontiff clasped his hands in an attitude of prayer. "There is also another matter," he said. "Alleged improprieties are going on at the archdiocese in Boston. On most accounts, I would say that most of these claims are bogus. But I need someone such as yourself who holds the judicial skills to wade through the facts and allegations and set matters straight."

"But I'm the secretary of the state," he said. "My duties lie here, at the Vatican."

"Your duties, my good cardinal, are whatever I see is for the good of the Church. You are being reassigned."

"To the United States?"

"To Boston, yes."

"And what about my position as the Vatican's secretary of state?"

"That position now belongs to Cardinal Angullo," he said. "He will make an excellent addition. And I'm convinced that he will perform his duties admirably."

"Why are you doing this?"

The pontiff looked him squarely in the eye. "I do what I do, Bonasero, because the Church needs a new direction. The direction God intended us to follow."

"Even God recognizes the right to defend oneself, or the right to defend those who cannot defend themselves."

"You leave for Boston the day after tomorrow," the pope stated immediately.

Obviously, the war of principles was over as far as Pope Gregory was concerned, so the cardinal labored to his feet.

"One more thing," said the pontiff, refusing to look up as he grabbed a pen and held it over a sheet of parchment. "I want the names of the five cardinals involved with this Society of Seven."

"Why?"

"I don't have to explain my intentions to you. I merely ask and you provide."

"Will they also be reassigned? Sent to some obscure place for punishment for doing what they believe to be the right thing to do?"

"Names, Bonasero. Now!"

The cardinal took in a deep breath and let it out as a gesture of his mounting frustration.

And then he gave the pontiff what he wanted.

CHAPTER FIFTY

Vatican City
The Congregation of the Clergy

Inside the office of Monsignor Dom Giammacio, the air hazy with cigarette smoke, Kimball sat in his rightful chair as the monsignor waited for him to galvanize the dialogue.

This had been the first visit since the incident in Necropolis when the point of the pick missed Kimball's heart by less than four inches. The tip, however, wedged deep and perforated his lung, causing blood to fill the sack as if it was a bladder. Along with his other wounds, he was incapacitated for weeks, moving in and out of fevers as infections came and went.

Now that he rebounded to the point of mobility, he still felt sore, his breathing sometimes labored. But it was his emotions that panged him more, the loss of Pope Pius and the betrayal of Ezekiel.

Kimball raised his hand and began to rub the throb in his forearm where the Chinese star broke the bone, which had to be pieced together by pins and screws.

"Are you still ailing?" asked the monsignor.

Kimball stopped rubbing. "I'll be fine," he told him. And then he fell back to his stoic manner.

"Kimball, I'm sorry about the loss of Pope Pius," he began. "His loss has struck all of us who knew him well. But you, in particular, appear to hold a deeper lament. We can talk about it if you want."

"It's not just him, Padre. There are other issues involved."

"Such as what went on in Necropolis?"

"That's part of it."

The monsignor leaned closer. "Are you sure it's not most of it?"

Kimball gave him a sidelong glance. "Have you ever been betrayed?"

The monsignor seemed to muse over this for a moment, and then,

"I'm sure I have been."

"Have you ever grown close to someone that you may have considered being a part of you as a son?"

"No."

Kimball looked away, his eyes growing distant, detached, his mind visualizing something only he could see. "Do you know what happened in the Necropolis?"

"I know you were severely injured down there. I believe you received a broken arm and perforated lung for your efforts in saving the good Cardinal Vessucci."

"The cardinal was never in jeopardy," he said. "It was all about me. I was being tested."

"By the one who tried to kill you?"

"By him, by God, by me—it was all about seeing if I had the true ability to change."

"To change?"

Kimball nodded. "The last time we met you told me that redemption was within my grasp because I had become something different than what I used to be. You said that I killed because I wanted to, but now I kill because I have to . . . And there lies the difference between the darkness and light."

"I remember."

"In the Necropolis, when I learned that I was betrayed by someone very close to me and that forgiveness was entirely impossible, I felt something very familiar."

"And what was that?"

Kimball faced him. "I learned that I hadn't changed at all," he told him. "I've only been hiding what was always there . . . The truth."

The monsignor grabbed his pack of cigarettes, shook a smoke free, lit it, and then waved the match dead before tossing it into the ashtray. "And what is this truth, Kimball?"

He hesitated, his eyes once again growing distant.

"Kimball, what is the truth?" he repeated.

"That I've been living a lie," he answered. "That salvation will never be within reach no matter how hard I try to obtain it because the fact is what it is."

"And what is the fact?"

"That I kill because I want to, not because I have to."

"Have you killed anyone because you want to?"

"No."

"But because you had to?"

"Yes. But it doesn't take away from the one thing I want most in my life right now."

"And what is that?"

"I *want* to kill Ezekiel," he said.

"Is this the one who betrayed you?"

"Yes."

"Have you looked deeper into yourself, Kimball? Have you looked far enough to realize that your emotional wounds run much deeper than your physical ones and that your anger over this recent betrayal is misdirecting your sense of logic and reason?"

"I won't justify what I feel, Monsignor, by saying that it's all right to feel the way I do because I'm angry. He murdered those close to me because of a personal hatred directed at me. He deserves what's coming to him."

The monsignor leaned back. "Are you going after him?"

"If I don't, then he'll come after me."

"Perhaps he won't."

"With all due respect, Padre, you have never felt the insatiable need to *want* to kill. I have it. He has it. And until we meet, it'll just feed until it drives us both crazy."

"And how do you think Pope Pius would have felt?"

Kimball's face dropped a notch, the beginnings of sadness and disappointment. "Amerigo's gone," he finally said.

"Do you believe he watches over us?"

"Don't do me like that! No guilt trips! I can't help what I am!"

"Then what about Cardinal Vessucci? Did he not see in you the man you failed to see in yourself?"

"I failed to see the man he saw because no such man exists! I kill, Padre. It's what I do. It's what I'm good at."

"For so long you have served the Church well. Now you have a conflict with faith and all of a sudden you're no longer virtuous because of the anger you hold so deep."

Kimball picked up on the Monsignor's tone. *Was that admonishment?*

"You sit there forgetting all the good you have done for the Church, the lives you have saved, and the restoration within yourself that there is hope beyond the darkness that had been your life. Now after a betrayal all the good that has become your life, the light that had become your path, is gone because you cannot let go of the rage that has consumed you like a dark shroud."

Kimball clenched his jaw, the anger working its way to the surface.

"Then perhaps you're right," the monsignor said, tilting his head and releasing a cloud ceilingward. "Perhaps the man in you is a killer. But do you want to know what I see? What Pope Pius and Cardinal Vessucci saw?"

Kimball's entire body tensed.

"We saw a man whose conviction to duty was far greater than his conviction to himself. Then one day he had an epiphany and learned that his need to reach the Light of Loving Spirits was not only a necessity but an attainable goal. What Pius saw in you, what Cardinal Vessucci saw in you, was the penchant to be what you truly are, Kimball. And that is a man who is lost and is trying to find his way."

Kimball was beginning to settle down.

"Yes, you were betrayed. And yes, it probably won't be the last time. But betrayal is a part of life's lesson, and we must learn from it and handle it with the will to forgive rather than the need for revenge. When you see that difference, Kimball, when the rage subsides, then I'm sure that you will once again see the Lighted Path."

Kimball sighed. "Ezekiel's not done with me. He'll come back to finish his agenda."

"Then if he comes, Kimball, his anger and hatred will surely doom him. For those who choose to remain in the dark will only find an unwanted refuge within its depths."

Kimball stood and walked to the window. People were milling by the hundreds through St. Peter's Square. "Losing Amerigo and Ezekiel at the same time is too much for me to handle right now," he said.

"Psychologically speaking, Kimball, there are many phases everyone goes through when dealing with loss such as anger, sadness, and disbelief—it's all a part of the grieving process. And you're not above that. It's obvious to me that you're going through the process right now. I guess that only makes you human."

Kimball considered this. The monsignor was right about the phases. In conjunction with his anger toward Ezekiel, he had taken the pick and smashed it down to indiscernible pieces of metal with a hammer before discarding it as scrap. The pick would never serve to harm anyone again.

"Kimball?"

He called back over his shoulder. "Yeah."

"Your time is almost up. Is there some other matter you wish to talk about?"

He thought about it but came up with nothing. "No, Padre. Nothing."

A knock came at the door.

"Excuse me," said the monsignor, and he went to answer the door.

Kimball could hear the hushed voices behind him. His eyes still fixed on the masses moving throughout the Square.

"Kimball."

He turned. The monsignor was standing by the doorway with a bishop who was dressed in proper attire.

"It appears that Cardinal Vessucci would like to speak with you in the Society Chamber. Do you know of such a place?"

The Society Chamber was the meeting area where the Society of Seven gathered, usually to brief him on missions. "I do."

"Then he'll be waiting for you there," he said.

As Kimball was leaving, he stopped by the monsignor. "Thank you," he whispered. And when he said this he did so with immeasurable gratitude.

"My pleasure," he said. "And if you don't remember anything else, please remember this: You're right when you say you are what you are. But it's usually the person in question who last sees himself as he truly is when others see him as he already is."

Kimball reached up and squeezed the monsignor lightly on the shoulder. "I appreciate you trying, Monsignor. I honestly do. But you're right about one thing: I am what I am."

When Kimball walked away with determination in his swagger and a cast-solid hardness to his face, the monsignor called after him.

But Kimball ignored his pleas as hot vendetta coursed through his veins.

I am what I am.

CHAPTER FIFTY-ONE

Vatican City
Chamber of the Society of Seven

In a restricted chamber situated deep in the lower level of the Basilica, seven chairs were situated on a marble platform rising four feet from the floor. The pope's chair was layered with gold leaf and beheld the ornate carvings of angels and cherubs across the framework. The second chair was smaller and less imaginative, the wood carvings around the framing not as aesthetic as that of the papal seat but were crafted well enough to draw the attention of an appreciative eye, nonetheless. This was the chair of the good Cardinal Bonasero Vessucci. The five remaining chairs, although less ornate by comparison, maintained detailed images of winged angels thrumming harpsichords along with the wood framing, the cherubs smiling, the images harmonious.

With a soft tracing of his fingertips, Cardinal Vessucci sat in his chair and guided them over the images. It would also be the last time he would ever sit in this chair again, he considered.

From the end of the long corridor, the large wooden doors held together by steel bands and rivets opened, the room sounding off with the hollow echo of the door closing behind Kimball as he made his way to the staging area.

He noted that Cardinal Vessucci sat alone, his shoulders slumped in defeat, the look of saddened dismay not a good sign.

"Bonasero," Kimball pointed to the empty chairs, "where are the others?"

The cardinal struggled to his feet. "There are no others," he told him. And then he labored his way to the pope's chair and ran his fingers lovingly over the throne. "Great men used to sit here," he added, "justifying the fates of good and decent people. Unfortunately, this chair will no longer be occupied ever again."

Kimball took a step forward. "Are you saying Pope Gregory is disbanding the Vatican Knights?"

"Not only is he . . . but he has."

The cardinal went to the edge of the staging area and held out his hand. "Please, Kimball, I need a helping hand down."

Kimball assisted the cardinal down the four steps, a laborious task for the aging cardinal.

When they were rooted below the stage they stared up at the empty row of chairs. And something awful like a mournful loss hung over them.

"During World War Two," began the cardinal, "a Nazi defector absconded from his regiment because he had witnessed unbearable atrocity after unbearable atrocity and took refuge within the shadows of the Vatican. When the Nazis began to invade the territory of Rome with the threat to reseat the papal throne to Germany under Goering's command, this one soldier swore that he would protect those who could not protect themselves. In time, as the Nazi regime was falling on all fronts, this man alone offered to protect the sovereignty of the Church and the welfare of its citizenry. He became the first Vatican Knight. And it was in this chamber that Pope Pius XII consecrated this soldier to serve the Church in the capacity that Loyalty was to be above all else, except Honor. Now with the passing of Pope Pius XIII, I'm afraid it all comes to a sudden end." He turned to Kimball, the hurt on his face obvious. "I just thought it fitting, my friend, that I see you here, in this chamber, where it all began."

Kimball stared up at the seats. It was odd to see them vacant. And the chamber held an odd and sepulchral quiet to it, something eerie and hollow.

"I thought it important that you hear it from me first," he told Kimball. "You are the best of the best. But more importantly, as a good person, you've come a long way."

Kimball felt ashamed. How does he tell a man who offered him the chance at redemption that his blood boiled with the underlying passion to kill Ezekiel? He was no savior. He was just a simple man whose dream of salvation came and went like a wispy comma of smoke. Ezekiel had shown him the truth. Underneath, there was darkness.

And if there was one thing Cardinal Vessucci was skilled at, it was seeing the insight of all people. Behind Kimball's brilliant cerulean blue eyes, he noted something dark. "You're still angry," he said, but not as a question. "The betrayal of the child you reared has consumed you with rage, hasn't it?"

"I tried to do the right thing."

"Of course, you did, Kimball. But the road to Hell is paved with good intentions."

"I had no idea he recognized me the day I saw him in the Boys' Home."

"Apparently he did. And by doing so he turned his rage into a crusade."

They began to walk away from the stage and toward the chamber doors.

"Kimball, he sees you as the betrayer of his grandfather. And now he holds the same animosity as you do. It's an ugly feeling. But you're better than that if you believe it or not."

"He killed Job and Joshua."

"And for that God will judge him for it, not you."

Kimball sighed; their steps small since the cardinal moved along with light footfalls. "You have become a good man, Kimball. Stay that way and let your anger go. Ezekiel has cast his fate in the eyes of God and will be judged thusly."

Still, something continued to smolder deep inside Kimball.

"And what will you do?" asked Kimball.

The cardinal stopped in his tracks. "It appears that I have been demoted," he answered.

"To what?"

"The good Pope Gregory saw fit that I am to be reassigned to a post in Boston where indiscretions are going on with alleged charges of fraud. The Pope sees me as the most judicious in handling such matters."

"And who will be the new secretary of state?"

"It appears that the good Cardinal Angullo will usurp my position."

Kimball ground his teeth.

"And what about those in the Society of Seven?"

"They will also be reassigned, as well."

So that's it. Everything about the Vatican Knights was being dispersed to all corners of the planet, broken and scattered like ashes cast to the wind.

"Kimball, you have earned the right."

"The right about what?"

Cardinal Vessucci faced him and smiled. "For redemption," he said. "It's yours. It has been yours for a while now."

For a moment Kimball could feel his heart skip a beat in his chest. It was a glorious feeling.

"You have earned it many times over," said the cardinal. "Don't let Ezekiel blacken your heart. Instead, fill it with forgiveness."

They were nearing the colossal door.

"So, what will you do now?" asked the cardinal.

Kimball shrugged. Good question. "I don't know," he said. "This is all I know what to do."

Kimball reached down and grabbed the wrought-iron ring of the door and opened it, the door whining on its aged hinges.

"The team is already gone," said the cardinal. "You are the last. But I want to say this." Both men stared through the open door, drawing a bead on empty chairs on the stage. "You have become a son to me. And I'm proud of you, as was Pope Pius and Pope John. You have always been a dear man and I will never forget you, Kimball."

Kimball could feel the sting of tears. He was losing his entire family in one fell swoop.

"So, I guess this is it?" said Kimball.

The cardinal stood there, staring, the stage a magnificent display where ideas were exchanged, and history made.

"Who knows," he finally answered. "Maybe you'll be pressed back into duty someday."

"But not likely."

The cardinal did not acknowledge him. Instead, he said, "Please . . . Close the door."

Slowly, Kimball closed the mammoth door until neither man could see the stage any longer.

EPILOGUE

Kimball did not return directly to the barracks to gather his gear. Instead, he walked the grounds through St. Peter's Square, through the Basilica, past the Colonnades, and sat by the Old Gardens until the late afternoon sky was turning into banded shades of red, orange, and yellow.

Here he had found peace unlike anything ever encountered.

Gathering himself for the short walk to the barracks, Kimball found himself vacillating between old emotions against new ones. Sure enough, he stewed underneath, but at the same time, he was warring over the fact that there was serenity, with each faction seesawing against the other.

Perhaps the cardinal's words were valid, after all, he considered.

But if questions remained regarding how he felt about Ezekiel, then he wasn't completely there. If anything, Ezekiel had become a much greater test on whether or not he should follow through and kill him to settle an underlying need or to find forgiveness and let him move on.

Either way, he needed closure.

Making his way to the barracks was almost a physically painful task; the empty rooms, the one-time laughter of Vatican Knights echoing off the stone walls after an off-key joke was told no longer, and the smell of baked meats wafting through the hallways from the Mess.

Now it was empty with a tomblike stillness.

Once inside his room, he sat on the edge of his bed and slightly grazed a hand over the soft fabric of the blanket, a loving caress.

He would take his military manuals, his military gear, and stuff as much of his life into a canvas duffel bag.

Everything I have to show for my life, he thought.

And this was not much.

After cramming his goods into the bag, he laid it next to the door and stood within the room's center. To one side was the small dais holding the Bible, as well as the votive rack and kneeling rail. To the other side were a super-single-sized bed, a nightstand, and bookshelves for his manuals. Comparatively speaking it was far from luxury, but it was his home. But he could not have been happier.

Kimball then moved to the mirror and stared at his reflection, noting crows-feet that were becoming longer and deeper. If there was one thing this man could not defeat, it was aging.

So, what will you do now?

He traced his fingers gingerly over his image.

And then he worked them down to the cleric's collar.

And then he worked his fingers further down to the patch of the Vatican Knights etched on the breast pocket of his cleric's shirt, the image of the powder blue shield and silver Pattée with the supporting heraldic lions holding it steady.

It was a nice ride, he told himself. And then he removed the band of the cleric's collar and held it in his hand.

For a long time, he stared at it, thinking what it meant to him: Loyalty above all else, except Honor. And then he placed it neatly on top of the Bible on the dais.

Grabbing the duffel bag, Kimball took one last look, absorbing everything. High on the wall was the stained-glass window of the Virgin Mother, her arms reaching out as a gesture of acceptance and the willingness to embrace those in need.

Although the light of the sun was beginning to wane, a thin beam of light cast from the Virgin Mary's hands alighted on the cleric's collar, giving it a glowing appeal that appeared ethereal in its effect.

In less than three steps Kimball crossed the room and looked at the collar, then at the image of the Virgin Mother.

The sun was going down.

And the glow of the collar was fading fast.

Kimball grabbed the band with a sense of homage and carefully placed it in his pocket.

Maybe someday you'll be pressed back into duty; he recalled the cardinal saying.

But Kimball knew this to be an unlikely scenario.

Straightening his beret to specs as a good Vatican Knight should, he grabbed his duffel bag and closed the door behind him, wondering what he was going to do with the rest of his life.